THE DREAMKEEPERS

A JAMES DILLAN NOVEL
BOOK 1

ANTONIO ZADRA

HIDDEN MOON PRESS

Copyright

Cover Art by Laura Boyle

For Mom, who taught me the importance of dreams.

CHAPTER 1

Santilli opened her eyes, gasping for air. Pain scorched her throat, spasms tore across her back. She tried lifting her head, but her body wouldn't respond. Her right leg was mangled, her left shattered. A memory swirled through her mind: she was falling feet-first through the air, arms flailing at her sides. One leg came crashing down onto a boulder. The sound of splintering bones echoed in her head.

As quickly as it had appeared, the scene vanished. Liquid was pooling in Santilli's mouth, but she was incapable of spitting or swallowing. She could, however, taste the metallic bitterness of blood as it trickled down her lip.

Santilli remained face down with her cheek to the snow, sprawled on the frozen ground. The shivers running though her limbs did little to warm the glacial winds deadening her muscles. Her socks, cargo pants, and thin top were no match for the elements.

As she lay there, laboring to breathe, she glimpsed a faint light shimmering on the horizon. The sun would soon emerge over the soaring, stone-faced cliffs. Vincente, her twelve-year-old son, would wake up within the hour and see that his mother was gone. The memory of kissing the boy goodnight a few short hours ago flashed by, but Santilli kept her emotions in check. Her next actions would be decisive, not only for her son, but also for countless others.

High above, the first rays of dawn pierced the gray sky. As the sun crept into view, a beam of light sliced through the morning haze, infusing it with a steel-blue sheen. Within minutes, the highest mountain peaks and towering spires were transformed. Dark grays gave way to muted silvers; deep browns were overtaken by fiery oranges. The Dolomites were waking up.

Santilli slid her head backward and examined the patch of bloodied whiteness before her. Pulling her right hand in toward her chest, she molded snow into four fist-sized balls. She curled her frozen hand under two of them and pushed them farther out, each about an arm's length from the other. Hoping for a momentary reprieve, she let her body go limp, but the pain continued to pound. She picked up the two remaining snowballs and, using her left elbow and hips as leverage, inched forward. She stretched out her arm as far as she could and carefully positioned the balls several inches above the first two, establishing the four corners of a square.

Almost all the bloodied snow had now been used to make the four orbs. Santilli reached below her hip, swept some clean snow toward her chest, and shaped it into a fifth ball. She smeared it over her nose and mouth, covering it with blood. This ball she positioned closer to her body, below the lower section of the square. The five reddish snowballs now formed a U-like pattern.

Santilli gathered more snow into a final heap. She bent her torso, reached down toward her ankle, and gripped her icy sock between her thumb and forefinger. In one swift move, she ripped it off her foot. Violent spasms sent globules of blood spewing from her mouth.

Breathing against the pain, she placed the sock by her lips and opened one side of it with her teeth. She stuffed the sock with snow and patted it into a round shape. She then lifted herself onto her elbow, aimed, and lobbed the sock. It landed where she had hoped. The pattern was now made up of the reddish U-shaped constellation, with the dark mass she had just fashioned out of her sock centered above it.

Exhausted, she laid her head on the ground and closed her eyes. She shoved her right hand under her left armpit, hoping for warmth, but found little. She forced her forearm down into her pants, toward her crotch. Better.

After she felt a little warmer, she removed her hand and pulled back the Velcro on the side pocket of her pants. She reached inside, wrapped her fingers around her multitool, and brought it up to her face. No need for the scissors, wire cutters, serrated blade, or screwdriver. The pliers would do the trick. She unfolded the multitool, exposing the stainless-steel pliers.

Santilli placed her weight over her injured hand and positioned the lower metal prong under her thumbnail. She stared at the pliers and took a steadying breath. Her jaw clenched as the cold metal prong penetrated her skin. Her thumbnail began to rise, slowly tearing away from the raw tissue beneath. She pushed the pliers as far as they would go, then ripped the nail right off. Santilli fought the urge to shriek and gritted her teeth as blood seeped from her thumb. With her nail still dangling from the end of the metal prongs, she reached out and embedded it on the top of the nearest snowball.

She raised the pliers into view and examined the grooves running down the metal spines. Using the same torturous technique, she ripped away, one by one, the remaining fingernails from her left hand. Each bloodied nail was, in turn, carefully pressed onto the surface of one of the four remaining snowballs.

The woman stared at her butchered fingers and plunged them into the snow to ease the bleeding and dull the pain. Almost done. She took her hand out of the white ground, and with the blood still dripping off her fingertips, she drew eight letters in the snow. The word was messy but legible: "INVICTUS." She rolled onto her back and reached for the silver chain she had worn since childhood. With the round medallion centered in her palm, she yanked the chain off her neck. Clutching the medallion, broken ends dangling out of the sides of her fist, she pressed her hand to her chest and stared up at the sky.

A wintry gust swept down the face of the mountain, but Santilli remained unaffected; no longer did she hear or feel the bitter winds swirling about her. Her body was blanketed by the numbing cold, and her mind had receded into a distant calm. A tear welled up in the corner of her eye. Before the cold could freeze it in place, it grew and drifted away down her frostbitten cheek. Santilli closed her eyes, took a deep breath, and welcomed the burst of icy air seeping into her lungs.

CHAPTER 2

I n almost every respect, Doctor James Dillan's one-bedroom apartment looked the same as it had when he was a student. The walls might have now displayed paintings that were unaffordable back then, and the bed was new, but otherwise the place remained unchanged. The same pine bookcase covered the far wall of the main room. The oak desk at which Dillan had spent countless hours studying, writing, thinking, and procrastinating still stood in front of the bay window overlooking Jeanne Mance Park. The wood flooring, revarnished a few years ago, still had the same planks that creaked under the slightest pressure. Even the recent coats of paint faithfully matched the living room's original sundrenched yellow and the bedroom's initial shade of evening-sky blue. And, of course, there was the oversized leather chair.

The doctor wasn't the only person who loved the big carmine chair. As he always did when visiting Dillan's third-floor apartment, Victor chose that chair, and he was now sitting in it, his muscular hands clutching the rounded armrests. But today was different; Dillan had rarely seen Victor so agitated. First pleading, then bellowing, Victor demanded that the doctor help him find Maria. Dillan certainly understood how important she was to him. After all, Maria and her whereabouts had been a focus of their conversations for over a decade, ever since their first encounter.

The doctor stood by the bay window, surveying the night sky. A trail of low-lying clouds glided past, their pale, moonlit contours contrasting with the black firmament. As he turned toward Victor, he noticed that the light from the Tiffany lamp on his desk was too faint for the late hour. Dillan walked over to the floor lamp in the corner and switched it on. The bulb flickered and died.

"Look, Victor," he said, trying to remain composed. "When I first met you, you couldn't even remember Maria's name. We've discovered lots of things together since then, but I don't know Maria or where she might be. I don't even know what she looks like."

"You have to help me," Victor said, his voice dropping to a whisper. "You're the only person who can help me." He searched Dillan's eyes for any sign of understanding. "Wasn't I there for you when you needed to talk about your own issues? What about your last case? You spent weeks trying to figure out how that couple could've died in their sleep like that. You and I both know you only solved it because of the clues I gave you."

"You've always been helpful, Victor. I know that."

"Then why don't you trust me?"

"I do trust you."

"So you do believe she's out there?"

Dillan searched for something to say that was reassuring yet truthful, but his moment of hesitation didn't go unnoticed.

Victor raked his hand through his coarse black hair. "Time's running out, Doctor, and I can't find her without your help. I'm telling you, our lives depend on it. *Your* life depends on it. The whole world's in danger."

"From what?"

"From forces surrounding us now and more powerful ones to come."

"These forces you're talking about, they don't exist."

Victor shook his head. "After all this time, you still refuse to believe me. Sooner or later, you're going to have to step outside that wall of yours. Until you do, you can't possibly understand the worlds we live in or the actions you need to take." Victor stood up, gave Dillan a long stare, and walked out of the apartment.

"Victor," he called, "come back!" But all he heard were the echoes of heavy footsteps on the stairs.

The doctor was shaken. He reached into the front pocket of his pants, took out a small bottle of pills, and popped open the snap cap. He looked inside; the bottle was empty. Dillan took a deep breath and gave the bottle a futile shake before slipping it back into his pocket. He then sat in the leather chair and ran his hands over the armrests, still warm from Victor's grasp. He gazed at the colors and patterns on the Tiffany lamp, lulled by their quieting, almost hypnotic effect. What if Victor was right? What if they did have to find Maria? What if the danger was not only real, but imminent?

After all these years, the doctor still didn't know why Victor kept visiting him. Victor had never been a patient of his. He came and went of his own accord, without warning or schedule. But Dillan had always welcomed his friend's unexpected appearances. He had been fascinated by Victor's unusual character, and the man had shown himself to be both insightful and caring. There was no denying that Victor's story was outlandish, but the details had remained consistent over the years. Dillan had never doubted Victor's love for Maria or his ever-pressing need to see her again. He only doubted that she existed.

CHAPTER 3

D illan fought off eye strain as he looked over his PowerPoint presentation. As much as he disliked finishing things up at the last minute, his schedule these past weeks had left him little choice. With his talk at Boston University less than forty-eight hours away, he'd tried to squeeze in extra prep time at the office earlier that day, but he'd had only a few breaks between patients. Now he was once again seated at his desk, but it was already one in the morning.

The doctor had been invited to speak about his work on sleep-walking, though Dillan had long considered the term to be inadequate given the range of behaviors sleepwalkers could engage in. His team at the Sacré-Coeur Center for Sleep Medicine had captured images of the brain activity of his patients during their sleepwalking episodes. These images revealed that, while some parts of the brain were asleep during these clinical events, others appeared to be fully awake. This was another example of how—as Dillan was fond of telling his students—being asleep or awake was not all black or white.

Dillan specialized in the study of unusual and aggressive behaviors that occurred during sleep: running into walls, jumping through windows, screaming, feeling paralyzed, leaving the house barefoot in the middle of winter, wielding knives or loaded shotguns, attacking bed partners. The doctor had seen all this and more in his sleep-disordered patients, and his expertise in sleep forensics made him a sought-after consultant in the growing number of cases involving bizarre and often violent sleep-related crimes and accidents.

But as he sat reading his notes, his thinking became sluggish. Time to call it a night.

* * *

The sound of the phone startled Dillan into partial wakefulness.

"Hello?"

"James, it's Michael. Michael Kohler."

Dillan emerged from his fog. "Michael ... it's been a while."

"Sorry to call you like this, but there's been a tragic incident. Giancarla just died. Giancarla Santilli. You remember her? I introduced you to her in Berkeley."

"What happened?"

"She was hiking in the Dolomites with her son. Her body was found at the bottom of a cliff. The police aren't sure what happened, but it looks like she died in the middle of the night. She had nightmares and may have suffered from some kind of nocturnal wandering. You know more about this stuff than anyone else."

"Michael, it's..." Dillan looked at his alarm clock. "It's almost three in the morning."

"Sorry about the time. I'm calling from Italy. Giancarla wasn't just a friend; she was a patient. Her death comes as a shock. It could have been suicide, but then there's her son. He's only a kid, but he might be implicated, up against murder charges."

"I never realized..." Dillan was seized by an overwhelming sense of déjà vu.

"James, are you there?"

"Yes. I never realized Giancarla was a patient of yours. What is it you want me to do?"

"I know this is asking a lot, but I was hoping you could come here. I told the chief inspector that one of the better-known experts in sleep forensics was an old friend, and he's interested in getting your input. I can take care of your expenses, and you're more than welcome to stay at my place. It wouldn't be for more than couple of days."

"I don't know what to say. I'm flying to Boston for a talk. Let me see if I can cut things short and get away in a day or two."

"Thanks. I know I've been lousy at keeping in touch, but this means a ton to me."

"That's all right. I'll get back to you as soon as I have the details."

Dillan hung up, lay back in his bed, and stared into the darkness. He thought back to his university days with Michael and how their different life experiences had led them to similar fields of study. Shifting his focus, Dillan revisited the time Michael had introduced him to Santilli. He recalled his conversations with the athletic, blue-eyed woman and her smart questions about the interplay between mind and sleep. Now Santilli was dead.

Dillan mulled over the few details he'd been given about the case, but this was not the time to engage in such musings. What the doctor most needed now was sleep. He turned onto his side, pulled the sheets up to his neck, and closed his eyes. The strategy was of little benefit. The ruminations zigzagging through his brain had gained too much momentum. Shutting them down would take some doing: a quieting of his mind and a conscious effort to let his thoughts dilute and dissolve, like ink drops in water.

He considered getting out of bed, if only for a few minutes, or maybe reading, but a better option came to mind. He reached between his home phone and digital clock and picked up his cell. Even at this late hour, there was a better than fifty-fifty chance that Liz, his close friend and colleague—and incorrigible night owl—was still awake and maybe even at the sleep lab.

R u still up? he typed with his thumbs.

Seconds later, his cell buzzed. *No. Texting in my sleep.*

The doctor smiled. *Something's come up,* he wrote. *Another trip after Boston. Think u could run things for a few extra days?*

U know I can. The real question is will I? :)

Dillan tried to think of a clever reply, but before he could formulate one, Liz had already followed up.

Where r u off to?

Italy.

Can I come?

Dillan imagined them sitting side by side on a train as they made their way through the Tuscan countryside. It was an appealing idea. *Afraid not,* he wrote after taking a moment to indulge in his reverie. *Appears u agreed to take care of things while I'm away.*

Serves me right for texting in my sleep. What's in Italy?

New case. Few details. How come ur still up?

Working on software.

Dillan shook his head in silent disapproval. *Don't know how you keep these hrs.*

The reply was immediate. *Good vampire genes.* Then another text: *Why r u up? Don't u have a flight in a couple hrs?*

Woken up by a call.

U should get back to sleep. Catching some zzzs will help u nail down your talk, don't u know?

So I've been told.

There was a pause.

Anything else Dr J? Late for u to be texting.

Dillan hesitated. *Not really. Thanks for helping out.* He hit "send" and immediately shook his head. In an ideal world, he would have told her that their simple exchange had lifted his spirits.

No prob. Sweet dreams Dr J.

The doctor released a sigh. *You too. Good night.*

CHAPTER 4

T he willowy flight attendant gave Dillan a smile as she closed the overhead bins. Although the doctor preferred to sit toward the front of the cabin, the Montreal–Venice flight was full, and the best he could manage was a last-minute spot near the very back, right by the lavatories.

He moved his knees sideways, trying to get comfortable, reached into his briefcase, and took out a paperback. After going over the same paragraph a few times, he realized he was too tired to read. His sleep debt had to be paid. He put away the book, leaned back, and drifted off.

* * *

The elevator began to rise. The entire contraption—walls, door, ceiling, and floor—was made of clear glass. Dillan strained his neck, looking upward, but couldn't make out the top of the skyscraper. The elevator was on the outside wall of the soaring edifice, allowing a view not only of the sky, but also of the receding pedestrians, cars, and buildings below. Dillan steadied himself as the carriage accelerated upward. Within seconds he was being propelled at horrific speeds. The floors of the skyscraper flickered by, a vertical blur. He glanced downward. The ground was thousands of feet below; the view made him sick to his stomach. He was trapped. His chest pounded, each thumping heartbeat resonating inside his head. He tried to scream, but no sound came. The glass walls boomed and shook as the elevator continued its terrifying launch. His legs buckled. Any second, the whole thing was going to break apart and send him plummeting to his death. He braced himself.

"Sir? Sir!" The flight attendant's hand was on Dillan's shoulder.

He sprang forward with open hands, steeling himself for impact.

"It's okay," the attendant murmured. "You were moaning in your sleep. Like you were having a bad dream."

"I was," Dillan replied, his heart still racing.

The attendant leaned forward, almost as if to kiss him on the cheek, and said, "I'm going to have to ask you to place your seat in the upright position and fasten your seat belt. The captain has turned on the seat belt sign because of the turbulence. We'll be landing shortly."

CHAPTER 5

The arrivals terminal at Marco Polo Airport was swarming. Dillan edged his way through the crowd and headed toward the baggage pick-up. At the carousel, he studied the stream of luggage pouring off the end of the ramp. A dark suitcase with a yellow ribbon tied around the handle appeared, slid onto the conveyor belt, and began making its way toward its owner.

Dillan cleared the large sliding doors and exited the baggage claim area. On the other side was a crowd waiting for the passengers to emerge. Off to one corner, the doctor spotted a tall, rail-thin man sporting a broad grin. Dillan smiled, walked up to his friend, and gave him a quick hug.

"Thanks for coming, James."

"Glad I could make it. You haven't changed a bit."

"That's because I never had much hair to begin with," Michael said with a smirk. "My car is on the other side of the building." He took his friend's suitcase. "Are you hungry?"

Dillan frowned. "My stomach's a little upset from the flight."

"Turbulence?"

"You could say that."

* * *

The black Lancia accelerated out of the curve and merged onto Strada Statale 4. Michael glanced over at his friend. "Still single?"

"Sort of," Dillan said. "Things are a little complicated."

"Are you telling me you've finally let someone inside your bubble? Complicated or not, that's progress!" Michael waited for a response, but Dillan remained silent.

"Oh, come on," Michael said. "I'm just having some fun. Besides, you know I'm right. So tell me, what's the problem?"

"For one thing, she's a colleague."

"Not another scientist, I hope."

Dillan shook his head. "She's a software engineer. She does all our programming, and then some."

"So she's smart, and I'm guessing cute too, right?"

"She is bright, and yes, I do like her."

"Name?"

"Liz."

"Well, my friend, I can think of other reasons why things with Liz might be complicated. Psych bubbles aside, I'm guessing either she's already taken, or you're not sure how much she likes you back. Either of these right?"

"She's single," offered Dillan. "But I'm the one who hired her. I don't think it would look too good."

"How long has she been at the lab?"

"Four years."

"And you're still worried about what people might think? Sounds to me like you're afraid of something else. Like ruining things by taking them to the next level."

Dillan wetted his lips. "Could be."

"Either that or you're pretty sure she never liked you to begin with," teased Michael.

Dillan smiled. "Always a possibility. What about you? Anyone new?"

"After everything that happened, I haven't been too keen on jumping into another relationship. Quite happy with things as they are."

Dillan sensed the bitterness in Michael's reply. It was understandable. Less than two years after leaving Montreal to be with a woman he'd met on a trip to Italy, Michael discovered she was seeing another man. There was no reason for the doctor to press further. "So tell me about Santilli," he said, changing the subject.

Michael overtook the vehicle ahead of him and moved back into the right lane before sharing what he had learned from Commissario Enrico Battista, Trento's chief of police.

"Monday morning, Santilli's twelve-year-old son, Vincente, put in a call to emergency services. He'd been hiking with his mom in the Dolomites, but when he woke up that morning, his mother was nowhere in sight. There were bloodstains on the ground and a set of footprints leading away from their campsite. The tracks came to an end by a drop down the side of the mountain. The thing is, he never found any footprints heading back to the tent, or in any other direction for that matter. According to what Vincente told the police, nobody else was up there but them. And whoever left those footprints walked right off the face of the mountain."

Michael paused, then said, "I know it sounds bizarre, but either she committed suicide, which I doubt—I mean, even if she had a reason to kill herself, why would she do it there and take her kid along, for heaven's sake—or there's some other explanation. That's where you come in. It happened after they'd gone to sleep."

"Footprints can be hard to make out," Dillan said. "And the fact they didn't see anybody else doesn't mean—"

"The police know they were up there alone."

"How can they be sure?"

"Santilli and her boy started their hike during the tail end of a snowstorm. When the investigators showed up, their tracks were still visible in several spots along their route. And there were only two sets of footprints leading to their campsite: those of an adult and those of a child. No other footprints within several kilometers."

"Any idea why they'd go up there on the heels of a storm?"

"According to the boy, Santilli told him it would be a 'unique' adventure. That the Dolomites look magical when covered in snow."

"Was the boy's other parent involved?"

Michael appeared to hesitate. "He died when Vincente was a baby," he said. "Santilli never remarried."

"Poor kid. Did they have any other children?"

"Just Vincente."

"Do you know if they'd backpacked in winter before?"

"Not sure, but they did trek a lot in the summer. Santilli was an avid mountaineer, and her son loved being up there with her."

The black Lancia decelerated and exited the highway. Michael took a narrow road and headed into the town of Seren del Grappa. The car pulled up to an old building, its straw-colored facade dulled by time. "Need an espresso," he explained.

Above the main entrance was a large wooden sign with the words *Pasticceria di Casa* carved into it, along with the outline of a steaming loaf of bread coming out of an oven. The moment the men walked through the door, they were enveloped by the aroma of baked pastries. They strolled up to the bar. "*Un caffè macchiato*," Michael said.

"*Due macchiati*," corrected Dillan, holding up two fingers.

The men collected their order and sat at a corner table. "Something else was odd," continued Michael. "Santilli and her boy slept in separate tents. The boy said it was his idea, that he wanted to sleep on his own like a grown-up." He pulled the demitasse toward him and downed the espresso in a single gulp. "He also said his mom snored, and the noise had kept him awake on previous trips."

"What's odd about that?"

"The tents were set up almost twenty meters apart."

Dillan raised an eyebrow. "What about Santilli? You mentioned she'd been a patient of yours."

"She came to see me a few months after I'd settled in Trento. Said she'd read a few of my articles on treating nightmares. She'd had nightmares herself, but that's not why she came. She wanted to learn more about dreams. And not Freud and Jung kind of stuff either. Giancarla was interested in rare and obscure work."

"Like what?"

"Achmet, Saint-Denys, Seafield, some of the older German theorists."

Dillan took a sip of coffee. "What was she after?"

"Theories about how dream characters are created and the processes behind what they say and do in our dreams."

"That's why you brought her to the conference in Berkeley?"

Michael nodded. "I told her that I could introduce her to some people there."

"Interesting woman, I'll give her that. What were her nightmares about?"

"Giancarla wasn't interested in talking about her own dreams. She did mention having had nightmares since she was a kid, but she felt they were valuable, had helped shape who she was. The few she told me about had her slogging her way up dangerous mountains. Sometimes she'd fall into giant crevasses. Other times, hurricane-like winds would blow her right off the mountain. That's about all I ever got out of her."

"So she never came to you for psychological issues?"

"Not once," replied Michael. "She did pay me a nominal fee for my time, but all we did was talk about dreams."

"When you called me, you said something about Giancarla suffering from nocturnal wandering."

"I think it's possible. She said she'd sometimes wake up from her nightmares after falling out of bed. And about a month ago, she asked me for your email. Said she wanted to talk to you about sleepwalking and insomnia."

Dillan looked surprised. "Did she say why?"

"Only that she wanted to hear your take on them."

"Too bad she didn't follow through. Maybe we'd have a bit more to go on."

CHAPTER 6

A final cluster of water droplets escaped from the showerhead and spattered onto the bathtub floor. Dillan tied the belt of the white terrycloth robe around his waist and trudged out of Michael's bathroom. His friend was on the living room couch, pouring himself another shot of whisky.

"Care for a refill?" Michael asked.

"No, thanks. I'm feeling the jet lag."

"Suit yourself." Michael took a sip of his drink. "Can I ask you something?" he said, still holding his glass.

Dillan walked over to the recliner. "Of course. What is it?"

"I know this isn't any of my business, but are you still taking those anti-anxiety meds?"

Dillan's stomach tensed. "Not that often. When I need to."

"You used to pop those things like they were Tic Tacs."

"That was a phase," Dillan rushed to say.

Michael grinned. "So was the ice age… Look, I worried about this back then, and now that you're here, I thought it'd be good to follow up. As a friend."

Dillan gave a slight nod but remained silent.

"I know you're all about brains and neurons, James, but I still don't think pills are the solution to whatever ails you."

Dillan rubbed the back of his neck. "I appreciate your concern. But really, it's under control."

"Happy to hear it." Michael raised his glass in a silent toast and gulped down the rest of his drink.

"Still keeping your dream diary?" Dillan asked, changing the subject.

"I stopped a while back. When things turned sour with Stefania. I didn't have the energy. Besides, it was taking up too much time. I still jot down the odd dream now and again, but that's about it."

"Too bad. You had a goldmine of information there." Dillan paused for a moment. "You remember my elevator dream?"

"Of course, the *glass* elevator dream. The perfect nighttime companion to your daytime vertigo. Don't tell me you stopped having it."

"I wish. I had it on the flight over here."

"You're serious?"

"Absolutely."

"Well, James, I told you then, and I'll tell you now. Unless you hit the ground floor button, the damn thing will keep taking off like a missile. And up, up and away you'll go."

Dillan cracked a smile. "I'll try to keep that in mind. Time for me to hit the sack. My brain's about to shut down."

* * *

Dillan stretched his legs like a cat emerging from a midday nap. He could tell from the darkness that he had awoken according to his biological clock and not the digital clock by the bed. He pulled the comforter up to his chin and closed his eyes, hoping to fall back to sleep. Images began to appear. He was in the middle of a vast, snow-covered meadow. To one side, peeking out from under the snow, were dozens of colorful crocuses. In the field there was a little girl, her blond hair and shimmering gown billowing in the wind. They had exchanged words—meaningful words.

Dillan lay still, trying to remember what had been said, but the words eluded him. Soon the child faded away, along with the flowers, snow, and meadow. His tenuous hold on the scene was lost, leaving him puzzled and sad. Strange how memories of dreams, even the most recent, can be so evanescent.

Dillan's thoughts wandered to Michael. For over twenty years, his friend had kept a meticulous record of even his haziest dreams, and now he had stopped altogether? Michael had once showed him his cherished dream diary, a series of leather-bound volumes containing anything and everything he had ever remembered from his dreams since age nine. The volumes were a treasure trove of ideas and accounts: over five thousand dream reports; hundreds of illustrations of scenes, objects, and characters; thousands of analyses and annotations. And now—no more time? Perhaps the break with the faithless Stefania had been more painful than Michael had let on. Even so, his apparent change of heart didn't feel right.

CHAPTER 7

M ichael pulled the car up in front of the old four-story building that housed Trento's police department, right on time for Dillan's meeting with Captain Battista. Dillan thanked his friend and strode up the stairs to the building's oversized doors. Waiting for him at the entrance was a stocky, fit-looking man in his early thirties.

"*Dottore* Dillan, it is a pleasure to meet you." The man gave the doctor a firm handshake. "Welcome to Trento. I'm Detective Riccardo Tramonte. Captain Battista wanted to be here, but he had an emergency."

Detective Tramonte led Dillan to his office. "Please, have a seat," he said before taking his place behind a desk. The detective looked through a pile of papers, rolled his chair over to the filing cabinet behind him, and took out a couple of folders.

Once Dillan was seated, Tramonte reviewed the details surrounding Santilli's death but had little to add to what Michael had already told the doctor. As the detective was explaining how Santilli's body was found, a familiar three-note guitar riff rang out: the Rolling Stones' "Satisfaction." Flustered, Detective Tramonte reached into his pocket and took out his cell.

"Good news, *Dottore*," he said after a brief exchange. "We have the okay to go see Vincente, Santilli's son. The boy's English is very good—his mother had him tutored for several years. But I warn you, we had a hard time getting him to speak to us yesterday."

* * *

The makeshift interrogation room had the feel of an abandoned shed and carried the distinctive smell of old books. Vincente, a slight and dark-haired youth, was seated, his head nestled in his arms on the battered wooden table.

"Good morning, Vincente. This is Doctor Dillan. He has come all the way from Canada to help us. He would like to talk to you for a little bit."

Vincente raised his head. His eyes widened, as if he recognized the man standing before him. He remained still, staring at the doctor, before burying his head back in his arms. He started to sob.

Detective Tramonte held out a box of tissues.

Vincente looked up, tears trickling down his cheeks.

Dillan moved toward the boy. "My name is James. I'm a medical doctor. I study things that happen to people during their sleep. I'm here to help us understand what may have happened to your mom. Is it okay if I ask you a few questions?"

Vincente shrugged and wiped his nose on his sleeve.

"I know you've already answered a lot of questions," Dillan said in a low voice. "If you don't want to repeat things, that's fine, just let me know. Maybe we could start with why you and your mom were hiking right after a snowfall."

"I, I don't know…. She picked me up at school and told me we'd be leaving the next morning. She was going to show me something important."

"Did she tell you what?"

"She said we'd have to hike for a few days and that I'd under-stand"—his voice cracked—"…that I'd understand once we got there. I believed her, but I don't understand, and now she's dead!"

Dillan reached out with his hand to comfort him, but Vincente swatted it away.

The doctor waited a few seconds. "I'm not sure you know this," he said, "but I met your mother once. About three years ago. We were at a conference on dreams. She seemed to be a fine and caring woman. We spoke about many things, but one thing she told me was that the two of you liked going to Bolzano to watch hockey. I'm trying to remember the name of the team there. The Wolves, was it?"

"The Foxes," replied Vincente.

"Yes, the Foxes. Your mom mentioned that you're a pretty good skater yourself. Is that true?"

The boy remained silent, his gaze fixed on the table.

"I'm curious because I spent part of my childhood playing outdoor hockey. It was just for fun, and I was never very good, but still like to go skating whenever I get a chance. Do you like North American hockey?"

Dillan waited for an answer, but none came. He tried again. "Can I ask you a few more questions about what happened?"

The boy gave a slight nod.

"From what I understand, you and your mom decided to sleep in separate tents. Is that right?"

"Yes."

"Did you do anything in particular with your mom before going to sleep that last night?"

Vincente hesitated. "Mama was quiet."

"And that was unusual?"

"Yes."

The boy appeared on the verge of crying again. Dillan took a second to think through his next question.

"Was she quiet during the rest of the trip as well?"

"She always taught me things on our hikes. But this time she said she needed to focus so we wouldn't get lost. But my mom never got lost! Not because of some stupid snow."

Dillan leaned forward. "What kinds of things did she like to teach you?"

"All sorts of stuff: the weather, the history of the mountains, how to tie knots, how to look for planets and stars…"

"What topic did you like most?"

Vincente chewed on his lower lip. "The mountain legends," he said finally.

"What kind of mountain legends?" Dillan asked.

The boy remained silent.

"There are many legends associated with the Dolomites," Detective Tramonte said. "Most come from the Ladin people. They have been in the Dolomites for centuries. My father is of Ladin descent."

Dillan waited a second. "Did the two of you talk about any of these legends on this trip?"

The boy nodded. "Before going to bed."

"Can you tell me a little about the story she told you?"

"It's called the *Monti Pallidi*."

"What's it about?"

The boy didn't speak.

"It's a well-known legend," said the detective. "It's about the origins of the edelweiss flower and why the Dolomites have pale, silver-like colors."

"I'd love to hear more about it," Dillan said. "Do you want to tell me the story, Vincente, or would you prefer the detective do it?"

"Detective."

"I will do my best." The detective pulled up a chair and sat next to Dillan and the boy. "Many years ago, in a kingdom in the Dolomites, there was a sad prince. He was in love with a woman who would visit him in his dreams. But she was from the moon, and he had no way to visit her. One day, an old man from the mountains granted him his wish and took him to the moon, but the prince could not stay long or he would go blind because everything there was so bright."

The boy sniffled, laid his head back down on the table, and closed his eyes.

Detective Tramonte glanced at Dillan, who motioned him to carry on. "The prince met the daughter of the Moon King and realized she was the woman from his dreams. They got married and came to live in the Dolomites. To help her remember her home, the Moon Princess took some white flowers from the moon and planted them in the mountains. But the dark colors of the Dolomites made her feel sad and ill, and soon she had no choice but to return home."

The detective stopped to look at Vincente. The boy still had his head down and his eyes closed. "The prince was *inconsolabile*. But while walking in the forest, he met a dwarf king who chose to help him. That night, the king and his dwarfs covered the Dolomites with thousands of threads of silver light made from the rays of the moon. The Moon Princess was able to return to Earth, and she and the prince lived the rest of their lives together in the mountains. That is why the Dolomites look pale like the moon, and why the edelweiss, the flower the princess had taken from the moon, is found in the Alps. Is that about right, Vincente?"

The boy raised his head. "A few things are missing … but yes."

"What a wonderful story," Dillan said. "The prince gets to marry the woman of his dreams, and the Dolomites are transformed by their love." He paused, then said, "Do you think our own dreams can be important, Vincente?"

"Sometimes. There's … there's so much you can do in them."

"Like what?" Dillan asked.

"Fly, visit new places, make friends with animals."

"You can do those things?"

The boy gave a slight nod.

"What kinds of animals have you befriended in your dreams?"

"Owls, bears. Turtles and butterflies too. I even got to ride on the back of a giraffe once. But butterflies are my favorite."

"Why's that?"

"Because they start off as caterpillars. And I like the way they fly around."

"Do you know you're dreaming during these dreams, like in lucid dreams, or do they just happen to you?"

The boy shrugged. "Both."

"Do you sometimes have bad dreams?"

"I used to have falling dreams. But Mama told me they were special and that I shouldn't be scared. She taught me things like how to turn falling dreams into flying dreams and how to land so I could see what was there for me." The boy paused for a moment. "I used to get really excited when I'd fly and wake up before I could land. The important thing is to stay calm and remember that nothing can hurt you."

Dillan had to shake off his sense of disbelief. The kind of dream-related knowledge the boy was describing was not only rare, but was usually possessed by older, more experienced dreamers.

"I like your advice," the doctor said. "For me, it's not only keeping my emotions in check that I find difficult, but also remembering that I'm dreaming as the dream unfolds. People talk to me or something happens, and bingo, I forget that I'm dreaming."

The boy gave the doctor a half-smile. "You need to keep practicing."

"Do you have any tricks to help you stay lucid in your dreams?"

"I look at my hands. I use them as a cue to remember I'm dreaming. I also spin my body when I feel I'm about to wake up. It helps me stay in the dream longer."

"How long do you spin for?"

"Not long. A couple of turns. I like to put out my arms while I do it." Vincente straightened his back. "I don't know why spinning works. Do you?"

"Maybe it stimulates something called the vestibular system," Dillan suggested, pointing to his ear. "The bones and liquids inside your ears that help you keep your balance or make you feel dizzy when you spin too fast. That system is involved in REM sleep, the sleep stage where most vivid dreaming takes place, so it may help keep the dream going somehow. I'll have to remember to try it."

The boy scratched the back of his ear. "That was a complicated answer."

"Sorry, I sometimes do that."

"I also spin my body clockwise," Vincente added. "Works better for me than the other way."

"You have this down to a science. Sounds to me like you've become quite the oneironaut."

"A what?"

"An oneironaut—an explorer of the dream world."

"That's a real word?"

"Yup."

"I like it," the boy said with a faint smile.

Dillan waited a moment then asked, "What about your mother's dreams? Did she ever talk about them?"

Vincente appeared unsure. "She dreamed a lot about mountains. Big mountains. Way bigger than the Alps or Himalayas. She had this one dream where she'd be climbing one of the tallest peaks. She was way above the clouds, and the top of the mountain was covered with snow and crevasses. But what scared her the most was the wind. She said it was so strong, it could blow you right off the mountain."

"I appreciate you sharing that with us," Dillan said. "Do you know if your mom had any problems with her sleep?"

"She slept okay."

"What about snoring? I was told that was why you and your mom slept in separate tents."

Vincente's eyes fluttered. "It would wake me up."

Dillan felt the boy wasn't telling the truth, but his suspicions would have to wait. "Do you know if your mom ever suffered from sleepwalking?"

Vincente shook his head. "She never mentioned anything like that."

"I know you've already told the officers about your last day in the mountains," Dillan said, "but can you tell me what happened after you woke up that morning?"

"I got out of the tent because I needed to pee. The sun was up, and Mama should have been making breakfast by then, but she wasn't there. There was blood on the snow, and I got scared. I started calling for her. That's when I noticed her footprints. They were from bare feet, not the kind you make with boots. I followed them till I got…" The boy swallowed hard. "To the *burrone*, the edge of the cliff."

"Is that when you called the police?"

"No… I yelled, hoping to hear her. I got down on my knees and looked over the edge, but all I could see were rocks and snow. I found her phone when I ran back to her tent."

"Thank you, Vincente," Dillan said. "That's very helpful. I know this isn't easy. If you think of anything else that might be important, or if there's anything I can help you with, let me know."

The boy stared long and hard at the doctor, tears welling in the corners of his eyes. "You really think you can help me?"

Dillan wasn't sure what surprised him most, Vincente's question or the hopeful tone in which it was asked. He pulled himself closer. "What I can promise is that I'll do everything I can to find out what happened to your mom. But I might need more help from you to do that. Is that okay?"

The boy wiped the tears from his face and gave a gentle nod.

CHAPTER 8

The black Mercedes decelerated, pulled up to the curb, and came to a stop. Michael, by now well acquainted with the strict protocol, stood on the sidewalk waiting for the chauffeur to step out. Seconds passed, then minutes. The door on the driver's side opened. A colossal man emerged and straightened up. He gave Michael a stern look and walked toward him. Michael, with his six-foot-two-inch frame, wasn't used to having people look down on him, not figuratively and certainly not literally. The man cleared his throat. "The Priorate is ready."

Michael's heart pounded as the driver opened the back door of the car. Michael stepped inside, catching a glimpse of the dark suede coat worn by the man waiting for him. The air was malodorous.

The driver climbed back into his seat. The vehicle drove away, made a sharp turn, and sped down a cobblestone road. All the while, the man sitting beside Michael stared straight ahead, his ire permeating the air. Michael lowered his head and out of the corner of his eye glanced at the man's lap. The man's right hand was resting on the suede coat. His fingers were long and emaciated and his skin translucent. At the base of his thumb was a wide silver ring, its surface studded with five rubies that formed a capital letter U. At the top of the U was a larger blue sapphire. Michael tried to swallow, but his mouth had gone dry.

"We had an understanding," the man said in an even, almost robotic tone. "You failed me. Now we've lost our only path to the stones and face much greater risks."

"I'm truly sorry. I don't understand what happened. I took the drug exactly as instructed but wasn't able to get anywhere near Santilli's dreams. I couldn't see a thing. It's like the drug didn't work. I don't know what pushed her to jump."

"You couldn't see a thing..." repeated the man, sotto voce. "You said you were up to the task. Santilli must have sensed your presence." The man gazed out his passenger window. "The fact is, Mr. Kohler, that the only person who could lead us to the stones is dead because of you."

Michael caught the driver staring at him in the rear-view mirror. "I did everything I could to make sure things went as planned. I've never let you down before, sir."

The man took a series of slow, forceful breaths, then said, "I was informed that your doctor friend has arrived. You have twenty-four hours to find out what he knows."

"It's possible he doesn't know anything. I mean, I'm not sure Santilli contacted him."

The man reached over and pulled Michael toward him by his chin. His fingers were as cold as icicles. "Look at me," he whispered.

Michael lifted his head reluctantly, knowing his hope of not having to look the man in the eye was about to be slain. Since the last time he had seen him, the man's drawn-out face had become more gaunt, his cheekbones more angular, and his skin an even more ghastly white. His irises, once forest green and overlain with golden filaments, had faded, replaced by a pale, silvery halo.

"Santilli *did* contact him," he said, squeezing his glacial fingers into Michael's jaw. "You have one last chance to make things right, Mr. Kohler. Find out what Dillan knows. And remember, I rarely forgive one failure, let alone a second."

CHAPTER 9

In the lobby of the police station, Dillan glanced at his watch as he waited for Detective Tramonte, who had been called away after their meeting with Vincente. The doctor was looking for the detective among a group of officers that had emerged from the main corridor when his phone rang. It was Liz Parks.

"James! Didn't you get my text? Someone's accessing your laptop. Do you have it with you?"

"Slow down. What about my laptop?"

"There's a keylogger on it."

"A what?"

"A piece of surveillance software."

"Give me a minute." Dillan walked to a quiet area of the hall. "Someone's monitoring my laptop?"

"Notes, pictures, email. Plus automated screen captures. Whoever's doing this can see anything you have up on your screen in real time."

"How do you know?"

"From the software I installed on your PCs."

"Any idea how long it's been there?"

"It's been on since five o'clock yesterday—so before midnight your time. It wasn't on your hard drive when you left. Did you use a USB charging station or a wireless connection at the airport?"

"I haven't used my laptop since leaving the office. I was going to write to you tonight."

"Where's your laptop now?"

"I left it at Michael's."

"Okay, here's what we're going to do."

* * *

Dillan went back into the main hallway. One of the traffic doors swung open, and out came Detective Tramonte.

"Sorry it took longer than expected. Everything okay, *Dottore?* You don't look well."

"Just got a call from the hospital. Problems with one of my patients."

"Nothing serious, I hope."

"Too early to tell."

"What did you think back there?" Tramonte said.

"About the boy or his story?"

"Both."

"I believe him," Dillan said. "Just not sure he's telling us everything." The men headed down the hallway.

"He was a lot more open with you than with the officers yesterday."

"Really?"

"He told you about his dreams, his mom being quiet, the mountain legends. All that was new. Maybe not much to go on, but it is a start."

The detective stopped in front of a large door with an opaque window and a black-and-white plaque that read, *Enrico Battista, Commissario capo.* He knocked on the commissario's door.

"*Entrate! Entrate!*" bellowed a voice from the other side. Battista, the district police captain, was a diminutive man with a round face and thinning hair slicked back. But it was his thick black moustache that caught Dillan's attention.

"*Grazie* for coming, Doctor Dillan," Captain Battista said in a gravelly voice. He gripped Dillan's hand like a vise. "My English is not very good, but I am sure we will understand each other," the captain said, rolling his *r*'s like an untuned engine.

"I'm sure we will." Dillan's fingers were still throbbing.

"You met *Ispettore* Tramonte," continued the captain, pointing his chin at the detective standing next to Dillan. "And this is *Direttore* Montella of Milano's national police." He turned to the svelte, silver-haired man standing behind him. Montella, impeccable in a dark gray suit, white shirt, and black tie, acknowledged Dillan with a tip of the head.

The captain signaled for Dillan and Detective Tramonte to sit. "You study sleep-related crimes. I did not know this field, sleep forensics, existed."

"Few police officers do. Even most doctors and lawyers aren't aware of it."

"I read a little about these cases," the captain said. "Some are hard to believe. People jumping out of windows, running into *traffico*, even murder and attempted murder."

"I'll admit that the more extreme cases can be challenging," Dillan said.

"Genuine occurrences must be rare, though," said Director Montella. "In many cases, claiming to have one of these disorders is probably a ploy. A way to avoid conviction. Would that be fair to say?"

"Yes, very fair."

Battista looked over some notes. "*Alora* ... the meeting with Vincente. Anything new, *Ispettore?*"

"The boy was more talkative today, Captain. Still the same account, but with more details."

"What did you think, Doctor Dillan?" the captain asked.

"He's distraught, which is normal, but he sometimes spoke clearly and calmly about the events. That's not unusual in children having just experienced a trauma. I also understand that his father died when he was an infant, so to lose his mother like this..."

Director Montella, still standing behind the captain, spoke up. "Giancarla and Signor Santilli lived in California for a few years before she returned here with the boy. Signor Santilli died in a car accident outside San Francisco. Vincente wasn't even a year old at the time."

Captain Battista handed Dillan a file. "*Le foto* of Santilli," he said. "She hurt herself good in the fall. Nothing to explain what happened. Only strange thing is that she had no shoes."

Dillan opened the folder on the captain's desk and examined the photographs of Santilli's body lying in the snow. He studied one of the close-up images. "Is there an autopsy report?"

"Yes, right here," the captain said. "Came in this morning. *Ispettore* Tramonte can translate."

The detective scanned the document. "Internal bleeding; fracture of the left femur and tibia; two broken ribs; contusion and laceration of the skull. Death is estimated between five and eight that morning, principally from exposure and internal injuries."

"Were there any toxicology tests?"

"Opiates, *cocaina, alcol, sedativi,* the usual," the captain said. "All negative."

"What about the blood by the tents? Was it only Santilli's?"

"Yes," the captain answered.

Dillan became perplexed as he inspected the files.

"Everything okay, Doctor Dillan?" asked Director Montella.

"Yes," came the white lie. Dillan had been through enough Montreal winters to notice the snow in the pictures was odd. A crust of crystallized snow coated with icy dimples covered the ground in the shots of the area away from Santilli's body. Dillan was familiar with the type of surface that forms when fresh snow begins to melt in the sun and then freezes again overnight. That same kind of crust was evident near the tent, as well as in the close-ups of Santilli's footprints leading toward the edge of the cliff. But not near her body. That snow was whiter and its surface inexplicably smooth, as if polished by more than winds. The doctor mulled over these incongruities and tried to think of a reason the snow around Santilli's body would be different from everywhere else.

Dillan felt the weight of his silence growing. "I was wondering if there are more pictures."

"More pictures?" repeated the captain. "Of what?"

"Close-ups of Santilli's clothing, her face, injuries, detailed shots of the tents, inside and out. That sort of thing."

The captain gave Dillan an inquisitive look, but it was the director who spoke up.

"Maybe you're forgetting that what we're dealing with here is a death in the mountains. This isn't some rural area where officers can take their time combing the scene for clues and taking pictures left and right. These rescue crews are flown in by helicopter, sometimes not knowing if the people they're supposed to save are still alive. I'm sure you can appreciate the dangers that come with such missions."

The director's tone may have been condescending, but Dillan accepted it and responded as best he could, with a forced smile and polite nod.

"What I think Director Montella is trying to explain," interjected Detective Tramonte, "is that the goal of a mountain rescue is to get everyone out as quickly and safely as possible."

"Exactly," continued the director. "Fatalities in the mountains almost always happen because of one kind of accident or another. Faulty equipment, poor judgment, changes in the weather, a loose foothold, the list goes on. But the Dolomites aren't exactly a magnet for criminal activity. In the case before us, Doctor, we know that Vincente and his mother were the only people anywhere near their campsite. So either Santilli herself was responsible for what happened, or her son was involved. Given your expertise, we hoped you could suggest possibilities for what may have happened to her—possibilities that would be unfamiliar to us."

"Of course," Dillan said.

While the director remained stone-faced, the captain piped up. "So what do you think of the pictures that *were* taken?"

Dillan took a picture out of the folder. "It's hard to make out the details..." He held the picture up to the ceiling light before bringing it down to eye level.

Detective Tramonte reached into his pocket. "Would you like a magnifying glass?"

"Yes, that'd be helpful." Dillan's eyes stayed fixed on the picture.

The detective handed over his iPhone. Dillan looked up. "A phone app?"

"Mirror, flashlight, and magnifying glass—all in one," the detective explained.

Dillan took the iPhone and, surprised by the app's efficiency, scrutinized the magnified picture before him. "Petechiae," he mumbled.

The captain leaned forward. "What did you say?"

"Puh-TEE-kee-ee," the doctor enunciated. "Facial petechiae. Tiny red spots. They form when capillaries or small blood vessels rupture and leak blood under the skin. There's a small cluster of them on Santilli's face."

The detective moved in closer. "What would cause that?"

"Could be lots of things," Dillan said. "Straining to move, a violent cough, prolonged exposure to the cold. Of course, they could have been there before she fell."

But that was not all Dillan had noted. Below Santilli's jaw line were faint signs of ecchymosis. The bruising was not diffused but showed what appeared to be a semicircular imprint. And surrounding Santilli's head was more of that overly polished snow.

"What do you think?" the captain asked.

"Since the blood stains near the tents belong to Santilli, she must have been bleeding before she headed toward the cliff. The question is why."

"She could have woken up with a nosebleed," Detective Tramonte said. "Not uncommon at altitudes. Or it could have been something more serious. Same for her injuries. Some of them could have happened before her fall. There is no way of knowing for sure."

Dillan was still examining the pictures. "I agree," he said. "The body's position, however, suggests that she was still alive when she landed."

Captain Battista sat up straight and cocked his head. "What makes you say that?"

Dillan flipped through the pictures and laid a few on the captain's desk. "See how her hand is resting on her chest?" He pointed to the middle photo. "There's almost no way for a body to come to a stop on its own with an arm in that position. Not after that kind of tumble."

"But not impossible," clarified the director, hunching over the captain's shoulder to get a better look.

"You're right. But here's something I think is impossible. See how Santilli's leg is perched on its heel at an angle? She couldn't have landed like that. We know from the autopsy that her left leg was fractured, both above and below the kneecap. The only thing that could have brought her leg back up like that was a voluntary, and no doubt excruciatingly painful, movement. So either Santilli landed on her back and tried to move using her legs, or she was in another position and managed to roll onto her back. Either way, these pictures indicate she was still alive after the fall."

The room fell silent.

Detective Tramonte reached for the folder and took out pictures of the mountain's upper ledge. "What do you make of these, *Dottore?*" he said, placing several pictures side by side. "If you look at Santilli's footprints, you see that the gaps between them get bigger as she moves farther away from the camp. The shape of the footprints also changes as she gets closer to the edge. When she first left her tent, Santilli was walking. But as she got closer to the cliff, she started to run, and by the end, she was practically sprinting."

Dillan examined the series of pictures. "I think we have to consider the possibility that not only did Santilli know there was a precipice in front of her, but she chose to jump off it."

Captain Battista looked up at Dillan. "Could it be an accident? Some kind of condition in her sleep?"

"The records show no history of night terrors or sleep-related epilepsy. Dr. Kohler thought that Santilli may have suffered from sleepwalking, but Vincente wasn't aware of his mother ever having had an episode. Other than that, I don't see how a sleep disorder could cause someone to make their way out of a tent and run dozens of meters like Santilli did."

Director Montella gazed at Dillan and fired his question point-blank. "What about the boy? Do you think he could have killed Santilli?"

Dillan processed the question and carefully weighed his words. "I'm not a child psychiatrist, but from a clinical standpoint, he's not behaving like he has killed his mother, and I see no compelling reason to doubt what he told us."

Director Montella leaned forward and planted his hands firmly on the edge of the captain's desk. "I'm not a doctor, but my years on the force have taught me that things aren't always as they seem. The boy could have injured his mother while she was asleep. Hit her over the head with her ice axe. He could have used an excuse to get Santilli to the edge of the cliff and pushed her off. He could have poisoned her water. There are several scenarios in which the boy could have been responsible for his mother's death. Would you not agree with this, Doctor?"

Dillan slowly rubbed his forehead. "Those scenarios are possible, but I don't see Vincente planning such a thing, let alone being able to pull it off. There are too many things that could have gone wrong. His mom could have fought back or survived whatever the boy had in store for her. If Vincente had wanted his mother dead, I think he would've come up with a much easier plan and place to do it. And he would need a motive. But you're right, Director. All options should be considered."

Captain Battista was twirling one side of his moustache with his fingertips. "What about suicide?"

"Can't rule it out," Dillan said. "But why hike up a mountain for two days after a snowstorm if all you're planning to do is kill yourself? Why do it barefoot in the middle of the night? And why drag your son into it? It doesn't make much sense."

"Well," said the director, "this has been very helpful, very constructive, Doctor. I'm sure your insights will be useful to us. But if I can be blunt, we're still left with only two possibilities. Either Santilli did this to herself or somebody did it to her. And the only other person up there that night was her boy."

CHAPTER 10

T he hand dryer in the men's room made a raucous noise, but Dillan barely noticed as he held his fingers under the stream of air. His mind was elsewhere, processing his meeting with the Italian authorities.

"*Dottore* Dillan!" called a voice from the hallway.

"In here," Dillan shot back.

The door to the WC swung open. Detective Tramonte waited for the racket of the dryer to stop. "Do you still want to examine Santilli's belongings?"

"That'd be good."

The detective led the way to a nearby elevator.

"Do you mind if we take the stairs?" Dillan said.

"Not at all."

They headed for the stairwell.

"Can I ask you something about dreams, *Dottore?*"

"Of course."

"Do you think it is possible for dreams to show things happening far away, or something in the future?"

"You mean like clairvoyant and precognitive dreams?"

"I don't know what they are called, but my mother believed in these kinds of dreams. She told me stories about people dreaming about things that later happened in real life, and about women during the war dreaming about their son dying in a battle at the exact same time he died far away."

"I've heard accounts like those as well. But these stories are largely anecdotal and can almost never be verified. And when you look at the dreams more closely, there's usually a rational explanation for them."

"So you don't believe these kinds of dreams can happen?"

"No, I don't think it's scientifically possible."

Once at the evidence room, Detective Tramonte said a few words to the security officer on duty, instructed Dillan to sign the registry, and walked through the metal doors. A clap resonated inside the room as he threw on the double light switch. Neon lights flickered overhead, then powered up to full force. Before the men stood rows of tall metal racks jammed with plastic bags, crates, and boxes. The detective walked down the center aisle, taking note of the numbers on the racks. He stopped and reached for a large box. In it was Santilli's tent, sleeping pad, boots, clothing, and sleeping bag.

"Could you unfold the sleeping bag for me?" asked Dillan, pulling out a narrow tube from the inside pocket of his jacket.

The detective laid out Santilli's red sleeping bag on the floor. "Is that an ultraviolet light?"

"Yes, it'll make most dried liquids stand out. Could you turn off the lights, please?"

The detective walked to the far end of the room. A loud clack echoed off the walls as the room went black. The detective used his cell phone as a flashlight to find his way back. He crouched next to Dillan and switched off his phone.

A purple glow engulfed the sleeping bag. Dillan moved the UV light from the top of the bag to the wider shoulder area, then all the way to the bottom. Nothing. He carefully flipped over the bag and examined the underside. Still nothing. The detective unzipped the bag and opened it up. Starting with the head area, the doctor inspected the inside of the bag. Halfway down, he stopped. Detective Tramonte moved closer to get a better look at the circular stain now visible in the center of the bag. "What's that?"

Dillan leaned forward and took a whiff. "Urine."

"Is that important?"

"It could be."

They scrutinized Santilli's sleeping pad, leather boots, gloves, wool toque, Gore-Tex jacket, and knapsack. Dillan spotted a few small stains, but nothing out of the ordinary. He inspected the flysheet and guy lines before turning his attention to the tent itself. That was when he noticed the small spots on the floor right inside the zippered entrance. "Could you hand me your flashlight, Detective—your smartphone?"

Dillan's eyes took a few seconds to adjust to the light, but there was no mistaking the dried blood inside the tent door. The detective came in closer.

"Santilli was already bleeding when she left the tent," he said.

"It would appear so…" The doctor wanted to tell the detective what was going through his mind but was worried about the consequences of doing so, especially for Santilli's son.

CHAPTER 11

The sun was low on the horizon. Dillan leaned against the back wall of the police station, trying to make sense of everything he had seen and heard since stepping off the plane in Venice some twenty-four hours earlier.

"Where to?" Detective Tramonte asked as the door behind him clacked shut.

Dillan had come to a decision. "Is there somewhere quiet we can go to talk?"

* * *

The tomato-basil bruschetta was simple but packed a mouthful of flavors. Dillan washed it down with a sip of wine. "What did you say this was again?"

"Teroldego. The vineyard is just up the road."

Dillan looked directly at the detective for several seconds. "I have something to tell you," he finally said. "I think Santilli may have been strangled."

Detective Tramonte narrowed his eyes. "Strangled?"

"The pictures taken at the scene and the stain in her sleeping bag support the idea of strangulation."

"Strangulation can cause involuntary urination," Tramonte said, "but there weren't any rope-like burns on Santilli's neck in any of the pictures we saw."

Dillan nodded. "I was thinking about manual strangulation. There were faint marks on her neck consistent with head-on strangulation. One of the imprints—I'm guessing from the aggressor's thumb—was right over Santilli's throat. Probably crushed her larynx."

Tramonte leaned forward. "You think the boy did it?"

"No, although I'm convinced he's not telling us everything. Whoever tried to strangle Santilli had to be very strong and must have done it while she was still in her sleeping bag. Santilli could have been injured while fending off the attacker. That would explain the blood stains we found inside her tent."

"There was nothing about strangulation or throat injuries in the coroner's report," Tramonte said. "Why didn't you mention this to the captain?"

"Because we have no evidence of an assailant, and I didn't want to risk incriminating the boy."

The detective stared down at his glass. "Reminds me of a story my dad told me around a campfire when I was a kid. He often told us stories after day hikes, usually to scare us. The strange thing about this story is that, even when I got older, my dad always insisted it had really happened. But I never believed him."

Dillan wasn't sure where the detective was going with this. "Is your father still alive?"

"Yes, but he's not well. He has Alzheimer's."

"I'm sorry to hear that."

There was a moment of silence. The detective glanced at his watch. "We should go talk to him."

* * *

The Casa di Cura was a thirty-minute drive away, ample time for Detective Tramonte to share the story his father had told him when he was a child.

The detective showed Dillan a picture of his father, Domenico Tramonte, as a young man decked out in climbing gear, and explained how his dad had volunteered a great deal of time to the Club Alpino Italiano, one of the world's oldest alpine societies. In addition to teaching mountaineering and taking care of the mountain huts owned by the Club Alpino, the detective's father had been a member of an elite corps specializing in mountain rescue.

Dillan understood the detective's need to present his father as he once had been: strong and courageous. That image was needed to offset the reality Dillan was about to witness: an older and, more importantly, brain-impaired man.

"When I was a young boy," continued the detective, "my dad worked in several *rifugios* in the Dolomites. One morning, before the sun had come up, he was woken up by a man yelling for help outside the mountain hut. The man was holding the body of his seven-year-old daughter in his arms. The girl was white as a ghost and gasping, and her mouth was covered in blood. The man had carried her in a desperate run all the way from their campsite. My dad took the girl inside and administered first aid. The man said he had been woken up in the middle of the night by his daughter's moaning—moaning that turned into choking. He tried to get the girl to sit up but could not wake her." The detective paused as he maneuvered his car through the main entrance of the nursing home.

Dillan remained silent, waiting for the rest of the story. The car came to a stop; the detective cut the ignition.

"When the man turned on his lantern, he saw his daughter was coughing blood and struggling to breathe. He took her out of her sleeping bag and noticed the girl had wet herself. He wrapped her in a blanket and took her to the *rifugio* as fast as he could."

The men sat in silence, a silence neither was in a rush to break, as they tried to grasp the meaning of the links—if links existed—between this story and Santilli's.

"What happened to the girl?" Dillan asked finally.

"She was transported to a hospital in the valley. My dad told me there were marks around her neck, as if she had been strangled. The girl survived but could not speak for days. My dad was convinced that the father, a man well respected by the locals, would never have hurt his daughter." The detective stared down at his empty hands. "He believed something he could not explain happened up in the mountains that night—something evil. And that something wanted the girl dead."

CHAPTER 12

A series of command prompts flashed across the screen. Although she felt a little rusty, Liz didn't miss a beat. Her eyes glued to the prompts and her fingertips ready to fire again, she dispatched a series of keystroke commands into the network. Minutes later, she was almost finished looking into what Dillan had asked, and then some. She closed one window, logged out of her anonymous account, and reverted back to typing in Linux terminal code. Almost immediately, the stolen files were forwarded to a secured server for retrieval through a secondary laptop.

Coroner Giuseppe Rossi's report on Santilli's death was brief. A copy and paste into Google Translate gave her a rough idea of its contents. Damage to subcutaneous tissue, compound fracture of the left tibia, two rib fractures, broken metacarpals. Injuries sustained during a fall down a rocky escarpment. Cause of death: exposure and internal bleeding.

Nothing appeared out of the ordinary given the events described and the pictures that accompanied the report. Nothing except Coroner Rossi himself. Liz had conducted a thorough search through public and private registries of accredited coroners. The name Giuseppe Rossi didn't figure in any of them.

It was almost two in the morning, and Liz would need to be back at the lab in a few hours. It was time to call it a night. She lay in bed, hoping to catch some sleep, but her brain wouldn't shut down. A far-fetched idea crept into her mind. She tried to ignore it, but the thought endured, like an itch in need of a scratch. She got out of bed.

Liz turned on two of her laptops and took a cyber shot in the dark. Her first log-in attempts missed the mark, but persistence and craftiness finally gained her unlawful access to an encrypted database. She had hit pay-dirt. Doctor Giuseppe Rossi was indeed a legitimate coroner, just not one that belonged to Italy's national registry.

Her illicit unraveling of digital information sent a rush of adrenaline through her veins. She poked her virtual nose further into the database. Her scripts uncovered dozens of documents referring to Giancarla Santilli, G. Santilli, and simply Santilli. Judging from its title, one file appeared to be a copy of the coroner's report she had retrieved earlier from a server belonging to the Polizia della Provincia Autonoma di Trento—except this file was over a hundred times larger than the one she had downloaded from the Trento police. She parceled the folder into smaller units, rerouted them to a directory on the Anonymous network, and covered up the digital footprints of her unlawful passage.

One laptop executed an additional set of commands, and a new directory containing the filched materials appeared on her screen. Liz clicked on the folder.

First up was the coroner's report. *What the hell?* This couldn't be right. She went through the entire file but still couldn't believe her eyes. She opened the dozens of digital pictures accounting for the folder's bloated size. She was flabbergasted. The shots she had retrieved from the Trento police system had been tampered with. Not only that, but many of the pictures hadn't been forwarded to the police, including several that were almost too harrowing to look at. Liz examined the close-up shots of the woman's mangled fingers, her bare frozen foot, the bloodied snowballs... What had James gotten himself into?

CHAPTER 13

Soft music played in the background while the two wall-mounted televisions played different stations. Some of the residents watched the screens; others stared at nothing. At one end of the room, a group of gray-haired men and women sat around a table, carrying on a lively conversation. A male orderly wearing matching off-white pants and shirt emerged from a side room, wheeling a fragile-looking woman toward the opposite end of the common sitting area. He noticed the detective standing by the entrance and motioned with his head toward the private rooms off the main hall. Detective Tramonte nodded a telegraphic thank-you and headed toward his father's room.

"Best you wait by the door," he told Dillan. "My father sometimes gets nervous around people he doesn't know."

The detective knocked on the door and walked into the unadorned room. Domenico Tramonte was sitting in a chair in the corner, holding a magazine. He was smiling but seemed only partially aware that the person standing before him was his son. The detective pulled up a chair and caressed the top of his dad's balding pate, where a once-thick mane of dark curly hair had receded into a thin band of gray frizz. The man's upper torso, however, had retained much of its muscular broadness, and he looked hearty and hale. Detective Tramonte patted his father's hand and spoke quietly to him. The elderly man's expression lit up as he appeared to recognize the familiar man sitting in front of him.

"You can come in," the detective said.

Domenico Tramonte's eyes followed Dillan as he made his way inside.

"He used to remember all kinds of things, especially from when I was a kid, but now those days are getting rarer."

Domenico Tramonte looked restless and he changed positions in his chair. His gaze, however, remained locked on Dillan.

"Would you mind putting on some music for him?" the detective whispered. "There's a CD player behind you. Music calms him and sometimes even clears his mind a little."

Dillan stared at the pile of Italian CDs on the table beside him. "Anything in particular?"

"There should be some by Adriano Celentano."

"The one of his hits?"

"That's perfect. When I was growing up, my dad used to sing these songs to us in the car, even though everyone but him thought his voice was terrible. I often joined in, and it sort of became a tradition."

Detective Tramonte said a few words to his father, knelt in front of him, taking both his hands in his own, and signaled for Dillan to hit "play." Celentano's catchy "Coppia piu bella del mondo" came on, and Domenico Tramonte started to smile. By the time the song ended, Domenico was asking his son how he was, and as he often did in error, why he hadn't come to visit him in such a long time.

As the detective explained to his dad that he had been there a few days earlier, the opening trombone sequence of Celentano's famed "Azzurro" pulsed out of the music player. Domenico's eyes lit up as soon as the first stanza began.

Domenico Tramonte looked happy as he and his son sang the refrain.

Dillan was moved but couldn't help thinking that the detective's father wasn't the only one in the family with a less than stellar voice.

As the waning notes of a ukulele announced the song's end, the father and son duo let out a collective cheer. Dillan turned down the volume of the CD, but let the music play on.

"*Riccardo! Che bello!*" the detective's father exclaimed.

Detective Tramonte smiled and introduced his father to the *dottore*.

Domenico took a long, inquisitive look at Dillan then whispered something to his son.

The detective smiled. "He says he's glad you're here, that you're a good man."

The elder Tramonte asked his son to repeat the man's name. His face turned solemn. He pulled his son close and murmured again. The detective appeared saddened by what his father told him.

"What is it?" Dillan asked.

"Nothing, he's confused. Keeps saying that he knows you, that you're a good man."

Even on his bad days, nothing lifted Domenico Tramonte's spirits like talking about his exploits in the Dolomites or reminiscing about his treks with his son. And this time, to the detective's relief, was no exception. A few well-planted questions and cues brought a smile to the man's face as he launched into his familiar stories. The detective waited for the right moment before asking his dad to tell him the story of the strangled girl.

Domenico began his tale as he always did, with how the sounds of a man yelling outside the mountain hut woke him one cold September morning. Domenico spoke as much with words and changing intonations as he did with his hands. Having picked up some rudimentary Italian, Dillan was able to follow the story's broad lines.

After his dad had finished recounting the events of that night, the detective asked him about the young girl and what had happened to her later. Domenico shook his head and gave a long, forceful explanation.

"He says the girl tried to speak to him but couldn't say anything. Her throat was injured and she had trouble swallowing the warm drink my dad gave her. A nurse at the hospital later told him the girl wasn't able to speak for several more days and that when she did, she could only whisper."

"Ask him if he knows what became of the girl."

The detective was listening to his father's answer, but his face grew sad again. "He's lost in his fantasies about the mountains."

"Do you mind telling me what he said?"

"He said the girl was taken away by some church people and schooled by a high priest. When the priest thought the girl was ready, he took her to the Himalayas, to Tibet, where she entered a monastery to be mentored by a monk ... a blind Tibetan monk..." Tramonte trailed off, his tone pained. "I'm sorry I brought you here. I don't know what I was hoping for. My dad is not well."

He kissed his father on the forehead and promised he would be back the next day. The elder Tramonte didn't seem to find solace in his son's words and pleaded for him to stay.

The detective was about to leave when Dillan said, "Did your dad ever find out the girl's name?"

Detective Tramonte hesitated.

"Please."

The detective walked back to his father's side and asked him, *"Papà, ti ricordi il nome della bambina..."*

Domenico Tramonte told his son that he did know the girl's name but was drawing a blank. He frowned and seemed frustrated at not being able to remember, but after a moment, his facial muscles relaxed into a quiet, empty stare.

"Now can we go?" the detective said.

"Of course. Thanks for trying. I know seeing your dad like this must be hard."

Detective Tramonte was about to get up when his father gripped his arm. *"Mi ricordo!"* he blurted. *"Santilli ... Giancarla Santilli."*

Dillan and the detective stared at each other.

Domenico Tramonte motioned for Dillan to come closer. He reached out, touched Dillan's cheek, and examined his face, as if piecing together a puzzle. The elder Tramonte smiled, turned to his son, and asked him a simple question. "*Riccardo perché non mi hai detto che avevi un amicizia con il dottore del sonno?*"

Dillan was bewildered. Even with his limited Italian, he had understood what the elder Tramonte asked his son. "*Riccardo, why didn't you tell me you were friends with the sleep doctor?*"

CHAPTER 14

The electronics store where Dillan had asked the detective to drop him off was a few blocks away from Michael's place. A short while later, he walked out of the store with a new cell phone in hand. He was standing on the stoop, texting Liz a quick message, when a deep, motorized purr drew his attention. On the opposite side of the street, a stylish car—its tinted windows blending with the sleek black exterior—hummed and pulled over up ahead.

As Dillan looked on, the driver—a tank of a man, decked out in a black-and-white uniform—stepped out. The chauffeur walked over to the opposite side of the car and opened the rear door. When Dillan saw who emerged from the car, he pressed himself against the side of the building. Nervous, he watched Michael exchange words with the driver. The chauffeur got back into the car and drove off. Dillan kept his eyes on Michael as his friend walked down the street, rounded a corner, and disappeared from view.

The doctor couldn't make sense of what he had seen. Was his friend in some kind of trouble? The idea that Michael might have owed money to the wrong crowd popped to mind but seemed improbable. He looked at his new cell and finished writing to Liz. *All OK, need 2 talk soon. Thanks for everything. Really miss u.* He stared at the text, overthinking the ways it could be interpreted. He deleted the last three words and hit "send."

* * *

"It's open!" Dillan heard Michael say after he had knocked on the door. Michael was sitting on the black leather couch, drink in hand.

"That was a long day," Michael said. He pointed to a scotch glass on the coffee table. "I poured you a drink."

Dillan made his way to the living room. "Thanks, but I think I'll pass."

"Oh, come on. I got us some Lagavulin. Used to be your favorite, right?"

"Still is." Dillan sat at the other end of the couch and looked at his friend. Michael's face was pale, almost sickly.

"To the good old days," Michael said, raising his glass.

Dillan joined him in the toast.

"And if not always good, then certainly simpler," Michael added before finishing off his scotch.

Dillan took another sip of his drink and returned his glass to the coffee table.

"So, how did it go?" Michael asked.

"Okay, I guess. Met Battista and some other people working on the case. Also got to speak to Santilli's son, but can't say we're much further ahead."

"How's the boy? Is he holding up all right?"

"I think he's doing okay under the circumstances. He basically repeated what he had already told the investigators."

"What about Santilli? Anything new?"

"Not really. We're supposed to go over the evidence again in the morning."

Michael appeared lost in thought, then he said, "I have an early meeting tomorrow, so unless you want to head out at six, I won't be able to drive you."

"No worries, I'll grab a cab."

* * *

Dillan was sitting on his bed with his laptop. A wave of trepidation rolled through him as he launched his browser. The very idea that someone was tracking his every keystroke was disconcerting. He opened his Gmail, trying to navigate what he saw. Liz, as promised, had cleaned out his mailboxes and reorganized his main directory. He opened the phony email she had sent him from a bogus account and wrote back an equally staged reply. Next up were a handful of genuine emails Liz had left in for show: a request to review a research article for a medical journal, a question from one of his lab technicians, and a few personal but unrevealing missives from friends and colleagues. He answered a couple of them as naturally as he could until a wave of uncontrollable sleepiness washed over him.

CHAPTER 15

T he park was dark and desolate. Dillan walked down the un-
paved trail and headed toward the only source of light.
Perched in a tree and visible through a thick tangle of branches
was an old metal lantern. Right beneath it, in the golden glow, was
a bench. Dillan sat down. The wood was cold, and the damp penetrated the backs of his legs. Wind whistled through the treetops.
It dawned on him that he might not be able to find his way back
to Michael's apartment.

Dillan saw something move by his feet. He leaned forward, intrigued, and watched a swarm of small shadows swirling on the
ground, their movements rapid and intricate, like a dance. He
gazed up as a gust of wind sent the leaves under the lantern into a
new, more frantic choreography that was matched by their twin
shadows below.

A twig snapped, splitting the park's silence. Dillan froze. Someone or something was making its way through the bushes.

He scanned the vegetation nearby, but the shapes merged into
blackness. Silence returned. Dillan got up and hurried back up the
trail. As he came to a turn, he glanced over his shoulder. A human
silhouette was emerging from the woods. He broke into a sprint.

"Doctor Dillan! Doctor Dillan!" a voice called out. But Dillan was
too caught up in his flight to make out the rest of the man's words.
He leapt off the path and darted behind a tree.

His pursuer was walking in his direction. "Doctor ... it's me."

The voice was familiar, but Dillan couldn't place it. He took a cautious step away from the tree. The man, now only a few feet in front of him, had stopped and was looking around, his back to the doctor. "Victor?" Dillan whispered.

Victor turned and let out a sigh of relief. "Thank God you're still here. I thought I'd lost you."

"What are you doing here?"

"There are things I need to tell you. I know why they went after Santilli. They're looking for a vase. An old vase, rather large, and with a family crest on it. They called it the Lost Cellini. You need to find out about it. That's what they're after."

Dillan's breathing quickened. "How do you know about Santilli?"

"That doesn't matter. What matters is that you find the vase before they do."

"Who are *they*?"

"It's hard to know who's out there now, but I think they're planning to go after Santilli's boy next. You can't let anything happen to him. He's waiting to help you."

Dillan moved closer to his friend. "How do you know this?"

"I overheard a man talking to someone I know, someone I've been keeping tabs on for a while now. There's no doubt they were involved in Santilli's death."

"What are you talking about?"

"Last night, I recognized an old man walking with a cane on the street, and I followed him into a bar. He sat at the counter, right next to the guy I've been keeping an eye on. I stayed close and listened in. I was careful. They never even realized I was there. I heard them talk about Santilli, about how she died, about the boy and the vase."

"How did she die?"

"I don't know the details. She was forced to jump."

Dillan thought he heard something behind him. He whirled around but saw nothing.

"Don't worry, we're alone," Victor said.

"How did you find me?"

"Never mind that, Doctor. I came here to help, to tell you what I know, what I heard the men say at the bar."

"You said you've been keeping an eye on one of the men. Who is he?"

"His name is Kohler."

Dillan felt sick. "Kohler?"

"Yes, Michael Kohler."

"Tall, thin guy?"

"Yes."

"You're sure it was him?"

"I was only a few feet away from him at the bar, with only one guy between us—some drunken fellow in a big black cowboy hat. Trust me, it was him."

"You're telling me Michael was involved in Santilli's death?"

"I know for a fact he was."

Dillan put his hand on the tree to steady himself.

"Listen to me, Doctor, you can't let yourself get bogged down in details. The Lost Cellini, the vase, that's the key. You have to find it, and soon. The boy will help you."

CHAPTER 16

A ray of light peeked into the bedroom through the gap between the curtains. Dillan opened an eyelid. All was quiet. The digital clock read 9:15. Was it possible he had slept that long? He felt hungover. His head hurt, as did the back of his neck. He reached for his cell phone and double-checked the time. A text message from Liz was waiting for him. *Urgent. U r being lied to.*

Dillan put on a bathrobe and lumbered into the kitchen. A handwritten note was taped to the espresso machine.

Bonjour, James. Hope you had a good night's sleep. Java is ready to go. Back late tonight. Call if you need anything. Michael.

Dillan called Detective Tramonte and left a message saying he was running late. He needed a quick breakfast: cereal and a dose of caffeine would do the trick.

He opened a cupboard, looking for a bowl, when a familiar object caught his attention. Standing out from the back of the top shelf was the yellow rim of a large mug. Dillan reached up and pulled out the oversized porcelain cup with *McGill T-House* written across it in green psychedelic letters. Dillan had owned the same mug back in his university days, although his had met an unfortunate end on some ceramic tiles. He glanced inside it. At the bottom of the mug lay a thick brass key.

Dillan tilted the mug toward him and let the key slide into the palm of his hand. Nothing in the kitchen seemed to need a key. He gave the living room a once-over, but nothing was a match either. He was about to drop the key into the mug when he remembered Victor's words from the previous night—the sinuous path, the bench, the lantern, the shadows. Dillan stood still, encouraging the torrent of memories pouring back into his mind.

He took the key, walked into Michael's room, and opened the chest of drawers, looking and poking inside them one by one. The antique two-door armoire was next. He pulled on the two wooden knobs, but the doors wouldn't open. He tugged harder, but there was still no give. He examined the cast iron hinges running down the sides of the doors and tried turning, sliding, and even pushing the unyielding knobs.

Dillan turned his attention to the nightstands on either side of the bed. One contained a pile of books, the other magazines, topped by a small headlamp. Resting vertically against the stack of magazines was a folded sheet of paper. He took it out. It was a list, handwritten by Michael, detailing all kinds of information about his ex: place and date of birth, name of her parents and their origins, where and how he and Stefania first met, the date they got engaged, her work history. Puzzled, Dillan put the sheet back in its place and stared at the large cabinet.

He pulled a chair from the corner of the room, stepped onto it, and inspected the top of the armoire. Right near the front was a slat nestled between identically colored neighbors. The slat was not whole, however; it was made up of two separate sections that met in the middle of the armoire, with the telltale junction point lying right under Dillan's nose. He pressed his fingers down on either side of the junction mark and slid the two sections apart. The beams glided away from each other, and he found what he was looking for—a brass metal slot. The key was a perfect fit.

After a clockwise half turn, the inside of the armoire gave a muffled clap. He jumped off the chair, wrapped his fingers around the knobs, and pulled. The doors creaked open.

Inside were five shelves, each holding a row of books bound in soft black leather. Across the spine of each book, the year was handwritten in white ink. The volumes were organized in chronological order, beginning on the left side of the bottom shelf and progressing to the right and then moving up to the next shelf, time flowing horizontally as well as vertically.

Dillan was dumbfounded. Although the collection had grown considerably since the last time he had laid eyes on it, the books were familiar to him. Long ago, he had even been invited to skim through one of the volumes. These were Michael's dream diaries. It was clear his friend had lied to him; he'd been keeping his precious diary all along.

Dillan pulled out the most recent volume and flipped to the last entry. That dream had been transcribed mere days ago. He started to read a few lines, but nerves got the best of him. It was time to go. But first, he needed to take some pictures.

Dillan was snapping quick shots of some of the pages with his cell phone when he heard somebody come into the apartment.

His heart raced. He put the book back inside and closed the armoire. How was he going to explain this to Michael?

He took a steadying breath and stepped out of the bedroom. A woman was in the hallway, holding a bucket filled with cleaning products in one hand and a pair of yellow rubber gloves in the other. "*Sono un amico di Michael,*" he explained in his accented Italian. The cleaning lady, visibly surprised by the presence of an unknown man before her, appeared to have understood, and he, in turn, caught the essence of her reply: that in the five years she had been coming to the apartment, she had never seen anyone other than *il signor* Kohler. She smiled, tilted her bucket ahead of her, pointing to the kitchen.

"*Si, si,*" Dillan said, motioning her to go on in.

He waited for her to disappear into the kitchen before stepping back into Michael's bedroom. He nudged the door shut behind him, got back on the chair, and maneuvered the key inside the hidden slot. With a muffled click, the doors locked.

His work wasn't done, though. He went to the kitchen, removed the portafilter basket from the espresso machine, dumped the coffee grounds into the trash, and started to prepare another shot of espresso. The tactic worked. The cleaning lady gave him a polite smile—one that failed to mask her annoyance—and moved to the washroom. Dillan took the oversized mug, put the key back inside, and lifted it back to where he had found it.

CHAPTER 17

The late-morning traffic wasn't all that bad, but that didn't prevent the taxi driver from weaving in and out of the lanes every chance he got. Dillan tried to relax as he went over his options before arriving at the police station. He knew what he was going to tell Detective Tramonte but was still unsure about the best way to approach Vincente. And he still had made little sense of what Victor had told him. He wished he had someone to bounce ideas off, someone who could offer him a fresh view of the evidence, someone he trusted. He wished Liz was there.

He took out his cell to send her a note and noticed that her last message had included a link. He clicked on it. The web page showed a single line of text with an empty text box below it. The line was the kind of question Liz was fond of including to protect Dillan's more sensitive electronic documents. He smiled as he read: *lightning's number + cap initials LPJD fave NFL teams.*

Dillan went through the items: the favorite number of Liz—known to some of her older online friends as Lightning Liz from her days as a hacker—was 7; and their two respective favorite teams in the National Football League were the Denver Broncos and the Green Bay Packers. Dillan typed in the final result: 7DBGBP.

A series of pictures appeared on screen. Dillan stared at his phone in disbelief. None of the pictures Liz had sent him had been in the file given to him by Captain Battista. Close-up pictures of Santilli's face, of a bare, frozen foot, of a small multitool lying by her body, of a silver chain dangling from her hand. The cab pulled to a stop in front of the police station.

* * *

"Buongiorno Dottore," Detective Tramonte said as Dillan walked into his office.

"Sorry for being late."

"I got your message. Take a look at this." He handed Dillan an eight-by-ten-inch picture. "You see the boulder off to the right of Santilli's tent? See how it leans to the side? The two small bulges on top? I recognize that boulder."

"From where?"

"A few years after my dad told me the story of the strangled girl—that's what he called it—he took me to the place where the girl and her father had been camping that night. About two hundred meters away from the trail was a large boulder. That's where they had pitched their tent. He then showed me something remarkable. On the top side of the boulder, embedded right in the rock, was a giant, heart-shaped tooth. It was from a megalodon, a prehistoric shark. I stared at it for a long time trying to understand how the mountains had once been underwater." Tramonte tapped the top edge of the picture with his finger. "This is the same boulder. I'm sure of it. Santilli set up her tent at the exact same place where she almost died as a kid."

"Why go back there now—and with her son?"

"I've been asking myself the same question. I think she was scared something might happen to Vincente. That's why she had him sleep away from her and why she headed up there with two tents to begin with."

"That's certainly plausible," Dillan said.

Tramonte got up to close the door. "There's something else, *Dottore.* There are things about the case that we haven't told you," he said, walking back to his chair. "Information I'm not supposed to share."

"I'm a guest here, Detective. I understand if there are things I'm not meant to know."

"That's the thing, *Dottore*. I think you should know about this. There is more to this case than you know, and probably more than I know as well."

"What do you mean?"

"Santilli may have had some very valuable art. Are you familiar with the works of Cellini?"

Cellini. That was the name Victor had mentioned. "Yes, vaguely," Dillan replied.

"I didn't know much about him before this case. He was one of Italy's greatest artists during the Renaissance. Did you ever see the bronze sculpture of Perseus holding the severed head of the Medusa? It's in the Piazza della Signoria in Florence."

"I've seen pictures of it."

"That's by Cellini. Today, any of his works would be priceless. Santilli's father was a lawyer. It's thought he received some art for representing a client who didn't have the money to pay him. We have reason to believe that at least one of the pieces may have been by Cellini. We don't know any of this for sure, but Santilli would have inherited these works when her father died."

"Do you know if she was aware of their origins?"

"I wasn't told, but I wouldn't think so. Santilli worked as a translator and lived a modest life. We don't think she ever tried to sell any of the works, and she didn't live like she knew she owned a treasure. But others may have known."

"Others?"

"One theory the captain mentioned is that Vincente knew about the Cellini and was involved in his mother's death. I don't think so myself, *Dottore*, but the possibility is being considered. Nobody seems to know where the artwork might be, but anything by Cellini would be worth a fortune—in the millions of euros. That's why Director Montella is here. These are national treasures."

"I appreciate you sharing this with me, Detective."

"There's something else I need to show you. I stopped to check up on my dad this morning. I found this on his dresser." He handed Dillan a four-by-six photograph.

Dillan fell silent as he eyed the picture. It showed Giancarla Santilli with Dillan standing to her right and Michael to her left. "This was taken at the conference where Michael introduced me to Santilli," he explained. "How did your father get it?"

"Santilli gave it to him a few weeks ago. That's how my dad recognized you. And according to the orderly I spoke to, that wasn't the first time she had gone to see him. My dad didn't remember much about her visits. Only that Santilli told him that you were a good and important man, and that he needed to help you."

"Help me with what?"

"He wasn't sure."

There was a quick knock. An officer poked his head into the room. "*Il bambino e pronto,*" he said to the detective.

"*Va bene,*" Detective Tramonte answered before turning to Dillan. "We're set to meet with Vincente again."

* * *

The air in the makeshift interrogation room still smelled of old books. Vincente was sitting quietly at the same table, his shoulders drooping, his eyes bloodshot.

Dillan sat down in front of him while the detective remained standing near the wall.

"How are you?" Dillan asked, turning on the digital recorder on the table.

"Tired."

"I can't pretend to understand what you're going through, Vincente, but I know it must be hard. I want to help. That's why I'm here. But I can't do it without you. Do you think you can help me as well?"

Vincente gave Dillan a long stare. "Yes."

"Last night Detective Tramonte and I went to visit his father, Domenico Tramonte. Does the name mean anything to you?"

"No."

"It seems your mother knew Domenico Tramonte quite well. According to an orderly we spoke to, she visited him at his nursing home a couple of weeks before your trip, and that wasn't the first time your mom had gone to see him."

The boy looked at Detective Tramonte. "I don't know anything about the detective's father, honest."

"I believe you," Dillan said. "There's another thing I was hoping you might be able to help us with." He took a photograph out of his shirt pocket. "On one of her visits to the nursing home, your mom left this picture with the detective's father. It shows your mom standing between two men, and it seems she went out of her way to make sure Domenico Tramonte understood who these two men were." He handed the picture to the boy. "Do you recognize them?"

"That's you on the right."

"What about the other man? Do you know who he is?"

"Yes." Vincente looked up at Dillan. "His name is Kohler. He's some kind of psychologist."

"How do you know him?"

"My mom ran into him in a store once. She introduced us."

"What else can you tell me about him?"

"I think he works at the university. My mom went to see him to talk about dreams."

"Your mom told you this herself?"

"Yes."

"Did she ever mention what they talked about?"

"All she told me was that Kohler knew a lot about dreams."

"This picture was taken at the conference I mentioned to you yesterday. It's the only time your mother, Kohler, and I were ever together. Do you have any idea why your mom would want to leave this picture with the detective's father?"

Vincente rubbed his hands down his pant legs then stared at the doctor. "Mama showed me the same picture. She told me to memorize your names and what you and Kohler looked like. She said that ... that if you ever showed up, it would be because something bad had happened to her." He brushed a finger over one of his eyes.

Dillan glanced over at the detective as he handed the boy a tissue. "This is helpful, Vincente. Is it okay if we go on?"

The boy wiped his nose. "Yes."

"I only met your mom once, so I'm trying to understand why she thought I would show up if something ever happened to her."

"She told me I could trust you ... and that you would help me."

Dillan extended his hand but kept it short of the boy's fingers. "What about Kohler? Did she tell you anything about him?"

Vincente glanced over at Detective Tramonte. "I can't say."

"It's okay. You can trust Detective Tramonte."

Vincente shook his head.

Dillan looked up at the detective. "You think you could give us a moment?"

Detective Tramonte appeared uncertain. "I'm sorry, *Dottore*, but I cannot leave you alone with Vincente." He softly walked to the table and paused the recorder. "Two minutes," he whispered.

The detective walked out of earshot.

Dillan closed his fingers over the boy's hand. "We don't have much time," he said. "I need you to tell me as much as you can, starting with what you know about Kohler."

"I don't know much more. Mama told me never to trust him, that he was smart and dangerous."

"I know Kohler from when we were both university students. He's the one who called me to come and help with the case. But I think your mom may have been right about him."

"I hope my mom was right about you too." Vincente squeezed Dillan's hand.

"You mean about trusting me?"

"Mama told me other things about you."

"Like what?"

"I can't tell you. Not yet."

Dillan considered pressing the issue but decided against it. "Did your mom ever talk to you about the detective's father, Domenico Tramonte, or about the detective himself?"

"No."

"So you don't have any reason to mistrust the detective."

"No."

"What can you tell me about the Cellini?"

Vincente wrinkled his face. "You know about it?"

"Very little."

"I don't know where it is."

"Is that why your mom was taking you to the mountains? To show you where it was?"

"No. She wanted to give me a special book."

"And this book was somewhere in the Dolomites?"

Vincente nodded.

"Do you know what it's about?"

Vincente looked Dillan in the eye and whispered, "A dream world that lies beyond this one."

For an instant, Dillan considered the possibility that the boy was psychologically unfit, or worse, that he'd been indoctrinated by some kind of sect. "What about the Cellini? Why is it so important to find it? I mean, aside from whatever it might be worth?"

"There's something powerful inside it."

"Do you know what it is?"

The boy looked unsure.

"Tell me, Vincente, have you ever seen the Cellini?"

The boy shook his head.

"But you're sure it exists?"

"Yes."

"And what does it look like?"

"It's a vase. It has two large handles on it. Each one is shaped like a screaming face. On the front is the family crest of the Medici."

Dillan was reeling. He closed his eyes and ran his fingertips over his forehead. *Victor was right about the vase. What if he was right about everything else?*

"Do you think you might be in any danger?"

Vincente looked concerned, as if he'd never stopped to think about it till now. "I don't know ... maybe."

"Who would want to hurt you? Kohler?"

"I don't know."

"Okay. Why were your tents set up so far apart?"

"Mama said we had to sleep away from each other. I didn't want to, but she insisted. She said it'd be dangerous for me if we didn't."

"In what way?"

"She didn't tell me. She promised she'd explain things on our way back."

"Was your mom wearing any kind of jewelry that day, like a ring or bracelet?"

"She had a silver chain on her neck. She always wore it."

"Was there anything attached to it?"

"A medallion of Sant'Antonio holding baby Jesus."

Dillan furrowed his brow. "Saint Anthony? Do you know where she got it or what it meant to her?"

"A priest gave it to her when she was little. It's a reminder that God looks over His children."

"Do you happen to know the priest's name or where he lived?"

"No."

"Anything else she may have been carrying with her that night? Maybe in her hand or pocket?"

"A headlamp maybe. And her multitool. She always had it on her when hiking, usually in the side pocket of her pants."

"That's very helpful. Anything else you can think of?"

"The helicopters ... they weren't normal rescue helicopters."

"What do you mean?"

"They were all black."

"There was more than one?"

"There were two. One landed near me, and the other went down below the cliff."

"Did the people in your helicopter tell you they had found your mom?"

"They were still looking for her."

"Okay. Anything else?"

"I lied about the cell phone. Mama left it outside my tent, along with this." Vincente reached into the front pocket of his pants and pulled out something between his fingers. It was a small double-sided card holder made of clear, soft plastic. The boy held it out for Dillan to see. Tucked into one side was a short, thick silver key. Vincente twirled the holder in his fingers, showing Dillan the other side. Pressed behind the plastic was an edelweiss.

"She'd always take this out before telling me the story of the Monti Pallidi. She'd let me hold it on my chest."

"Do you know what the key is for?"

"She said that one day it would help open my eyes, and that this flower was the granddaughter of the first edelweiss. She also wrote something in the snow. I never told the police about it," Vincente said, catching the detective's gaze for a moment. "When I didn't see her anywhere, I stomped all over it."

Dillan leaned close to the boy. "What did she write?"

"The letters *D* and *T*."

"Do you know what they stand for?"

The boy shook his head. "She wrote something else," he said. "Closer to the tent. *Due beni.*"

"Two loves?"

"It's something she often said before putting me to bed. It means her love for me, and my love for her..." Vincente bit at his lower lip.

"It's okay," Dillan said.

The boy looked up at the doctor, his eyes welling. "I ... I keep seeing these pictures in my head. They scare me, but I can't make them stop."

"If you think talking about it might help. I'm here for you."

"It can't be, Doctor. What I see in my head, it couldn't have happened."

Dillan remained silent, waiting for the boy to gather his thoughts.

"I see myself going into her tent. I can still hear the zipper as I pull it open. But there's something else, another picture. I'm ... I'm standing over my mom. She looks panicked. It's me ... my hands are around her neck ... I'm the one strangling her."

There was a knock at the door. Dillan quickly hit the "record" button. "I understand, Detective," he pressed to say.

Then came a second, more forceful knock.

"*Un momento!*" Detective Tramonte said before opening the door. Standing before him was an officer. They exchanged a few words, after which the detective turned toward Dillan and Vincente. "I'm sorry, but I've been called to a meeting. We're going to have to stop here for now. Is there anything you wanted to add, Vincente?"

"Will I see you again?" he asked.

"Of course," Detective Tramonte said. "Both of us. I promise."

The boy looked at Dillan. "Please come back soon."

CHAPTER 18

T he wind gusting behind the police station was unseasonably cold, but the path there was the safest place within walking distance for Dillan and Detective Tramonte to talk.

"Santilli had to know what she was doing," the detective said, stuffing his hands into his coat pockets as he headed down the trail. "She took the time to leave her phone by the boy's tent and write those words in the snow. She could not have been fighting anyone off. So how do we explain the blood and marks on her neck?"

"I don't know, Detective. The more clues we find, the bigger the puzzle becomes."

Detective Tramonte looked pensive. "Any idea what the letters 'DT' might stand for?"

Dillan gave a half-smile. "Maybe he wanted to make sure you were called in on the case. You *are* Detective Tramonte."

The expression on the detective's face remained serious. "Maybe not me," he countered, "but those are my father's initials." He paused. "Santilli went out of her way to show my father and Vincente that picture, but how could she be sure you would come? The only person linking the two of you is Kohler. Santilli had to know that Kohler would call you if something happened to her and that you would come. And how could she know you would meet my father? It doesn't make sense."

Dillan had considered the same riddle but was no closer to an answer than was the detective.

"I mean no disrespect, *Dottore*, but why is your being here so important?"

"I only came at Michael's urging, to help with the case. I hope you're not thinking—"

"What? That you are here to steal the Cellini?"

"Yes."

"I did consider it, of course. But if Santilli wanted you to find it, she would have told you herself. There has to be another reason."

Dillan slowed. Something was buzzing against his thigh. "Excuse me a second." He reached into his pocket for his phone.

"Liz … yes, I'm all right… Slow down… I'm not alone, but I can talk… Yes, I got them… You're sending me what? But how did you… Okay, I'm listening… Got it. I'm sure."

Detective Tramonte gave Dillan an inquisitive look.

"A colleague from work," the doctor explained. "Looks like one of my patients is sicker than we thought. Can you give me a moment? She's sending me some files I need to look at."

"Would you rather go back inside? It is freezing out here."

"It's still balmy by Canadian standards. I'll meet you inside."

Dillan clicked on the link Liz had sent him and typed in the code she had given him over the phone. ITTRL?ITJF? Simple enough to remember when you know your Queen lyrics. *Is this the real life? Is this just fantasy?*

With his jacket flapping in the wind, Dillan stood still and waited for the batch of pictures to appear on screen. Despite Liz's warning, Dillan wasn't prepared for what he saw. The troubling photos were more than enough for him to understand Liz's concerns and to heighten his own.

CHAPTER 19

The midday sun was beating down on the barren, rust-colored land. The man, tall and lanky, walked gingerly across the powdery soil, his feet uncomfortable and hot inside his leather boots. He stopped, examined the billows of dust kicked up by his footsteps, and studied the floating particles as they settled back to the ground. He wiped his forehead with the back of his hand and peered into the distance. His eyes narrowed against the glare as he searched for his rendezvous point. The wooden hut came into view. Within minutes, if all went well, he would be inside.

Overhead, a bird squawked. The man looked up, expecting to see a raven or a crow, but instead, circling high above, was a vulture, its black silhouette gliding against the bright cerulean sky.

The man trudged onward. The hut now looked more like an old ramshackle barn, its weather-beaten planks crooked and riddled with cracks and holes. He approached warily. The wood grain on the barn's rickety door formed a swirling, paisley-like pattern of grays and blacks. The door had been left ajar.

Pressing his spindly fingers around the handle of the gun tucked into his belt, the man stepped up to the wooden door and, with the tip of his boot, gave it a shove. To his surprise, the door opened without the slightest creak. He stepped inside. Sitting at a table in front of him was a bald bear of a man, his round jawline sporting a band of wild gray hair that fused into his bushy sideburns.

"You're right on time, Mr. Lee," the man said in a deep baritone. "Happy to see you found the place. Not everyone does, you know." He leaned back in his chair, his steel-blue eyes twinkling. "Don't worry, I really am Ivan Mihalovitch. The one and only. Please, have a seat."

Lee walked to the table and pulled out a chair, dragging its legs along the wooden floor. He sat down. "Eight plus thirty-eight?" he called out, as if ordering a strange drink.

Mihalovitch smiled. "Hmm. Forty-six."

"Twelve times nine?"

The smile on Mihalovitch's face grew wider. "One hundred … and eight."

Lee continued. "Seventy divided by five."

"Come on, Mr. Lee, do we have to do this?"

"Seventy *divided by five*."

Mihalovitch chuckled. "As you wish. Seventy divided by five … let's see … that would be fourteen."

Lee stared at the man. "Any for me?"

Mihalovitch shook his head. "Enough with the child's play. Tell me what you know."

"Your sources were right. The lab exists. It's outside Heidelberg."

Mihalovitch let out a roaring belly laugh. "The affable Germans, of course. Where are they in their testing?"

"The drug is almost ready. About a dozen people have been run through the latest protocol. From what I was able to find out, all but one of the subjects realized they were dreaming within seconds of entering REM sleep. I don't think any trial has gone on for more than a few minutes, though."

"What kind of tasks were they asked to carry out?"

"Simple stuff. Counting, flying, engaging dream characters in discussions, making objects appear or disappear—the basics."

"Were any of them able to venture beyond their dreams?"

"You mean into the other side?"

Mihalovitch nodded.

"One of the last volunteers, maybe. Her brain signals went haywire minutes into her dream. She died of heart failure while she was still dreaming."

"Because of the drug?"

Lee frowned. "Maybe not."

"Then what?"

"There are rumors, Ivan. About the *taurines*. That they might be back. I don't think it's possible, though ... I mean, they haven't been seen in ages."

Mihalovitch leaned forward and rested his thick forearms on the table. "Maybe not by anyone known to you."

Lee glided his hand over his gun. "What are you saying, Ivan?"

"What I'm saying is that it's not what we know that we should fear the most, but what we don't know."

"So you think it might be true?"

"The question was never if they would return, but when. Either way, the mission continues. As does our agreement."

Lee scratched his forehead with the tip of his thumb. "Excuse me, but if there's even the faintest suspicion that the *taurines* might be back, that they're crossing over into our dreams, then that changes everything."

"It does and it doesn't."

Lee jumped up, pulled out his gun, and fired it into the wall.

Mihalovitch ducked as the deafening boom hit his ears. "What are you doing!" He turned and saw a bloodied mouse lying on the floor, its tiny legs stricken by spasms. "Are you crazy? Put that damn thing away!"

Mihalovitch marched over to the corner of the room, slid his fingers through a crack in the wall, and snapped a plank in half. He lifted the broken board over his head and swung it down onto the animal's head; its jittery dance came to a splattering halt. "What the hell were you thinking?" He tossed the piece of wood onto the floor.

Lee stared at the dead creature, tucked his gun under his belt, and sat back in his chair. "I'm sorry. Something about the way it scurried across the floor... It had me scared for a second. Thought it might have been..."

"What? Possessed? For Christ's sake!" Mihalovitch shook his head. "Get a grip and focus on why you're here." He sat down, leaned back in his chair, and folded his arms over his sizeable gut. "What else?"

"I don't think the drug is being developed solely for lucid dreaming. These people were scared, Ivan. And not just for their own lives. Whatever they're working on is big. Bigger than what I was able to find out."

"That's most interesting, Mr. Lee. A wily fox like yourself, however, must have some idea as to the nature of this work." Mihalovitch interlocked his fingers over the table. His knuckles cracked.

"I'm not sure if or how it ties in with the drug trials, but I think they're working on something unprecedented. And with dire consequences. Maybe ... maybe something to do with the *taurines*." He glanced at the splattered mouse, then back at Mihalovitch. "I've told you everything I know, Ivan. I swear."

"Everything except the name of whoever kindly shared this information with you."

Lee swallowed hard. "You know I can't reveal my sources. That was part of our deal. I mean no disrespect, Ivan, but I have a reputation to protect."

Outside the barn, a cow lowed mournfully.

Lee gave Mihalovitch a worried look. "Are you sure we're safe?"

"From the cow?" Mihalovitch said with a laugh. "Stop and think where we are for a second, will you?"

Lee went to the door and poked his head outside. A scrawny brown cow was walking by. Under the thin flap of skin dangling from its neck was a brass bell. He watched the cow stop and lower its nose to the ground, but the bell made no sound.

"Tell me, Mr. Lee," Mihalovitch shouted from his chair. "How good are your chances of getting hold of the drug once it's ready?"

Lee stepped back inside "Very good to excellent."

"Well, then, looks like we'll be meeting again."

CHAPTER 20

D illan was in Detective Tramonte's office, explaining how his quick research online had led him to Professor Luigi Antonielli, director of the Accademia di Belle Arti and, more importantly, a leading authority on Cellini.

"Go ahead," the detective said, turning the phone on his desk toward Dillan.

Dillan dialed. The line rang, once, twice, three times. *"Accademia di Belle Arti, Dipartimento del direttore,"* answered a male voice.

"Excuse me, sir. *Mio italiano non e molto buono.* Do you speak English?"

"Of course."

"My name is James Dillan. I'm a doctor helping Italian authorities with the investigation of a possible murder. I was hoping to speak to Mr. Luigi Antonielli."

"The police want to speak with the director?" the man asked, his Italian accent now more noticeable.

"No, not the police, just me."

"Signor ... er...?"

"James Dillan. I'm calling from Trento."

"I do not want to appear impolite, Mr. Dillan, but Mr. Antonielli is a very busy man. Perhaps I could arrange for you to speak to somebody else, someone other than Mr. Antonielli. Perhaps I could be of assistance."

"Thank you, but I was hoping to speak to the director himself. Given his expertise, he may have some knowledge that would be of help to us."

"You said this is a murder investigation, *si?*"

"Possible murder. The death we're investigating may be related to a lost artwork by Cellini. Possibly a vase."

"Yes, we often get calls from people thinking they have found a priceless artwork. Almost always turns out to be worthless. And often ugly."

"I understand, but I'm not interested in having the value of anything assessed. Could you at least give him the message, please?"

"Very well. I will see what I can do."

Dillan left him his number and handed the phone back to the detective. "I don't think I was taken too seriously."

"It was worth trying," Tramonte said. He collected some papers scattered across his desk. "Vincente mentioned there being two helicopters," he said, picking up a pencil and pointing to a column of numbers on the top sheet. "I looked through the phone records and spoke to some friends at the Alpino Soccorso. One of them was working the night of Santilli's death. Vincente called 118 at 6:24 that morning, and the call ended under three minutes later, at 6:27. At 6:28, Emergency Services contacted the Alpino Soccorso to inform them that a rescue was needed for a young boy and his missing mother. Two minutes later, however, my friend took a second call—this one from the Caserma Ederle military base. They said sensitive materials were involved and that they would be taking care of rescue operations. When my friend objected, he was told that this was a matter of national security and that the orders came straight from the Ministry of Defense."

"You think this is because of the Cellini?"

The detective twirled the pencil between his fingers. "You need to understand, *Dottore,* this has never happened before. The Alpino Soccorso is an elite group of mountaineers and medical officers. They are trained for these kinds of rescues. It doesn't matter if it's the pope who is stranded. That's who gets called."

"I need to ask you something, Detective. I don't want you to take this the wrong way, but are you sure you can trust everyone involved in the case?"

The detective put down his pencil. "I trust Captain Battista."

Dillan needed to make a decision, and he knew that whatever he decided, the consequences would be both immediate and grave. "There's something I need to show you." He took out his cell phone.

The detective reached across the table. "What do you have there?"

"The files of my sick patient."

It didn't take long for the detective to recognize the bloodied constellation close to Santilli's body. "Why the emblem of the Medici?"

"I might have an idea about that, but there are pictures I can't explain." The doctor scrolled to another series of images.

"*Mannaggia!*" the detective cursed. "Who did this to her?"

"I don't think anyone did this to her. I think Santilli did it to herself. Take a look at these close-ups."

Dillan scrolled down further. "One of her fingernails is on top of each snowball, and right next to her body is the multitool Vincente said she'd been carrying. You can still see the blood on the pliers."

"Where did you get these?"

"Let's just say I have a resourceful colleague."

The detective appeared sullen. "So the photographs we were shown were falsified?"

"Some of them were altered, others withheld."

The detective stared at one of the pictures. "It looks like a ritual of some kind."

"Whatever it was, she was determined," Dillan said. "Most people would pass out after tearing off one fingernail, let alone five."

"You really think she did it to herself?"

"The footprints leading to the edge of the mountain were hers, and there aren't any tracks near her body. Looks like she was alone down there."

"What's this in the snow?" the detective asked, turning the phone to Dillan. "It looks like she used her blood to write ... 'INVICTUS.' "

"That's what it looks like to me."

"Isn't that Latin for, what is the word, *invicibile?*"

Dillan nodded. "Yes, invincible, or unconquerable. It's also the name of a famous poem about surviving adversity. I looked it up. The last two lines are 'I am the master of my fate, I am the captain of my soul.' "

"Sounds like a message of confidence," the detective said. "Maybe even defiance."

"Could well be. The question is, a message for whom?"

"Maybe she knew who would find her body first."

Dillan's phone was vibrating. He put his cell to his ear and answered. It was Professor Antonielli returning his call. He said he had been intrigued by the doctor's query and went on to explain that while he was aware of the myths surrounding Cellini's vase, he remained skeptical as to its actual existence. The men agreed to meet the following day at the professor's office in Florence.

* * *

The clouds grew thick as darkness fell.

As he neared the apartment door, Dillan recognized the album playing inside as Pink Floyd's *Dark Side of the Moon*—it had been one of Kohler's favorites. Dillan, his heart now beating like a snare drum, knocked at the door and let himself in.

"James!" Michael called out from the living room. "How did it go?"

"You mean with your cleaning lady?"

"Sorry about that. Completely slipped my mind."

"No worries. I was getting ready to leave when she arrived."

"Anything new?" Michael asked.

"We went over the files again," Dillan said, fighting his nerves. "But we're no further ahead. I don't see how sleep figures into this."

"Sorry to hear that."

"I wish I could've been more helpful. I might take a few days off before heading back, though. Maybe spend a little time in Rome or Venice."

Michael gave Dillan a quizzical look. "When?"

"I was thinking of heading out in the morning." In truth, Dillan would have been glad to leave immediately.

"So soon? We haven't had a proper night out together since you got here."

His heart skipped a beat, but Dillan forced himself to smile. "You're right, we haven't."

CHAPTER 21

The train was Dillan's favorite way to travel in Europe, and today's route only reinforced that preference. A little over an hour had passed since the train left Trento: there were still two and a half more hours till Florence, plenty of time to gather his thoughts.

The little sleep Dillan had gotten before catching his train had been anything but restful. All night long, his mind had replayed scenes from his conversation with Michael at a corner table at the bar—and the tape wasn't finished playing back. He reanalyzed the ebb and flow of their exchanges, the questions they'd asked each other and the tone in which they'd been answered.

Early in the night, well within their first round of drinks, Michael had surprised Dillan by revisiting some of their first exchanges on the nature of dreams and admitting that his views at the time were probably wrong—and wholly unscientific. It was only later, after they'd reminisced about their university days and had several more drinks, that Michael began firing questions at him about his recollection of Giancarla Santilli and their conversations in Berkeley, about his impressions of Vincente and the boy's version of the events, and about what Dillan thought might have happened in the mountains. Dodging these psychological salvoes had taken a toll.

Had Michael bought his story? Had Dillan succeeded in keeping his body language from betraying his words? Though he replayed the conversations, he couldn't see any major slip-ups, but there was no way to be sure.

One thing he was sure of, however, was that he'd caught Michael in a lie, the ramifications of which he'd only begun to piece together. They had been about to call it a night when Dillan, returning to a prior discussion, said, "You were right about my being scared of ruining things with Liz. At least you had the guts to pack up and make a move to be with Stefania. I admire that."

Michael kept his eyes on his glass of scotch and after a moment said, "You can plan and hope all you want, but you never know how things will work out. One day you wake up, regretting that you took a chance, or that you didn't. Either way, it's too late. It's just too fuckin' late." He drained what was left of his scotch, looking dejected. "All you can do," he added, "is act while the choice is still yours. After that, you're basically screwed. Simple as that."

Maybe it was something in Michael's tone, or the glum look in his eyes, but Dillan was sure Michael had been referring to something other than his three-year-old separation from Stefania.

Michael reached for his stein of beer and gulped half of it down. "We should head back," he said, placing the mug back on the table. "Can't have you leaving all fogged-up in the morning."

It was at that moment, after he'd wrapped his fingers around the handle of his own beer mug, that Dillan said, "You've got yourself a nice flat. Glad I got to stay there and spend a bit more time with you."

"I guess it is nice," Michael said.

"Did you move in there when you first got here?" *Boom.*

Even as he sat on the train, with the benefit of hindsight, Dillan wasn't sure whether he had intended to test his friend, or if the seemingly innocent query had come out on its own. Either way, the question caught Michael off guard. There was no mistaking the sudden tightening of his lips and the quick shift of his eyes. "No," Michael had finally said. "I moved there after the breakup."

Dillan, remembering what the cleaning lady had told him, listened as Michael spun a convincing tale about how he and his ex had shared a lovely two-story condo outside Trento, and how, after discovering she was involved with another man, he had moved into a tiny studio, "a real dump" he called it, and only later into his current apartment.

Dillan's mind had flashed to the folded sheet of paper he had found in Michael's nightstand. The list it contained—everything from Stefania's birthplace to her work history—had been nothing more than a memory aid: a way of keeping past lies straight. How could someone he had known so long prove to be so duplicitous? He listened to Michael and for the first time saw his former friend for what he had become: a cold, calculating liar. The realization chilled him.

Sitting there on the train, he pondered the possibility that the entire story had served as a cover-up for another, likely darker reason that had brought Michael to Italy. But what?

Dillan leaned back in his seat and took out his phone, debating whether to send Liz another text. It was a little past four in the morning in Montreal. He decided to wait until the train rolled into Florence. His phone buzzed. *Call me at this number asap*, read Liz's text. Dillan didn't believe in telepathy, but he sure welcomed this synchronicity.

"Liz. I was getting worried."

"Sorry, I couldn't take any chances. Had to have my electronics inspected by a pro." She paused. "What's that noise?"

"I'm on a train, on my way to Florence."

"Florence? What for?"

"I'm meeting an expert on Cellini."

"You serious?"

"I'll explain later. Did you find out anything else?"

"Yeah, the pictures I sent you of Santilli's body, the light in them isn't right."

"What do you mean?"

"If you look closely at the snow, you can see direct sunlight reflected on the surface. I Google Earthed the coordinates of where the body was found and factored in the time when the pictures were taken. Turns out the sun would have been too low on the horizon to be shining directly over her. The whole bottom part of the cliff would have been in shadow till later that morning."

"I get the Google Earth part, but how'd you figure out the rest?"

"I looked up the local time for sunrise and ran a topographical simulation to see what areas would have been in direct light as the sun moved over the horizon."

"How do you even come up with these things?"

"That's what I'm trained to do."

"I doubt they taught you that in engineering school. What about the pictures taken by the tents?"

"The light pattern checks out."

"That's great, Liz."

"Think of what I could do if I had more time to work on this."

"You've already been more than helpful. I don't know where I'd be without you on this one."

"Let me join you then."

"Here?"

"Yes! You promised to let me in on a case. I mean, really in."

"Not this one. There're too many things I haven't—"

"Please. There's always a reason why you won't let me get my hands dirty."

Dillan considered the options, along with the risks.

"I think I've earned it," she said. "Just for a few days." Liz waited a few moments. "Are you there?"

"Yes ... I'm thinking." Although Dillan had indeed promised Liz a hands-on experience in sleep forensics, this wasn't the kind of case he'd imagined her jumping into. One thing he couldn't deny, however, was that he wanted her here with him. He needed his ideas to be validated, refined—even challenged. But that wasn't all. He also wanted to share the growing doubts and unsettling feelings the case had provoked.

"You're right," he said. "Book your ticket."

CHAPTER 22

The black Mercedes decelerated, pulled up to the curb, and came to an abrupt stop. Michael stood on the sidewalk, waiting for the chauffeur to step out. The tinted front window on the passenger side slid down. "Get in," growled the driver. Michael opened the back door of the car and stepped inside, his eyes catching a glimpse of the Priorate's dark suede coat. The putrid smell had gotten worse.

"We have things to discuss, Mr. Kohler," the man said. "Urgent things."

Michael kept his eyes glued to the headrest in front of him. "I'm here to help in any way I can."

"Of course you are," the man replied. "Now tell me what you found."

"There was nothing in the documents taken from Santilli's house. We went over everything else again: hard drives, email, backups, browsing history. She didn't leave a trace. We also went through Dillan's files, his hospital network, university server. And I've been monitoring his online activity since he got here. There's still no evidence that Santilli reached out to him or that he knows anything more about her death than what the police told him."

"Evidence?" the man said. "My telling you that Santilli did contact him is the only evidence you need." He stopped, as if to rein in his anger, then said, "Is the tracker operational?"

"I injected it exactly as you asked," replied Michael. "It's working as we speak."

He handed the Priorate a small black receiver. "He mentioned he'd be leaving in a few days, though."

"I'm sure he did…" The man slipped the receiver into his coat pocket. Then he said, "The boy knows more than he's letting on. I must speak to him."

"What are you suggesting?"

The man put his skeletal hand on Michael's thigh. A cold wave shot through his pants and into his flesh. "I'm not suggesting anything. I'm telling you. I *need* the boy."

The man lifted his hand from Michael's leg. He leaned forward toward the chauffeur and whispered something into his ear.

Michael's stomach tightened as the car exited the highway and turned onto a rough gravel road. Clouds of dust billowed around the car as it sped down the rutted path and entered a forested area. He clenched his hands as the car veered to the side before grinding to a halt.

The driver stepped out, walked toward the back of the car, and swung open the door. "Get out."

Michael glanced at the man in the suede coat but knew better than to argue or plead. He did the only thing possible: he did exactly as he was told.

The driver reached inside his jacket and pulled out a dark piece of cloth. "Put this on."

Michael spread open the bottom of the hood and slipped it over his head.

The driver took out a piece of twine and wrapped it around Michael's neck, securing the base of the hood.

Michael struggled to breathe through the dense woven mesh. The darkness alone was asphyxiating. He tried to remain calm as the air around his face thinned. Then came the jab to his neck.

CHAPTER 23

P rofessor Antonielli led Dillan into his wood-paneled office at the far end of the museum.

"Thanks for the tour," Dillan said.

"I'm glad you enjoyed it," answered the professor, closing the door behind him. "Most people come here to see the original *David*, not knowing about our other masterpieces."

The professor gestured to a pair of matching brown leather chairs. "Please, have a seat. As I started telling you, the Medici weren't nobility. They rose to power through banking and commerce. Giovanni di Bicci de' Medici, the founder of the Medici bank, used his wealth to turn Florence into the cultural center of Europe. His descendants kept his legacy going, acting as patrons of the arts. Even Michelangelo and da Vinci spent part of their lives in their residences. And several generations of children born into the Medici family were lucky enough to have Galileo himself as their personal tutor."

"I didn't know the Medici were interested in science."

"They weren't interested in science so much as being associated with one of the greatest scientists of their time. The Medici understood the importance of the family's image, not only for the masses they ruled, but also for other people with power."

Dillan leaned forward in his chair.

"For most artists," Antonielli continued, "working for one of the most influential families in Europe was a privilege. The Medici dynasty was in power for almost three centuries and during that time they amassed an astounding collection of artwork. Much of the art here and at the Uffizi came to us through the Medici."

"And where does Cellini fit in?"

"I'm going to have a *grappa*," the professor said, getting up from his chair and walking over to the liquor cabinet in the corner. "Would you like a drink? *Grappa*, scotch, *eau-de-vie...*"

"I'll have whatever you're having, thank you."

Antonielli returned with two elegant glasses and put a bottle of straw-colored *grappa* down on the table before them. "Cellini worked for Cosimo di Giovanni de' Medici, Giovanni's son, but he was also commissioned by Pope Clement VII—one of the Medici popes—as well as by his successor, Pope Paul III. And this is, maybe, where your question fits in. What do you know about Cellini—not as an artist, but as a man?"

"I know he was unpleasant."

Antonielli laughed. "That's a polite way of putting it, and also a great understatement. Cellini was exceedingly talented, a true genius. But it wasn't for nothing that he became known as *l'uomo terribile*, the terrible man. He was egotistical, vindictive, and prone to violence, with men and women alike. He engaged in sodomy with young boys, dabbled in necromancy, and confessed to three murders—although many suspect there were more."

"Was he ever jailed for the murders?"

"He was imprisoned on several occasions for brawls, embezzlement, and sodomy. Except for one daring escape, he was always saved by interventions from people in power."

"I still don't see how this connects to the vase," Dillan said.

"As I told you, I'm not even sure the vase exists, but if it does, I think his temperament is likely part of the story."

"In what way?"

"I first heard about the vase while working at the Capitolini museum in Rome. The person who told me the story was Giuseppe Falcone, a professor of art history. Falcone specialized in the

Renaissance. He spent most of his life tracking down lost works of art and, to his credit, he recovered several invaluable pieces, including some that had vanished during the Sack of Rome. He was convinced that the story of Cellini's vase was true. He told me he had evidence that Cellini had been convened to a meeting in Rome, and at this meeting, powerful intermediaries asked him to create a special work of art, one that would conceal an important secret."

"Intermediaries for whom?

"I don't think anyone really knows, but according to Falcone, several highly placed figures were behind the plan, including Pope Clement and Cosimo de' Medici. The work they commissioned, however, wasn't meant for public display. In fact, no one was to know about it. The Medici had apparently come into the possession of something priceless, although what it was remains a matter of speculation. Some believe it was the key to a great treasure. Others think it was a long-lost document from biblical times. Some of the more far-fetched ideas include an ancient cryptogram capable of giving the finder the power of immortality or the ability to summon the dead, maybe even the devil himself. Whatever it was, the Medici decided that the secret was to be kept and protected for centuries to come."

"Protected from what?"

"That I don't know," the curator said, swirling his grappa in his glass. "But I imagine they didn't want the secret to fall into the wrong hands, or maybe even be used."

"And why Cellini?"

"He'd already worked for the Medici and was indebted to several people in their inner circle for their help. Professor Falcone believed they chose Cellini because they had the power to blackmail him. They knew he would do as they asked."

"Did Cellini know what the secret was?"

"I doubt the Medici would have shared that sort of information with him. But he certainly knew it was gravely important to the people who hired him and that his job was to create a piece of art in which to hide it."

"And that would be the vase?"

"Yes. Falcone called it 'the Lost Cellini.' One odd thing, however, was that although Cellini earned his fame working with metals, he decided to make a vase."

"Maybe easier to hide the secret?"

"That's one explanation. Another has to do with Cellini himself. He certainly wouldn't have taken kindly to being blackmailed. It's possible his animosity to those who were threatening him played a role in his choice of artwork. Falcone was convinced this was the case. Be that as it may, once the vase was finished, it was supposedly hidden beneath the Basilica di Santa Maria in Trastevere, where it stayed undisturbed for almost a century. One day, however, three men broke into the basilica and stole the Cellini. They were hunted down, not only by the Medici, but by papal forces and hired assassins. Even the Borgia, sworn enemies of the Medici, were hired to track them down."

The professor poured them another shot of *grappa*. "Less than a week later, one of the men, a Franciscan friar, was captured outside Padova and tortured for weeks, but he kept silent until he was killed. It took the Medici, or whoever was working for them, two more years to find the second man, and another year after that to find the third one. The last two were also Franciscans, but from different orders. They too were threatened and tortured, but neither ever said a word about the vase or their supposed accomplices. And that's as much of the story that Falcone pieced together before he fell ill."

"From what?"

"This is something I hoped you could maybe explain. Falcone became unable to sleep and then went mad."

Dillan narrowed his eyes.

"It's not that he didn't want to sleep," continued Antonielli. "But that he couldn't. What started off as insomnia turned into a complete inability to sleep. It didn't matter how tired he got. The doctors tried different medications, including sleeping pills and anti-anxiety drugs, but nothing worked. His health quickly deteriorated. He lost weight and started having panic attacks. He thought that malevolent forces had gotten into his brain. His family had him hospitalized, but his condition only got worse. He died a little over a year ago. Have you ever heard of anything like that, Doctor? A man who goes mad and dies from a lack of sleep? He was only fifty-eight."

"There is a genetic disorder called fatal familial insomnia. The symptoms include the kinds of things you said Falcone experienced. The disorder is rare and always fatal."

"Do we know what causes it?"

"A cerebral infection. Abnormal proteins start eating away a part of the brain, leaving little holes in it, like those in a sponge."

"Do you think Falcone could have had this?"

"The disease usually starts earlier in life, and at least one of his parents would have needed to have the disorder."

"I met his parents at his funeral," Antonielli said. "They were aged but appeared to be in good health."

"How long did he suffer from this?"

"A couple of months maybe. I visited him near the end. There was not much left on him but skin and bones. What troubled me most, however, was the expression on his face. He looked terrified."

"Did he recognize you?"

"I think so. He spoke to me. Whispered, in fact. Repeated a phrase twice. I'll never forget it."

"What did he say?"

"*Il diavolo e qua.* The devil is here. He died a week later."

"Do you know if anything was wrong with him—physically or mentally—before the insomnia set in?"

"Falcone may have been obsessed with the lost Cellini, but he wasn't crazy. If anything, he was meticulous. That was his reputation, and a big reason for his success in tracking lost artworks. But his illness did taint his legacy."

"In what way?"

"It led some people to view his later ideas, including those about the lost Cellini, as the delusions of a madman. In any event, even before he became ill, most art historians viewed the whole story as nothing more than an old legend, probably started for political reasons."

Dillan leaned forward in his seat. "Is that what you think?"

"I think there's some merit to the idea."

"What about the vase then? Do you think it exists?"

"I really don't know what to think. Frankly, until you called, I hadn't thought about it for some time."

"But your colleague, Professor Falcone—what made him so sure?"

"While doing archaeological excavations near a castle by Lake Bracciano, his team found a scroll he believed was an account of the capture and torture of the three men accused of stealing the Cellini. A few months later, one of his students working at a nearby site found a box containing something mentioned in the account. Falcone saw this as proof of his thesis."

"What was in the box?"

"The bones from three pairs of hands."

"What?"

"The scroll Falcone found said the three men died the same way. When they were about to die from being tortured, their captors tied them down, heated metal prongs over a fire, and used them to rip off their fingernails."

Dillan felt a jolt. "Their fingernails?"

"Yes, one at a time. And when the torturers were done, they cut off the men's hands with a sword and left them to die. Their hands, however, were kept as mementos."

CHAPTER 24

The hood over Michael's head was damp from the warmth of his breath. He reconstructed the route he and the others had been forced to take, single file, to the underground chamber. There had been three doors before the tight, angular staircase. The first door, leading into the building, had been locked with a heavy metal chain that rattled as it was pulled through a metal cylinder. The second door, this one unlocked, came twelve steps later, in a straight line from the main entrance. Four steps forward, and then eleven more to the left, had brought him and the others in front of him to a stop. The final door was small and narrow, forcing Michael to crouch to pass through.

On the other side of that last door, there had been a series of steep steps down to the floors below. He'd noted how the sound of people's footsteps resonated off the walls. He thought they might be inside a tall concrete shaft, its walls flush with the staircase. Ten steps had been climbed down before they reached the first landing. From there, they had turned 180 degrees to the left before taking the next flight down. Michael had dragged his feet across two such landings. The crisscross pattern of rivets rubbing against the soles of his shoes had confirmed his assumption: the staircase was made of steel. In all, he had descended six landings—the equivalent of three stories —before entering a cold, dank chamber.

Once inside the room, he had walked down six shallow steps before a door—it sounded like heavy wood—closed behind him.

He had then taken a dozen steps, all in a straight line, before someone grabbed him by the arm and forced him into a chair.

Now sitting, Michael cautiously lifted one of his legs. After a few inches, his knee hit something. He was at a table. Nearby, a man coughed.

Michael tried to wiggle his fingers behind his back, but the rope around his wrists had been wound too tight for too long. His hands were numb. The heavy door creaked. Michael sat up, alert, as the sound of footsteps echoed off the walls. Four to six people, he guessed, had entered the room, which, based on the echoes, must be cavernous. Then, in unison, they stopped. Silence filled the air. After a brief moment, someone walked toward the men, and judging from the snapping sound, that person was wearing high heels.

Another person, this one with a heavy tread, walked past Michael and continued to the opposite end of the room.

"Listen carefully," came a man's voice from across the chamber. "What you're about to hear won't be repeated. Do not speak unless you're instructed to do so. Do not move unless you're told to do so. Do anything stupid after we free your hands, and I'll chop them off myself. Remove your hood, and the last thing you will ever hear will be the sound of my sword hacking off your head."

The crisp clacks of the high heels grew louder as a person walked closer to Michael's right. A woman spoke.

"Apologies for the manner in which some of you were brought here, but rest assured, I'm most delighted to have you at our communal table. This is the first time I've laid eyes on all ten of you—and it will certainly be the last. I do hope this meeting will be half as instructive for me as it will be for you."

Michael studied the woman's intonations, her choice of words. The voice was appealing and mature, its accent vaguely familiar. But he couldn't be sure where, or even if he had heard it before. Someone approached the table and slashed the ropes around Michael's wrists. Blood rushed back into his hands, and numbness gave way to waves of pain.

"I know the associates who hired you—the same associates, I might add, who make sure your considerable earnings always arrive on time—were supposed to be your only contacts. But what would our lives be without surprises ... without disappointments? It was brought to my attention that some of you have lost sight of the rules under which you were hired. How thoughtless. You were forbidden to talk to anyone about this. Even to a young, innocent daughter."

One of the men at the table began to hyperventilate.

"Something wrong, Mr. Devanch?" the woman asked. "Don't be afraid to speak up now. You weren't fearful when you decided to have your little chat with your daughter. Maybe living in such a remote corner of the world gave you a false sense of security."

"It's not true!" pleaded the man. "I didn't tell her anything. She knows nothing, I swear!"

"That's not what your lovely daughter told us, at least not on the second day of—how shall I put this?—of attending to her physical discomforts. How unfortunate for her to undergo such unkind, albeit effective procedures."

"No!" yelled the man called Devanch. Michael heard the man's chair topple over and blind, running steps. His body made a thump as it smacked into a wall. The man started to sob.

The sound of a sword being pulled from its metal sheath sliced across the room. Footsteps. Devanch screamed. There was a splattering sound, and instantly, the man's shrieks were reduced to a short, agonizing groan. Something heavy hit the floor and rolled a short distance. In the darkness of his hood, Michael closed his eyes, but that didn't keep the image of a decapitated corpse from flashing through his mind.

"All of you, hands on the table!" ordered a deep voice. Michael put his clenched fists on the table. He froze as the cold edge of a blade was placed against the back of his neck.

With his hands on the table and his head immersed in obscurity, Michael listened to the woman accuse someone of lying about what he had seen while out on a mission. Moments later, someone at the table was dragged from a chair. His cries were muffled, as if he had been gagged. There was an odd sound, like a giant flint being struck, followed by a second or two of crackling.

The thumping of the man's legs, his cries, and above all, the acrid smell of something burning left little doubt as to what was happening. A sword was again pulled from its metal sheath and ended the ordeal. The man's horrific screams, along with the stench permeating the room, made Michael sick to his stomach. He gagged as acid bile rose to the back of his throat. The screaming stopped.

"Don't let this bother you," the woman said. "I know a team-building exercise that's bound to get you focused on the tasks at hand. There are only eight of you now, four on either side of the table. You have an assigned partner sitting across from you. Slide your hands forward until your fingers touch your partner's."

Michael slowly reached out until his fingers were met by thin, trembling digits.

The woman took a few steps. "If we're to succeed, as I know we can, we must be able to trust each other. And each one of you must do exactly what you're asked. Go ahead and grab your partner's hands. Make sure you get a good, strong grip."

Michael interlocked his fingers with those of the stranger before him. The unknown person's hands were emaciated and cold. Michael grasped firmly, his partner tentatively.

"Stay seated," the woman ordered. "Keep your forearms on the table and pull your partner toward you. Pull hard."

The man who had been paired with Michael was clearly smaller—smaller and weaker. His grasp was tenuous, his fingers spindly and frail.

The woman, unhurried, kept walking. She seemed to be moving in a circle around the table.

Some of the people were panting from their efforts. Others grunted.

The woman stopped. "Whatever happens, whatever you do, never let go of your partner's hands. *Never.*"

Michael tightened his grasp around the man's clammy, bony hands.

The woman continued. "Each of you possesses a talent of one sort or another. That's why we came to you. Before leaping head-first into the void, even the greatest trapeze artist must believe someone will be there to catch them."

Michael fought hard against the man's increasingly slippery hold.

"In your hands," she continued, "lies your fate. You must trust us, as we need to trust you. Break this trust, and nobody will be there to catch you." She took a few steps away from the table. "Under no circumstances were you to communicate with anyone else involved in this. Your recruiters were to be your only contacts. If you remember this fundamental rule, lower your head."

Michael bowed his shrouded head, his focus still on his partner's hands. A bead of sweat trickled down his forehead and onto the bridge of his nose.

"Well, it looks like all of you remember this simple rule, as you should," the woman said. "So why would some of you try to meet up behind our backs? Because you thought you were too clever to get caught? Is there a better place to arrange a clandestine rendez-vous, to carry out your own furtive plans, than in one of your own dreams?"

The sound of heavy footsteps indicated that two men were approaching, one on either side of the table. The two men stopped.

"I must admit I was surprised at how easily some of you were able to enter each other's dreams," added the woman. "But did you think you could keep such things from us? There are perils in believing you can outsmart people you've never met. I'm certain that, at this very moment, Mr. Lee and the other fools seated at our table would agree with me."

The table shook as two swords came crashing down one after the other. High-pitched shrieks pierced the air. Something warm splotched over Michael's arms as he went tumbling backward in his chair, hitting his head on the stone floor. Other men had also fallen backward in their chairs: there was a man screaming on his right and others on the other side of the table.

"Kill the bastards," ordered the woman, "but keep their hands as souvenirs."

The squeals turned to yells, to grunts, to silence.

Michael was still on his back when the woman walked up to his head. He squirmed as she pressed the heel of her shoe through his hood and into the side of his face.

"Of the ten of you, Michael here had the most important assignment of all." She twisted the end of her heel deeper into his jaw. "But he failed—miserably. The only reason he's still with us is because I wanted to see him alive, at least for the time being. For the rest of you, understand that there will be no second chance. Do exactly what you're asked. No more, no less. Unless you wish to meet with me again, that is."

The woman pulled her heel off Michael's face. "I must give you credit for one thing, Mr. Kohler. I've led this sort of team-building exercise before, but you're the first one smart enough to follow my instructions to the end. You can let go of your partner's hands now. I'll be taking them with me."

CHAPTER 25

T he Tiffany lamp was in the usual place, diffusing its usual melody of lights. But the pattern in the stained glass ... how could he not have noticed it before? How many hours had he spent sitting by that very lamp? Hundreds? Thousands? How many late nights had he whiled away in its glow? But there was no denying the evidence. Dillan ran his fingertips over the stained glass, tracing the lead ridges that separated red, yellow, and blue. The pattern was unmistakable: five red orbs and one blue, on a shield of gold. It was the Medici coat of arms.

"Interesting, isn't it?" Victor said.

"You've noticed it before?"

"Last time I was here."

Dillan kept his eyes fixed on the lamp. "I can't believe I never saw it before."

Victor moved closer. "Amazing the tricks the mind can play."

Dillan didn't know if it was the sight of the Medici coat of arms, the coolness of the lamp's silvery veins, or something in Victor's voice—maybe all three—but he now realized a fact that, mere seconds ago, he had been unaware of. He was dreaming.

Dillan turned to Victor. "This is a dream, right? I shouldn't be asking you. I know this is a dream. That's why the lamp is different."

Victor looked puzzled. "Why shouldn't you be asking me?"

"Because you're part of the dream. Because I don't need you to tell me where I am."

"And where are you, Doctor?"

"I'm in Florence, sleeping at Professor Antonielli's house. In his guest room. I'm lucid. I know this is a dream."

Victor walked over to the bay window and stared outside. "You're right," he said. "This *is* a dream, and you and I are both perfectly lucid. You know who probably isn't lucid right now? That young couple walking hand in hand down there. And those kids running around in the park. You have to listen to me, Doctor. We're at a critical pass."

Dillan joined Victor at the window. He studied the couple as they continued their romantic stroll down the street, and he listened to the happy cries of the children in the park chasing an errant ball. A dog walked up to a tree near the sidewalk, lifted its hind leg, and relieved itself. It then gave a high-pitched yelp and darted away. Everything was exceptionally vivid.

"I'll listen to you," Dillan said. "Only this time, I know I'm listening to someone created by my dreaming brain."

"What are you talking about?"

"You, Victor. You're not real. You never have been."

Victor took a breath and looked around the room. "Do you think I can draw?"

"What?"

"Do you think I can draw?"

"I don't know … maybe. Why?"

"If I'm a creation of your mind, you should already know why I'm asking. But you don't, do you?"

Dillan tried to keep his focus. "You're right, I don't."

"Well, I know for a fact that I, supposedly a figment of your imagination, have a distinct talent for sketching." Victor slid open the top drawer of Dillan's desk and took out a pencil and few sheets of paper. "I don't know why I've never thought of this before. Or, since you say I'm a character in your dreams, I don't know why *you've* never thought of this before. I'm going to draw you a portrait of Maria."

Taking a binder off the desk and sliding it under the sheet of paper, Victor sat in the big carmine leather chair and set to work.

Dillan took a few steps toward him. He knew he could do things to prove to Victor, and to himself, that he was indeed dreaming. But doing so could change the course of the dream—its setting, its mood—or worse, cause him to wake up. This dream was too valuable for him to take such a risk. He needed to observe Victor, to study his words and actions. But Dillan was teetering on a cerebral tightrope. If he lost his mental footing, he could tumble back into nonlucid dreaming. If he got too worked up, the tightrope could snap and jolt him into wakefulness.

He looked at his watch. The digital display read 0.7734. He smiled, took a moment to study the room, and glanced at his watch again. This time it read 5:33. He turned and faced Victor. "All this," he said, waving his hand, "is a virtual world. A convincing world while we're in it, but a made-up world just the same. But you told me things in other dreams, about Santilli and the vase. Things I didn't know. Things I couldn't have known. How did you do that?"

Victor kept his eyes on his drawing. "I found out some things, and then I told you about them. Now, if you could be quiet for a second, I'm almost done."

Dillan remained standing and studied the pencil in Victor's hand as it glided over the page. Its movements were swift and graceful. Victor was right: he was good. Better than good, in fact. The doctor looked on as layers of details were created, superimposed and interconnected before his eyes. He couldn't make out the actual drawing, though. The top portion resembled a small metal bowl with blurry contours, sitting over some kind of lid. Victor continued, producing a myriad of additional lines and shapes, before coming to a stop. He rolled the pencil back and forth between his thumb and forefinger, imprinting a small, dark gray dot in the bottom left corner of the page. "Take a look."

The doctor kept his eyes glued to the drawing as he came closer and crouched by Victor's side. Every stroke, line, and curve was exactly where it had been drawn. The fuzzy bowl morphed into thick, undulating hair flowing down the sides of a woman's head. A series of tightly woven lines beneath it fused into a shawl wrapped around the woman's shoulders. To the woman's right, rising in the distance, was a broad, commanding mountain, the top of which appeared to be layered in snow. To her left, fading into the background, was a single row of tall wispy trees, their trunks curved by the force of time, their leaves agitated by a silent breeze. The portrait was that of a woman in motion, her eyes staring back at Dillan. He examined the mountain's soaring peak, the movement in the trees, the intensity in the woman's eyes. Her presence was ethereal. The entire scene, in fact, felt otherworldly.

"It's beautiful," he whispered.

"She's beautiful," corrected Victor. "Now you know what she looks like. Except her eyes. I could never do them justice. You'd need to see them for yourself to understand, to feel their pull. Now that you know what Maria looks like, you won't forget, will you?"

Dillan picked up the sketch and gazed at the woman peering back at him. "No, I don't think I will…"

He looked up from the pad as Victor slowly took it from his hands and placed it on the desk. Victor turned, leaned in, and gave him a firm, unexpected hug. Dillan felt the strength in Victor's arms as they wrapped around his shoulders and back. Surprised, Dillan stood motionless, then put his arms around his friend.

"I knew I could count on you," Victor hushed. "You'll help her, I know it. She must be feeling it too now. She'll come looking for us … for you."

Dillan tried to make sense of his emotions, of Victor's words, of the dream itself.

Victor stepped back but kept his hands on Dillan's shoulders. "Look at me, James. You're right about this being a dream. Your dream. But I'm not like other people in your dreams. I'm real. I always have been, from the first time we met at your apartment, to when I came looking for you in your dream of the park the other night. I don't always remember it, but I too once lived in your waking world. Now I'm trapped here. There are others like me, fated to live within other people's dreams. Some mean well, most don't."

"You're incredible," Dillan said, his gaze still locked on Victor. "You almost had me going again, but I haven't forgotten this is a dream. All of it, including you. You don't exist outside my dreams, but I do."

"I'm afraid you're only partly right. Most places you've ever dreamt of have come from your mind, from your 'dreaming brain,' as you like to call it. And you may have created almost every person, animal, and creature you've ever dreamt of as well. But there are forces that live in people's dreams and have done so for millennia. They're locked in a battle over the dreams of humankind. These forces don't come from your mind or even from the outside world, at least not as you know it. But they do exist."

"What are you talking about?"

"I'm talking about the fact that people spend a third of their lives sleeping, including over fifty *thousand* hours immersed in REM sleep. Think about that for a moment. Even if most dreams are forgotten—or never remembered to begin with—they leave indelible traces in people's minds, in their subconscious. Now, imagine the power you would have if you could shape people's dreams. You could instill foreign ideas and fuel feelings of injustice, anger, or hatred. You could direct people's behaviors, heighten divisions, encourage fanaticism, social uprisings, even wars."

"But no one can do that."

"How can you be so sure? Every person to have ever walked the earth has been pulled into that ancient state you call sleep, bathing in waters whose forces your science has yet to uncover, let alone understand. And while sleep cradles our minds, cutting us off from waking spheres, old, powerful worlds open up to us. People have become oblivious to the realities within them, James. But make no mistake, dreams have the power to shape who we are and what we become."

"You're trying to trick me again."

"This is no trick. If what you're after is a world ruled by fear, anger, and madness, is there a better, more accessible portal to the unconscious than one's dreams?"

Dillan pursed his lips but did not answer the question.

"I need you to remember what we've talked about," Victor said. "There's so much at stake here, and everything I'm telling you in this dream—your dream—is true."

The doctor remained silent, pondering the vagaries of the dream, when the image of an ominous purple sky appeared in his mind's eye. And through this image emerged a faint yet vital recollection. "Dreamkeepers," he muttered, grasping at the remnants of the distant, long-faded dream. "You once told me about the Dreamkeepers."

"I've told you about them on several occasions. Don't you remember?"

"I only remember the name and that they were important." Dillan closed his eyes, hoping to breathe life into the faint traces of the decade-old reverie. "They were like guardians," he said, straining to remember. The forgotten dream was inching its way into his awareness, yet it remained achingly out of reach, like a sought-after name on the tip of one's tongue. "Tell me again, please."

"They're sentinels and warriors," Victor said. "They're custodians and stewards. They protect the worlds that lie deep within sleep, the inviolability of dreams, the freedom of the human soul."

Dillan fought the impulse to dismiss what Victor was saying as nonsense, for his words had struck a chord. He felt they were harbingers of some kind of truth, a sentiment he could not brush away. "What do they protect us from?"

"From vile powers bent on infiltrating our dreams."

"In order to manipulate us," Dillan said, finishing his friend's sentence, "and the world we live in. Is that right?"

Victor gave the slightest of nods.

"So the Dreamkeepers are…"

"The guardians of sleep. And the defenders of dreams."

Dillan's thoughts were pulled in different directions, his mind torn between a desire to regard Victor's story as nothing more than absurd iterations and a yearning to consider the possibility that his words carried a measure of truth. "And if they were to fail?" he asked hesitantly.

"Then *we* will have failed."

Taking a step back, Dillan felt Victor's hands fall from his shoulders. He walked over to the Tiffany lamp and stared down at the patterns, at the Medici coat of arms. "Amazing the tricks the mind can play. That's what you said, Victor, when the dream began. You're so right. It is amazing."

"More than you know. Just think, while you're here talking to me, checking to see if the patterns on the lamp have changed since the dream began, thinking back to the things we've told each other in this and other dreams, you're lying in bed. Your eyes are closed, and your brain is fast asleep. But there's something even more extraordinary. If I try," he said, squinting, "I can *see* your other physical body, the one that at this very moment is lying in bed in Florence. You're sleeping on your right side. Your legs are bent at the knees, and both your hands are tucked under your pillow."

Victor opened his eyes. "Unfortunately, your dream is coming to an end, and I don't know when we'll see each other again. You must listen to me, James. The Dreamkeepers exist, and they will need our help. You, me, the boy, even Maria—we all have vital roles to play. Especially you."

Dillan looked around him, then back at his friend. "I'm trying to make sense of everything you've told me, Victor, I truly am. But there are no forces lurking within our dreams. No secret realms beyond this dream, and certainly not beyond the real world."

Victor gave a sigh of sadness and discontent. "The *real* world," he said, shaking his head. "How wrong you are. How presumptuous of you to even think you know what is real, what may be possible, and what has yet to be discovered."

Dillan smiled, refusing to be taken in by another one of his friend's tangents. Admittedly, the doctor had wrestled with Victor's ideas, had almost lapsed into believing that his friend was telling the truth. But this time he had held his ground without losing his awareness of the dream, or worse, waking up.

Victor fixed his gaze on Dillan, his eyes pleading to be taken seriously. "There's a storm on the horizon, James. It will get here, and with it, ancient creatures whose wickedness you cannot begin to fathom. Its first gusts are already upon us. You can see it in children's nightmares, in the world's restlessness, in people's hatred and intolerance of others, and in their growing inability to sleep. People's minds are being envenomed. That is the truth."

Victor's words sent a shiver up Dillan's spine.

"You're about to wake up," Victor said calmly. "I need you to do me a favor. I need you to close your eyes and touch the Tiffany lamp. Please."

Dillan extended his hand, sliding his fingers over the lamp's surface.

Victor came up behind him. "Tell me what you feel," he murmured.

"I feel the warmth of the lamp, the ridges of the strips of lead running down its sides, the texture of the stained glass. It all ... it all seems so real."

Victor put his hand on Dillan's shoulder. "I'm sure you can also feel my fingers as I press them into your muscles."

"Yes, but I'm not sure I—"

"Shh…" Victor breathed into his ear. "You've done great. I've never seen you so clear-headed, so focused. You have to believe me. Everything I've told you is true. *Everything.* We only have a few seconds, so I need you to listen carefully. I need you to remember my words. You must help Vincente find the vase. But the people who killed his mother are about to go after him. The boy is in imminent danger, James. You can't let anything happen to him. You just can't. Trust what lies inside you."

Dillan winced as Victor pressed his fingers into the side of his neck. "Keep the boy safe, and find the vase. The secret it holds was meant for you."

CHAPTER 26

Dillan woke up with a start. He ran his fingertips over the side of his neck: the pain was gone. He noted the position of his body. He was lying on his right side with his legs bent at the knees; his hands had been tucked under his pillow. A maelstrom of angst and confusion churned inside him.

He grabbed a pen off the nightstand and riffled through the top drawer looking for something—anything—to write on. The few sheets of printer paper he found would do. He sat up in bed and started with the beginning of the dream, as he remembered it: seeing the emblem of the Medici on his Tiffany lamp. His writing became frantic. There was so much to remember, to order, to transcribe.

Only once he had reached his third page of notes did Dillan's rhythm slow and become interspersed with pauses. He searched for moments, clues, or exchanges he might have forgotten and, once convinced there was nothing left for him to recall, he lay back down. He closed his eyes and replayed scenes from the dream in his mind's eye, partly out of a desire to relive the experience, partly out of a need to grasp its significance.

Although the dream had left him perplexed, there was one thing about it he knew without a doubt: Victor wasn't real. His dream friend, no matter how fascinating and clever, was nothing more than a creation of his imagination. Knowing that, however, did little to diminish his wish to understand why his dreams of Victor kept recurring and what meaning they held. He thought about the pain when Victor dug his fingers into his neck and the words he'd been told to remember. Those very words had created a knot in his stomach that was tightening with each passing second.

He looked over at the alarm clock. It was two in the morning. He took out his phone and brought up Detective Tramonte's number. He stared at the screen. His mind was telling him he was being foolish, but his gut had him thinking otherwise. What would he tell the detective? That he was calling in the middle of the night because of a warning from a dream? But what if something happened to Vincente? Could he live with himself? After all these years, could he go through something like that again? He had to make the call. *Just tell him the truth. Tell him about the knot in your stomach.* He hit dial and hoped the detective would answer.

CHAPTER 27

Two men in dark uniforms worked quickly in the moonlight, steering their long-arm cable cutters over one high-gauge metal wire and snapping it, then moving on to the next. Within minutes, the first part of the job was finished. They peeled back the chain-link fence behind the Trento police station, scuttled through the hole they'd created, dashed across the yard, and pressed their backs to the wall of the building, well away from the spotlight shining over the back entrance. There they put on their police caps. The man closest to the door unzipped the side pocket of his pants, took out a metal ring holding four keys, and flipped to the one with a hole at its base. He slid the key into the metal door and gave it a forceful turn clockwise. The deadbolt clacked open.

As planned, the guard normally stationed at the end of the hall had been called away. The men moved swiftly and unlocked a second door, this one leading to a temporary holding area. One of the men took a large cotton bag, a gag, and a roll of duct tape from under his vest while his partner inserted a double-sided key into the barrel lock of the special cell. With one full turn of the key, the door snapped open. The men rushed inside and grabbed at the bed but only caught hold of handfuls of a wool blanket and rumpled linens. The boy they had been sent to kidnap wasn't there.

A siren blared. The men took out their handguns and bolted for the exit. They were sprinting across the field when two armed officers ran out of the building in pursuit, ordering them to stop. The intruders dropped to the ground and scurried through the hole in the fence. Shots rang out. The men ran to a car waiting nearby, climbed in, and sped away.

CHAPTER 28

As usual at this time of night, the stretch of highway between Trento and Riva del Garda was deserted. Detective Tramonte, however, kept an eye on his speedometer, making sure he stayed well within the speed limit. Thirty minutes had passed since he had taken the wheel, yet his heart was still racing. He pushed the turn signal lever upward, moved into the right-hand lane, and with clammy fingers wrapped around the stick shift changed gears and took the exit for Lago di Garda. He drove past the lake's northeastern shore and turned onto a narrow, sinuous road leading into the hills. After a while, he brought the car to a crawl and turned toward the empty back seat. "Are you okay?" he shouted.

"Yes!" came the muffled answer from the trunk of the car. "Can I come out?"

"Soon. We're almost there."

Tramonte continued up the windy road and, after entering a pine forest, made a right onto a dirt lane. He drove another kilometer before pulling over on the gravel shoulder and turning off his headlights.

The detective reached down by his seat, popped open the lid of the trunk, and got out of the car.

"You can come out," he said, extending a hand to help the boy.

Vincente climbed out and rubbed his legs.

"I'm sorry," Tramonte said. "I couldn't take any chances. You can sit up front with me if you want."

"You think it's okay?"

Detective Tramonte opened the passenger door. "This area is pretty quiet, especially at this time of night. Just put your head down if you see anyone."

Tramonte got back into the car, turned the headlights back on, and continued along the dirt road.

"I'm thirsty," Vincente said.

The detective reached behind him and grabbed a thermos from the back seat. "Here," he said, handing Vincente the flask. "I also have a panini if you're hungry."

Vincente took a gulp of water. "Who were they?"

"I don't know."

"Do you know why they wanted to take me away?"

"They must have thought you knew something of use to them."

"About the Cellini?"

"Probably."

"Where are we going?"

"To a small mountain hut. My dad built it when I was about your age. You'll be safe there."

CHAPTER 29

Despite his delight that Liz would be joining him imminently, Dillan could not shake a deep sense of unease. He'd chosen a seat beside the window on the train but kept an anxious eye on the door. An elderly couple with a small suitcase in tow arrived and ambled to their seats at the opposite end of the carriage. Dillan pulled out his phone and reread the message Liz had texted him. *About to hop on! C U in a few min.*

Dillan took a deep breath. He was eager to see Liz, of course, but his mind was still troubled by last night's dream about Victor. He checked for a text from Detective Tramonte. Still nothing. The train lurched forward, leaving Florence's Santa Maria Novella Station behind.

Liz appeared in the doorway to the carriage, her red hair backlit like a nimbus. She flashed Dillan a smile as he stood to greet her. They gave each other a long, gentle hug.

"I misread the departure board," Liz said, slipping off her backpack. "Almost ended up texting you from Vienna."

Dillan smiled. "Let me help you with that." He lifted Liz's backpack onto the overhead luggage rack.

Liz glanced out the window. "Do you mind if I—"

"Of course not," Dillan said, extending his hand toward the window seat.

She sat down and stared at the countryside and rolling hills before turning to Dillan. "We're really here…"

Dillan considered touching her hand but decided against it. "It's a nice place to be ... I mean for us, for the case." She gave him a mischievous look, one that left Dillan mesmerized by her gold-flecked green eyes.

"So," she said, breaking the spell. "Did you meet up with the museum director?"

"I did. It was quite instructive, but there's something else I'd like to talk to you about first."

"All ears, Doctor J."

"I've been mulling over some dream-related questions, sort of related to the case."

"Fire away," she said.

"Have you ever had the same fictional character appear in more than one of your dreams?"

"You mean like in a recurrent dream?"

"Not the whole dream, just the imaginary person—more like a recurrent dream character."

"I don't think so. Why?"

"I've had a series of dreams, going back to when I was in med school, involving the same dream character—a man named Victor. I had a few unsettling dreams about him this week."

"Unsettling in what way?"

"I'm not sure how to describe it. There's this continuity from one dream to the next. It's as if Victor—the dream character—picks up where he left off the last time I dreamt about him. Sometimes, he even remembers our past conversations better than I do."

"Are these like bad dreams?"

"Not at all. But Victor's unlike any character I've ever dreamt about. He was in one of my dreams last night, probably one of the most vivid dreams I've had in years." Dillan's tone was more fraught with emotion than he'd intended.

"Mind telling me what it was about?"

"I've been asking myself that question all day. We talked, about him, me, and the nature of dreams. I was lucid throughout most of it, but he tried to convince me he was real."

"That sounds so cool."

"It was ... I've never spoken to anyone about these dreams." Liz flashed him a reassuring smile. "I'm flattered then. This Victor guy, does he remind you of anyone?"

Dillan wavered. As much as he wanted to be truthful, he wasn't ready to share what he thought Victor represented. "I can see parts of me in him," he said, "but I could say that about other dream characters." He paused for a moment, as if to gather his thoughts, then said, "Victor's unusual. In my first dreams about him, I thought he was a psychiatric patient. He claimed he was searching for a woman—Maria—and said I needed to help him find her—still does."

"Any idea why?"

Dillan shook his head. "It sort of makes sense when he's explaining it to me in my dream, but once I wake up, the logic fades. I know he considers Maria to be the love of his life and that they somehow became separated. He needs to find her because she's the only one who can set him free, although from what I'm not sure."

"You have to admit this is pretty weird."

"I know," Dillan said. He couldn't imagine what Liz might be thinking.

"Tell me more about Victor. What does he look like?"

"He's my height, maybe a couple of years younger. Very fit."

"You think he's smart?"

"I would say so. His explanations can get convoluted, even melodramatic, but there's always a line of reasoning behind them."

Liz grinned. "So he is like you, only with added theatrics."

Dillan took the lighthearted jab in stride. "He's also helped me with some forensic cases."

"What do you mean?"

"There've been a few times when he pointed out options I hadn't considered."

"That's odd, even by dream standards," Liz said. "Still, he's a reflection of what's on your mind. Thoughts and ideas your brain hasn't finished processing."

"I know, but it still feels strange. Even in my lucid dream last night, there were times I wasn't sure what was real and true and what wasn't."

"When you consider everything you know about dreams, doesn't it make sense that your mind would come up with a character that embodies these interests? I think your brain is having some fun, kind of teasing itself."

"Maybe … but Victor's also told me things about the case—things I had no way of knowing—that turned out to be true."

Liz frowned. "Like what?"

"You're right," Dillan said after a few moments. "Victor's a product of my imagination. And he's told me some silly things as well."

"I would hope so. They are dreams, after all. Even if they're yours."

Dillan rested his head on the back of his seat. "Yes, they are…"

* * *

As he waited for Liz to return from the washroom, Dillan thought about the information she'd uncovered before leaving Montreal: how coroner Rossi, who had produced the report on Santilli's death, was actually a Swiss physician who worked for the European Union; how his unusual license gave him jurisdiction in over two dozen member countries; and how the secret pictures of Santilli had been encrypted on a server in Lugano, a city in a predominantly Italian-speaking region of Switzerland by the Italian border.

"You look lost in thought," Liz said, scooting in beside him.

"I was thinking about the pictures of Santilli and why they ended up where they did."

"Join the club." Liz looked out the window, then back at Dillan. "Antonielli said that Cellini was chosen because he could be black-mailed. But I don't think I'd trust someone known for sodomy, rape, and murder."

"You forgot about the necromancy," Dillan said.

She gave him a tap on the shoulder. "I'm serious. And why a vase? Something about it made it most suited for what he needed to hide."

"Assuming the vase actually exists."

"You said Vincente told you the vase was real. Don't you believe him?"

"I think he's been telling the truth, but believing it's real may be a way for him to make sense of what happened."

"So you're not sure there is a vase?"

"Not at this point. Although a lot of people are acting as if there is." He smiled. "And since Victor also believes it exists, maybe at some level, I do too."

"That's why I wanted to work hands-on with you, James. Nowhere in any textbook would I have learned that a key principle of sound forensics is heeding the advice of people in our dreams."

"I let you in on one of the greatest secrets of the trade, and you make light of it? I'd be careful if I was you."

Liz laughed, which pleased Dillan.

"Look," he said, leaning closer to her while pointing at something through the window. "Above those vineyards, there's a castle."

"It's beautiful," Liz said. "Like something out of a storybook."

"Maybe when this is done, we could look into taking a tour of the area." He made the suggestion naturally, spontaneously. This also pleased him.

"That'd be nice," she said, her eyes fixed on the high-perched castle.

After a moment, Liz turned to Dillan and said, "You never told me much about Michael. You two were good friends, right?"

Dillan nodded. "We met when I was starting my residency. He was doing his thesis on the uses of lucid dreaming to treat nightmares. We often got together to talk about sleep and dreams, especially over drinks. We had different views about science, though, and what it meant to understand dreams."

"How so?"

"He believed there was little to be learned about dreaming from studying the brain. To him, the answers to questions about how and why we dream didn't lie in neuroscience or in the use of scanners and polygraphs, but in the subjective experience of the dream itself."

"Are you saying he didn't believe in science?"

"I wouldn't go that far. He believed science was better suited to describing how things worked rather than explaining."

"So what happened?"

"Nothing, really. He just became increasingly distant—isolated even. I tried to call him a few times, but he never returned my messages. Next thing I knew, he'd finished his thesis and was getting ready to move to Italy, to be with a woman he'd met on a trip there. I didn't see him again till the conference in Berkeley."

"Where he introduced you to Santilli."

"That's right." Dillan held up his left index finger while reaching inside his shirt pocket with his other hand. His cell phone was ringing.

"*Dottore*, it's me, Tramonte."

Dillan's heart began to race. "Is everything okay?"

"Sorry I didn't call earlier. You were right to call me last night. I got there in time, but now we have a problem. I'm going to call you from Battista's office in a minute with bad news. Pretend we never spoke. I need you to trust me."

"I do," Dillan said, trying to make sense of the information. "Where are you?"

"I'm on my way back from Florence."

"Fine. Wait for my call. I have to go."

"Detective, is he safe?"

"Yes."

"Thank you." The doctor ended the call.

"What is it, James?"

"I'm not sure. It was Detective Tramonte. There's some kind of problem. He's going to call back."

"Something to do with Vincente?"

Dillan answered with a tentative nod.

His cell rang.

"*Dottore* Dillan, it's Detective Tramonte."

"How are you, Detective?"

"I'm calling from Captain Battista's office. There was a break-in at the station last night. Vincente was kidnapped. The police are still combing the area, and we have set up roadblocks, but no leads yet."

Dillan was thunderstruck.

"*Dottore.* Are you there?"

"Yes, sorry. I don't know what to say."

"Where are you now?"

"On a train near Verona. I'm on my way back to Trento."

"We'll need to see you later today. The captain would like to speak to you now."

"Of course, put him on."

"Doctor Dillan," growled Battista. "Tramonte said you were in Florence yesterday, visiting some art professor."

"I was. Luigi Antonielli, the director of the Accademia di Belle Arti. I spent the evening with him at the gallery."

"At what time did you leave?" The suspicion in Battista's voice was plain.

"We finished late, and Antonielli insisted I stay the night in his guest room." Dillan was certain Battista would make sure his story checked out. Despite knowing he'd done nothing wrong, the doctor was glad he had a sturdy alibi. He agreed to come to the station later that afternoon.

"One more question," said Battista. "When did you last see Kohler?"

"The night before last. We went out for drinks."

"Any idea where we can find him?"

"He mentioned having an early meeting yesterday morning. Otherwise, I assume he'd be at work."

"*Va bene.* Here is Tramonte."

"*Dottore*, Mr. Kohler missed his appointments with his patients yesterday and didn't show up at the university clinic this morning. We also got word that someone broke into his apartment last night. The place is being secured. You stayed at Kohler's the other night, so the captain wants you to go there with me. Help us see if anything is missing."

"You think he could have been involved in what happened?"

There was a pause. "It is too soon to tell," Tramonte answered. "I must go. We will see you when you get here."

Dillan put away his cell.

Liz's hands were folded together, as if in prayer. "What happened?"

"It's Vincente. He was kidnapped."

"Oh my God! From the police station?"

"Apparently."

"By whom?"

"They don't know yet. It happened last night."

"We need to tell the police what we know, right?"

"Probably…"

Liz put her hand on his arm. "There's something you're not telling me."

"I called Detective Tramonte last night. It was two in the morning. I was worried that Vincente might be in danger and insisted he go and check up on him."

"Did he?"

"Yes," Dillan replied. "But he never called back. Not until now. He was cryptic on the phone, but I think Vincente's okay."

"I don't get it. You said he was kidnapped."

"That's what the detective told me now—when he had Captain Battista with him."

"You think he's hiding something from the captain?"

"I don't know."

"What made you call the detective in the first place?"

Dillan wavered for a moment. "Victor warned me that the boy was in danger, that the people who had killed Santilli were going after him next."

"It was a dream, for heaven's sake."

Liz was right. But Dillan's rational thinking was no longer in the driver's seat. His mind was being governed by a gut feeling— a most unpleasant one.

"I know, but I had to do something."

"You're telling me you called the police and insisted that they act on ... on a tip from an imaginary friend?"

"Not the police. Just the detective."

"Shit, James. I'm sorry, but that's... Why would you do such a thing?"

"Because of what happened to my brother."

"I thought you were an only child."

Dillan stared at his feet. "He died when I was young."

"I'm so sorry. I had no idea."

"You couldn't have known."

She laid her hand gently on his knee. "You don't have to say anything."

He raised his gaze to meet Liz's. "There's no reason to keep it from you." He took a quick breath. "My dad had taken us ice fishing. He had this big ice auger. I loved watching him drill holes through the ice with it. He wanted to check some of the holes he'd made earlier and asked me to keep an eye on my brother. I felt something pull on my line and got all excited. Usually we'd yell something like 'Got one!' or 'Here!' whenever we felt a bite, but I didn't say anything that time. I didn't want my brother asking me to pass him my line, which he often did when I caught something. I wanted to keep that catch for myself. I could feel the fish twisting as I pulled it closer to the surface. When I saw its silver body through the hole, I looked up to call Daniel, but he wasn't on his stool. He was maybe twenty feet away, walking across the ice with his back to me. I called out to him, and as he turned around, the ice beneath him gave way. He sank under the ice. My dad ran over to him, but it was too late. We never saw him again."

Liz gasped, covering her mouth with her hand. "How old were you?"

"I wasn't even eight. My brother had just turned six. They said the current probably carried his body out to sea."

"I'm so, so sorry, James. I didn't mean to open a wound."

"That's okay," he said, although he felt anything but okay. "I haven't talked to anyone about Daniel in ages. One of the reasons I got interested in dreams was because of the nightmares I had after he died. They were sickening... When I woke up from my dream last night, Victor's warnings kept repeating in my mind. I could still see the look on Vincente's face when he asked me if I could help him. I promised I would. If something happened to him and I hadn't ... I couldn't take that chance, Liz. I had to make the call."

CHAPTER 30

M ihalovitch was sitting alone in the opulent room, his gaze fixed on the intricate patterns sculpted in the molded plaster ceiling. He did his best to get comfortable, but his wide back and sizable bottom were a poor match for the delicate eighteenth-century armchair. The familiar sound of crisp and steadily paced clicks rang out from the hallway behind him. He folded his arms over his watermelon-sized gut and closed his eyes. The woman in heels was on time.

"Hello, Ivan," she said, closing the door behind her.

Mihalovitch remained seated with his back to her. "Always a pleasure to hear your voice," he said.

The woman took a few steps toward him. "I thought the get-together went rather well, didn't you?"

"I think it went better for some than others," Mihalovitch said, breaking into a chortle. He kept his eyes closed and listened to the woman walk past him on the right, then stop.

"How much was Lee able to find out?" she asked.

Mihalovitch pressed his fingertips together over his distended belly. His knuckles cracked. "More than I expected. He knew the lab was in Heidelberg, that none of the trials had gone on for more than a few minutes, and that the drug would soon be ready." He waited for a moment, then said, "Lee was confident he could get hold of the drug once the testing was over. Whoever spoke to him was no underling."

"Anything else?" Iris said, sounding unsurprised.

"Indeed there is. Lee believed one of the test subjects might have been able to venture into the other side. She apparently died of heart failure before she could wake up."

The woman remained silent.

"So it's true?" he asked.

"The drug was tested on a top-tier lucid dreamer," she said. "Oshima insisted his team was ready. *I* authorized it."

"Who else knew about it?"

"There were four people working that night. Three scientists, including Oshima, and a technician. The subject had over a dozen nights of training with the new drug. She was five minutes into her second period of REM sleep when she started to convulse and choke on her own blood. Less than fifteen seconds later, she was dead."

"Details, my dear."

"Oshima and his team tried to snap her out of her sleep, but she wouldn't wake up. Their attempts to revive her proved unsuccessful. Her carotid arteries had been ruptured, her retinas seared, and her throat crushed."

Mihalovitch shifted slightly in his chair but kept his eyes closed. "For a *taurine* to take her out like that, she had to have made it into the hidden realm—or have gotten tantalizingly close. That's quite the breakthrough."

"Indeed." The woman took a few steps, then turned on her heels. "Any idea who the snitch might be?" She was now facing him, no more than five or six feet away.

"Not yet, but I'd look beyond the lab itself. Just to be safe."

"Of course," the woman said, as if this were a given. "Anything else, Ivan?"

Mihalovitch cleared his throat. "Things are moving rapidly, Iris. I'm delighted to hear of the progress with the drug, but we still don't have the stones, and without them, we'll be no better than parched seeds blowing across barren land."

"We *are* closing in on the vase." The woman's voice was self-assured, practically defiant. "A matter of days. A week at most."

"Music to my ears," Mihalovitch said, savoring the thought. "Centuries of searching, of leads and dead ends. And you, my dear, may well pull off what none of your ancestors, generations of the mightiest Medici, ever had the courage to attempt."

Mihalovitch opened his eyes and stared at the woman before him. Iris, as always, looked stunning. She wore a slinky, coral-red dress that highlighted her thin waist and small, shapely breasts. Her matching stilettoes and dark cuff bracelet bolstered the dress's contrast with her milky skin and cropped, jet-black hair. But, as in their previous meetings, it was her piercing, mismatched eyes that inevitably drew Mihalovitch's gaze—and caused him to feel uneasy.

"Once the stones are yours," he said, focusing on her pale, ice-blue right eye, "you'll rule over more than mere people—you'll rule their dreams."

"My forefathers were stubborn and weak," she said, seemingly unmoved by Mihalovitch's flattery. "They didn't embrace the stones. They turned away, frightened by the idea of true power. That mistake is about to be corrected."

"By the stones' rightful heiress, no less," he said, now looking at her left and exceptionally darker, copper-blond eye.

"What about my uncle?" she asked. "You think we can still trust him?"

"As much as a rat can trust a starving snake."

"Maybe bringing him into the fold was a mistake. We should have disposed of him when we had the chance."

"The Priorate did help you get rid of your parents, and his group was years ahead of anything your scientists had going on. It was the smart thing to do."

"I've heard stories, Ivan."

"About?"

"About where he's been, about newfound powers he's said to possess. Rumors have him not only entering the *anumia*, but also forging allegiances with forces within it."

Mihalovitch let out a roaring belly laugh. "That troglodyte? I may have it in me to believe that after all the concoctions he's tried, he may have stumbled on a way to access a shore of the hidden realm of dreams. But the *anumia*? And allegiances? Puh-lease. The man has the acumen of a goat and the skills of a lemming."

"That may be so, but even he could rule supreme if the stones were in his possession."

"I have my doubts. First, your uncle would need to get his hands on the vase. Easier said than done. Then, he'd have to figure out a way of getting the stones back into the *anumia*. Good luck with that! He'd also need to know how to use the stones, and even then, they would need to be in the right hands, and his remaining hand is far from right. All in all, a pretty tall order, even for a shrewd lemming."

The woman did not respond, but Mihalovitch hoped he had managed to allay her concerns, at least for the time being. "He may have learned more than we gave him credit for," he added. "But the day he crosses the line, I'll have him flopping and gasping like a goldfish out of water."

"I hope you're right. Now if you'll excuse me, Ivan, I have a rat to catch."

The woman headed toward the door, but Mihalovitch extended his arm, gently stopping her. He gazed up at her. "If I were you," he said, "I'd be looking for rats, plural."

The woman gave him a tense stare and then smiled. "I always do."

CHAPTER 31

D illan and Liz exited the train from adjoining cars and, as planned, went their separate ways. Liz stopped by the row of prominent cement columns framing one end of the Ferrovie Stazione di Trento, took out her cell phone, and studied the local street map. The hotel she had booked for herself and Dillan was less than a twenty-minute walk away. She buckled the waistband of her backpack around her hips and headed off.

One street corner away, Dillan was about to hail a cab when a chorus of church bells rang out in the near distance. He turned to an elderly woman walking past him. "*Che chiesa e?*" he asked, inquiring about the name of church responsible for the tuneful chimes.

"*Il Duomo di Trento,*" she answered, gesturing toward an area behind some buildings to his right. Dillan, captivated by the oddly familiar dinging and clanging from Trento's cathedral, felt a need to see the church for himself. Judging by the loudness of the melodic rings, he couldn't have been more than a few minutes away.

As he followed the simple L-shaped route the woman had indicated, the ringing diminished to a few bell tones, then stopped. Moments later, he noticed a blue sign on a street lamp. On it, in white lettering, were the words *Duomo di Trento*, and immediately below them, an arrow pointing to the right. What struck Dillan, however, were the two capital letters that stood out on the sign: DT.

* * *

The fountain of Neptune stood in the cobblestone square facing the north entrance of the cathedral, a vision of coral-colored marble. At one end of the imposing structure was a bell tower, its gray stone facade crowned by a dark metal dome. Dillan walked along the cathedral's high marble walls to the main entrance.

The cathedral's interior was grand yet solemn. The aisled nave, with its soaring bays and clustered piers, led to a baroque canopy under which stood a high altar. A number of people were inside, some walking about, some sitting—seemingly in contemplation—on the wooden pews facing the altar, others kneeling by white pillar candles. Everything was surprisingly quiet.

Dillan opted to walk down the aisle to his right. He stopped along the way to admire a series of frescoes, a sumptuous wood carving of the Virgin Mary, and, separated from the rest of the church by a wrought iron railing, a small chapel. Moving to the south transept, Dillan approached the high altar and studied the angels, cherubs, and emblems adorning it. Not knowing what, if anything, he was looking for, the doctor studied the faint light coming through the large rose window at the back of the cathedral and started up the other aisle.

Built high into the stone walls was a sharply angled staircase, the far side of which was too high up to make out. Immediately below the angled steps was a large fresco. Dillan was overcome by a sense of déjà vu. The larger-than-life size painting showed a young Saint Anthony kneeling by a wooden table, his arms nestling the Baby Jesus. The Child appeared to be explaining something to the holy man who was looking at Him with a deep, almost pleading gaze. Not only was the scene familiar to Dillan, but even more eerie, he knew what he was about to see next.

On either side of the fresco was a narrow, vertically oriented metal-and-glass display case, the inside of which was lined with red velvet. Pinned onto the fabric was a column of forged metal medallions, each shaped like a heart. Intricate designs, ranging from paisley-like swirls to forged angelic wings, edged the hearts, while a flaming torch crowned their tops.

At the base of the fresco was another distinctly familiar display case, this one horizontal and lined with bright sapphire-blue cloth. Behind the thick glass lay a row of similarly forged hearts, but their shinier appearance suggested they were newer. The feeling of déjà vu vanished. Perplexed, Dillan took out his cell phone and snapped several pictures of the medallions as well as of the fresco, the altar, the rose window, and the angled staircase.

CHAPTER 32

Battista was still barking orders in the hallway when he stepped into Detective Tramonte's office. "Where is he?" he asked Dillan. "He was supposed to be here one hour ago!"

"I haven't heard from him since we spoke in your office, Captain."

"I'm here, *Commissario*," called a voice from the corridor. Tramonte strode into the office. "Sorry I'm late," he said, catching his breath. "There was an incident with my father."

Captain Battista, still fuming, appeared to think over his response. "No reason not to return calls, Detective. *Chiaro?*"

"Yes, Captain."

* * *

The wheels of the police car squealed as Tramonte took a right-hand turn too late and too abruptly. "Sorry," he said, slowing down. Dillan took his hand off the dashboard and leaned back in his seat.

"Want to share what happened?"

Tramonte kept his eyes on the road. "After you called, I went to check on the boy. He wasn't sleeping. He was terrified. He said he was in danger, although he could not tell me from what. He begged me to get him to another room. I took him to an unsecured section of the wing and promised to stay with him till morning. Minutes later, we heard gunshots. I got a call that there had been a break-in, that intruders had made it to the boy's holding cell, and that Vincente was missing. That's when I decided to get him out."

"Why are the police still looking for him then?"

"I haven't told anyone. Not even the captain."

They stopped at a red light. Detective Tramonte gave Dillan a searching look. "How did you know someone was coming for him?"

"I didn't. I know this sounds crazy, but the warning really did come to me in a dream. I woke up thinking something might happen to Vincente. The feeling was so strong, I had to call."

The light turned green. "It's a good thing you did."

"Can I ask where he is?"

"I took him to a valley on the east side of the Dolomites. My dad has a *baita* there. It's a small hut in the middle of nowhere."

"Why didn't you call me sooner?"

"I needed to think about what I did. Then there's my father. He's been agitated. It's happened before, but never like this. He injured an orderly trying to force his way out of the nursing home. I had to go see him."

"Any changes in his medications?"

"No, but he's stopped sleeping."

"Since when?"

"He's been complaining of insomnia for some time, but these past few nights, he said he did nothing but pace the corridors. The night staff found him wandering around, looking for a way out. That's when he became violent. When I went back to see him this morning, he begged me to take him out of there. He said he had to go to the mountains, and that if he didn't, he would die." Tramonte's voice grew quieter. "I could not bear seeing him like that."

"Has this—the complete cessation of sleeping—ever happened to him before?"

"My dad was never one to sleep in, but he's always slept well."

"I don't want to alarm you, but it could be serious. I could speak to the doctors if you like."

"That would be helpful." Detective Tramonte made a right-hand turn. "We're almost at Kohler's apartment."

"There's something I need to tell you, Detective. When I showed you the pictures of Santilli, I told you I'd gotten them through a colleague. The same colleague who uncovered the coroner's original report. She's discovered more since then, and thought she could be more helpful if she was here. I agreed. She's now in Trento."

There was an awkward silence. "I'm not sure that was a good idea," Detective Tramonte said.

"I've known her for years, Detective. She's smart, careful, and trustworthy. And she's taken her fair share of risks in this case already."

Detective Tramonte pulled over to the side of the street and stopped the car. He turned to Dillan. "What do you plan on telling her?"

"The truth. That you got Vincente out of harm's way."

* * *

As soon as the two policemen in the apartment had finished relaying their findings to Detective Tramonte, they let him and Dillan examine the place. On the coffee table was a half full bottle of scotch and two empty shot glasses.

"We had a couple of drinks before heading out that night," Dillan said, motioning to the scotch glasses. At one end of the leather couch was Michael's laptop, its lid shut and its charger still plugged in. "That was there too," he added, pointing to the computer.

Dillan walked into the kitchen. The portafilter was exactly where he had left it on a paper towel next to the espresso machine. In the metal dish drainer by the sink were the small spoon and cup he had placed there to dry before leaving for Florence.

"Everything looks the same," Dillan said. "Is it okay if I open the cupboards?"

"The officers are done taking fingerprints. Yours are probably on most of these things anyway."

Dillan started with the ones to his left that contained a selection of spices and stacked bowls and plates. He reached for the cupboard to his right, the one that held cups and glasses. Peeking at him from the back of the top shelf was the familiar yellow rim of Michael's T-House mug.

Dillan and the detective walked over to the guest room. The doctor examined the surroundings. Nothing appeared out of place.

He and Detective Tramonte then walked into Michael's bedroom, where Dillan's eye was instantly drawn to the armoire. Its wooden doors were slightly open. He gently pulled on the two knobs. His heart skipped a beat. The armoire was empty. "Do you know if it was found like this?"

The detective called one of the officers, and the two of them exchanged a few words. "He says they found it open, and the shelves empty. Why?"

"They used to be full."

"With what?"

"Books. Diaries to be exact."

"Michael's?"

Dillan nodded. "There were dozens of leather-bound diaries in here. Michael kept a record of his dreams in them. They were still here when I left."

"Why would anyone want to take his dream diaries?"

"I don't know. Maybe they contained more than just dreams."

* * *

Detective Tramonte parked the car near the entrance to the doctor's hotel.

"What do we do next?" Dillan asked.

Tramonte sat in the dark and stared straight ahead. "The boy wants to see you. If it's okay with you, I will come and pick you up in the morning and drive you there." He fell silent, as if gauging something. "Do you think your friend will want to join us?"

"I'm sure she will, unless you have any objection."

"She would be taking a big risk. As you are."

"As we all are…" Dillan said.

"You never told me her name. Or what kind of work she does."

"Her name is Elizabeth Parks. Likes to be called Liz. She's a software engineer. Does much of the programming at our center."

"How did she get hold of the pictures?"

"She's a former hacker."

"Not that former, I would say… I will be back around five thirty. Make sure you pack your things. You might be at the *baita* for a few days."

"One more thing, Detective. The risk you took last night … I don't think I would have had the courage to do what you did."

Tramonte smiled. "Well, I don't think I would have had the courage to call a detective at two in the morning because of a dream."

"You did more than check up on Vincente. You put your neck on the line to save his."

Sitting in the silent darkness, Tramonte cleared his throat. "I don't think I had a choice."

CHAPTER 33

Dillan collected the key to his hotel room. As he walked past the elevator, he placed his hand over the small bottle of pills stuffed inside his pants pocket, then took the stairs, made his way to Liz's room on the third floor, and gave the door a gentle tap. He heard footsteps.

"James?" Liz whispered.

"Can I come in?"

Liz opened the door. Dillan stood there awkwardly.

"You're still up," he said.

"Of course. I've been waiting for you."

They stepped into her room, closing the door behind them. Liz, wearing a blue flannel T-shirt, matching pajama bottoms, and white slippers, looked at him. "Well?"

"The boy is safe. Detective Tramonte's the one who took him."

"What?"

"Vincente was in danger. People broke into the station looking for him. That's why the detective got him out of there."

Liz stared at him in disbelief. "The police know about this, right?"

"Tramonte was afraid someone on the inside might be involved. He hasn't told anyone, not yet anyway." Dillan could feel his heart pounding, but his voice came out sounding calm and confident.

"So where's Vincente now?"

"In one of the mountain valleys. The detective's father has a hut there. That's where he took Vincente. And that's where he'll be taking me—or us, if you want to come along."

"Of course I do. Is that okay?"

"I'm good with that, and so is Tramonte. But you'd be taking a big risk."

"You and I both." She walked over to the bed, propped up a pillow against the headboard, and sat cross-legged, her feet tucked under her thighs. "What else?"

Dillan approached the side of the bed but remained standing as he told her about his visit to Michael's apartment, about the missing diaries, and how nobody had seen or heard from Michael since the last night he had spent with him. Then he took out his phone.

"After we got off the train," he said, "I heard some church bells. They were coming from a cathedral, the Duomo di Trento."

"DT," Liz said.

"How'd you get that so fast?"

"I also heard those same bells," she said. "Only I was too tired to visit the *duomo*."

Dillan had always enjoyed her spunk, but rarely more than at this moment. "I went and took a look inside. There's some pictures I want to show you." He handed her his cell phone.

"I came across a painting of Saint Anthony holding the Baby Jesus, much like on Santilli's medallion. There were these display cases around it with forged metal hearts."

"Some of these are pretty dark," Liz said, flipping through the pictures. "Mind if we look at them on my laptop?"

"Go ahead."

She transferred them onto an encrypted USB key, plugged it into her laptop, and examined the enlarged pictures. "Any idea what we're looking for?"

"Not really. The whole arrangement felt strange. As if I'd seen it before."

"Look here," she said, zooming in on one of the shots. "Some of the medallions have numbers and letters etched in them."

Dillan took a look. "Could they be dates?"

"It's not the right format," Liz said.

Dillan became aware of the late hour. "We should get some sleep," he said. "We need to be up in a couple of hours."

"You go ahead. I'll look these over for a bit."

"Don't lose track of time, Lightning."

"Don't worry. I'll be ready. Me and my vampire genes."

Dillan smiled and headed for the door.

"James."

He turned around.

"Sweet dreams."

* * *

Dillan was sitting up in bed wearing a loose terrycloth robe. He picked up his cell phone and thumbed his way to the pictures he had taken of Michael's dream diary before the cleaning lady had surprised him. He turned his phone horizontally and enlarged the pictures. According to the dates in the top right corner of each page, the half-dozen dream reports he had photographed had all been written recently, the latest one having been drafted the day after Michael picked him up at the airport. He chose to start with that one.

He skimmed the dream and shook his head, frowning. It couldn't be. He read through the dream again, slower. It was impossible. He scrolled back several lines and reread one key passage, this time focusing on each word. The second he actually digested what he'd read, he almost dropped the phone, as if the words on the screen had scorched him.

Dillan was stunned. His heart was racing, his breathing labored and shallow. He glanced at the wall on his right, up at the ceiling, and back at the text. The words were still there, unchanged.

Something had to be wrong with the dream. He racked his brain for some explanation, anything to make sense of this. Maybe he was dreaming. He looked at the digital clock by the bed, closed his eyes, then looked at the clock again: the readout was the same. He got out of bed, hurried over to the switch on the wall, and turned off the overhead light. Except for the narrow band of light shining from under the washroom door, everything was dark. He listened. Silence.

He then walked into the washroom and examined the things around him: the towel hanging on the rack, the bottle of shampoo on the far corner of the bathtub, the small bubbles on the bar of soap he had used to shower, the droplets still clinging to the showerhead. This was no dream.

Dillan ran cold water in the yellowed washbasin and splashed himself with both hands. He stood there, staring at himself in the mirror. There had to be an explanation. Some kind of trick, maybe. He walked back into the room, stopped by his bed, and picked up his phone again.

The dream Michael had recorded in his diary was straightforward, the evidence unequivocal. He had been sitting at a bar, having a drink while waiting for someone. Sitting to his far left was a man, obviously drunk, wearing an unusually large black cowboy hat. The man he had been waiting for arrived and, steadying himself with his walking stick, took the empty stool to Michael's left. Although Michael's account included only cursory details as to his conversation with the man he referred to as "old M," the two had discussed Santilli's death, the fate of a young boy, and the whereabouts of a vase—by Cellini.

There was no mistake. This was the same scene Victor had told Dillan in his dream two nights ago. And although he couldn't fathom a rational explanation for it, Victor had in fact spied on Michael after following an old man into the bar—into one of Michael's own dreams.

Dillan's mind was adrift and his head whirling. He lowered himself onto the bed, hoping the spinning would stop. It didn't. He closed his eyes. The spinning got worse. His body was in it now too. And the room. He kept his eyes closed and his body still. The faint knock on the door jolted him. He wasn't sure if the sound had been real or imagined.

The spinning slowed.

He heard it again: three faint knocks. He slid his phone under his pillow and got up. His legs were rubbery as he made his way to the door. "Who is it?"

"It's me," Liz said.

Dillan, still dazed, opened the door. Liz had her laptop tucked under her arm.

"Did I wake you up? You look a little lost."

"I'm fine," blurted out Dillan, his mind still wading in a sludge of unfinished thoughts. In the dim light by the doorway, Liz's eyes looked more gray than soft green.

Dillan took a step back. The room started to spin again.

"I need to lie down."

"What's wrong?"

"My vertigo," he said, faltering toward his bed. He lay on his back then slid his hand under the pillow. "There's something I need to show you."

CHAPTER 34

The elevator began to rise. The entire contraption—walls, door, ceiling, and floor—was made of clear glass. Dillan strained his neck, looking upward, but couldn't make out the top of the skyscraper. The elevator was on the outside wall of the soaring edifice, allowing a view not only of the sky, but also of the receding pedestrians, cars, and buildings below. Dillan steadied himself as the carriage accelerated upward. Within seconds he was being propelled at terrifying speeds. The floors of the skyscraper flickered by, a vertical blur. He glanced downward. The ground lay thousands of feet below; the view made him sick to his stomach. He was trapped. His chest pounded, each thumping heartbeat resonating inside his head. He tried to scream, but nothing came. The glass walls boomed and shook as the elevator continued its launch. His legs buckled. Dillan collapsed on the glass floor. Looking up at the wall next to him, he saw a panel with columns of white buttons flashing in chaotic runs. Using his hands to steady himself, he crawled over. At the center of the circles were the numbers one through ninety-nine, and on the lower right-hand corner of the panel was what he had hoped to see: a button marked G. As soon as he hit the ground floor button, the elevator began to decelerate, the rumbling dissipated, and the panel stopped flashing. All was quiet as the glass contraption came to stop. Then, almost imperceptibly, it commenced a slow and steady descent.

Dillan leaned against the wall and let himself slide to the glass floor. He glanced at the buildings, cars, and pedestrians coming into view beneath his feet, then closed his eyes. Not once since first being petrified by the glass elevator dream as a child had he managed to halt his blastoff toward certain death. Michael had been right; hitting the ground button had altered the course of the dream. Dillan kept his eyes closed and breathed deeply as he listened to his slowing heartbeat.

The walls rattled. Something heavy had landed on the elevator with a thump. Dillan looked up. Crouched atop the glass ceiling was a gigantic beast, its outline amorphous, its eyes leering, its pupils fueled by a blazing substance churning like lava. The creature let out an ear-splitting shriek. Viscous, yellow-green vomit dribbled down the sides of its mouth and onto the elevator. The thick glass beneath the drool began to steam and liquefy. A massive fist appeared out of nowhere, hammering the elevator. Dillan squatted in a corner, cracks spiderwebbing across the glass cage. The beast wound up as the doctor crouched in a ball, shielding his head with his arms.

The creature's fist smashed through one of the walls, shattered glass raining down on Dillan. Thick, powerful fingers grabbed at him, but the doctor shot to his feet and threw himself against the wall to his right. The lift swayed, but the creature held on. The beast let out another ear-piercing shrill and unleashed a fury of blows. Glass shards flew in every direction as the elevator broke loose and began to plummet to the ground. Dillan tried to hang on as the world around him spun out of control. Cold, leathery fingers snatched him by the ankle, pulling him out. He punched and kicked and braced himself for impact.

Dillan's right forearm was first to hit the carpet, followed by his torso and legs. A light went on.

"Are you okay?" Liz cried, dashing toward him.

Dillan took a few breaths to quiet the pounding in his chest. Lifting his head, he noticed the couch behind him. The right side of his ribcage was hurting. He pulled his bathrobe over his legs and tried propping himself up on his right arm. It too was hurting.

"Yeah," he said, unconvincingly.

Liz hunched over him, her hand on his shoulder. "You let out this bloodcurdling scream. It freaked me out."

"I'm sorry. I was having a bad dream."

"What were you doing on the couch anyway?"

"You fell asleep on the bed with your laptop still open. I thought it best to sleep here."

"That wasn't necessary."

Dillan grimaced as he got up.

"What is it?" Liz was still wide-eyed.

"I think I hurt my arm ... and maybe a rib." He tried to pump his right fist, but a sharp pain shot through his forearm and into his elbow. Liz helped him back onto the couch and sat next to him.

"What were you dreaming about?"

"It's a recurrent dream," he said, staring at the rug. "I'm stuck inside an elevator, except it's made of glass and hangs outside of a giant skyscraper. The thing shoots upward, and I get dizzy and scared."

"Your vertigo."

"It gets worse. The thing keeps going faster and faster until everything breaks loose. I usually wake up as I'm about to hit the ground."

"What about this time?"

Dillan told her the rest of the dream.

"This is another recurrent dream of yours?" Liz said with overdone effect.

"The first part was. And the falling to my death at the end. The parts with the panel and the monster were new."

"So let me get this straight. For years you've been telling me how important dreams can be, but not once do you mention all the stuff going on in your own sleep?"

"You know the story. Nobody wants to hear about other people's dreams," he countered, trying to make light of the situation.

But Liz, who was now wearing a coy smile, wasn't about to let the doctor off the hook. "I would have liked to have heard about them. Just saying."

Dillan considered all the years he'd kept his nightmares to himself. "Maybe I should have told you. I always thought that if I studied these things long enough, the pieces would fall into place ... but they never did."

"Not sure science is the best place to turn to for answers to personal questions," Liz said. "One thing that strikes me, though, is how steady your dreams sound. They're not as shifty as most people's dreams, don't you find?"

"I do have dreams that are all over the place, but I get what you're saying. Particularly with my dreams of Victor..."

"And what about Victor being in Michael's dreams?" she said. "You have to admit, that's more than a little freaky."

"I'll admit that all right."

"Maybe these dreams you're having," Liz suggested, "are your brain's way of guiding you through the case, suggesting new ways of looking at what you already know."

Dillan gave a half-smile. "If my dreams have given you ideas about the case, I'm all ears."

"Do you mean that, James?"

"Of course. Why would you even ask?"

Liz appeared to hesitate. "I don't think you're always open with me."

The remark, although probably true, saddened Dillan. "Like when?"

"Just yesterday on the train, when I asked you if Victor reminded you of someone you knew. Your answer was pretty high on the BS scale. 'He reminds me a little of myself, but so do other dream characters.' This from a sleep expert? About his own dreams?" She flashed Dillan a knowing smile. "I'm glad you felt comfortable enough to tell me about your brother, I really am. And I appreciate everything you trust me with at work. But if you think these dreams are important, you have to give me more to work with."

Dillan looked at her in silence, grateful for her presence. "You're right," he finally said. "I wasn't particularly forthcoming. I'm sorry about that."

Liz touched his leg lightly with her fingertips. "I'm the one who's sorry. I didn't mean to be pushy. We all have things we'd rather not talk about."

"There are things hard for me to discuss..." He let his words drift and his hand come to rest on Liz's. Her skin was soft and warm. "You asked me good, legitimate questions, including about Victor. I spent many nights thinking about him and the timing of the dreams."

Liz turned her hand over, interweaving her fingers with Dillan's.

"One thing I noticed was that the dreams always appeared during times of stress, of self-doubt." There was a long pause, but not at all uncomfortable.

"I think Victor represents a side of my father I longed to see more of." Dillan's stomach tensed. "My dad wasn't one to give out praise. I don't know if he'd always been like that, or if what happened with Daniel had something to do with it. He always focused on my shortcomings, never on what I did right. Deep down, I think he never forgave me for what happened. That's how I felt. How I still feel today ... that I was the one to blame."

Liz waited a moment. "What about your mom?"

"She kept a brave face, but part of her died that day. She fell into a depression which she battled on and off for the rest of her life. Even as I got older, I couldn't shake the feeling that I'd let my parents down, that I'd ruined their lives."

"But it wasn't your fault," Liz said, gripping his hand. "You were just a kid."

Dillan shook his head. "No... I was the older brother who'd been asked to do something very simple, even for an eight-year-old. I wasn't the kid. Daniel was."

Liz's eyes welled up. She made no attempt to hide it.

"Victor's longing for Maria … I think it's a metaphor for lost love, for the little brother that I'd still have today, if only…"

Liz brushed Dillan's cheek with her thumb. "I'm always here for you. You know that, right?" She slowly leaned her head toward him and pressed her lips softly against his.

Dillan closed his eyes, losing himself in the moment.

Their warm, shallow breaths fused. Their lips lingered in unison, their movements slow and effortless. Dillan became aware of the tenderness of her lips, the delicate scent of her skin, the steadiness of their interlocked hands. He wished for time to stand still, but the rhythmic beats of his heart continued to mark its passage.

When their lips parted, Dillan found himself gazing into Liz's eyes. Together they reveled in a long, almost ethereal silence.

"I'm here for you too," Dillan finally said. "I have been for a long time, even if I don't always act like it."

Liz raised their interweaved fingers to her chest and gave him a gentle nod.

"We'll have to talk about this again," Dillan said. "But not today. We need to focus on what happened to Santilli and find a way to help her son."

Liz took a slow breath. "You're right," she whispered, gently squeezing his hand. "No reason why this lovey-dovey stuff can't wait till tomorrow." Her lips curved into a playful smile.

Dillan felt his muscles relax. He hadn't realized how tense he'd become.

"So," continued Liz. "Let's think through what we know then. Victor told you that there are others like him, people living in others' dreams. He also said most of them had bad intentions."

"That's right," Dillan said, thankful for the ease with which Liz was able to help him shift gears.

"We also know that something likely happened to Santilli while she was still asleep. And that she then chose or was forced to jump off the cliff." After a short moment, she said, "What if Santilli was running away from something in her sleep? Or in a dream. Something that could have also harmed Vincente. What if the only way for her to escape the threat was never to sleep again?"

"She would have fallen asleep eventually," Dillan said, "whether she wanted to or not."

"Only if she remained alive. What if her falling asleep could have endangered not only her own life, but also the lives of others, including Vincente? Jumping to her death may have been her only option."

"What you're suggesting is—"

"Crazy, I know. But so is plenty of other stuff we're trying to piece together. I was on to something before I fell asleep and you fell out of your elevator dream."

Liz got up from the couch. "Come see," she said, picking up her laptop and walking over to the corner desk. Not bothering to sit, she opened her laptop, entered her password, pressed her thumb against the fingerprint scanner, and called up the pictures taken at the Duomo di Trento.

Dillan walked over to the screen. His right arm and ribs were still aching.

She flipped through the pictures of the medallions and clicked on two close-up shots revealing the small letters and numbers engraved at their base. "I think I know what they are," she said, pinning the pictures in the upper left corner of her screen. She opened a text box and typed in a series of commands.

Dillan watched as successive lines of code appeared on the screen. "I put the letters and numbers through some algorithms," she explained. "Everything from simple Caesar shifts to statistical translation techniques."

"And?" Dillan said, not even pretending to understand.

"I think they're codes from the WGS."

"The what?"

"The World Geodetic System. It's what GPS coordinates are based on."

"You're saying they're locations?"

"I was only able to make out the engravings on three of the older medallions. Two of the coordinates point to areas in the Himalayas. One in Bhutan, the other in Tibet."

"What about the third one?"

"I had to check it twice. It's the plateau where Santilli and Vincente had set up their tents."

The doctor took a moment to process the information. "You're sure about this World Geographic System?"

"It's World *Geodetic* System, and yes, I'm sure. The info on each medallion converts to a specific coordinate."

"What about the newer medallions? The ones pinned on the blue cloth?"

"Only three of them had markings. The first one had the same coordinates of Santilli's camp."

"And the others?"

"That's what I wanted to check before I dozed off," she said, copying and pasting one of the coordinates into Google Maps. Her eyes narrowed.

"What is it?"

"This one points to another area of the Dolomites," she said. "At lower altitude, in a forest. I can show you on Google Earth." An image of a small clearing surrounded by conifers appeared in her browser.

Dillan examined the circular meadow. "Any idea what these places might have in common?"

"Not yet," she said, still typing away.

The doctor looked on as Liz entered the coordinates from the last medallion and hit "return."

She froze.

Incredulous, Dillan moved closer and stared at the map on the screen. It couldn't be. A red arrow was pointing to an address all too familiar to them. Liz switched to Street View. There was no possible confusion. On the screen before them was a three-story graystone building facing Jeanne Mance Park. It was Dillan's apartment.

* * *

Dillan was alone in his room and packing his toiletries when the phone rang. It was a quarter to five in the morning.

"*Dottore*, it's me. There has been a change of plans."

"What's wrong?"

"It's my dad. He took a swing at one of the orderlies again. They managed to calm him, but when I got there he begged me to take him to the mountains. I told him I could take him to the *baita* instead."

"Where are you now?"

"On my way to pick you up. We will be there in about ten minutes."

"I'll be ready. My friend wants to join us. Is that still okay with you?"

There was a moment of silence. "If you see no problems with this," said Detective Tramonte, "then yes, it's okay with me."

* * *

The detective's father was doing better since he had left the nursing home, according to his son, but Dillan was still concerned. The old man had lost a noticeable amount of weight in only a few days, his voice was scratchy, and the dark bags under his eyes were now the size of small plums.

As the car pulled away from the hotel, Liz and Dillan smiled at each other in the back seat, still amused that the elder Tramonte had referred to them as a married couple.

"You can catch up on your sleep," Detective Tramonte said. "The sun won't be up for a while."

"Actually, Detective," said Dillan, "I think I'd rather stay awake."

Detective Tramonte reached into a small compartment between the two front seats. "Do you mind if I put on some music?"

"Not at all," replied the doctor.

The opening trombone sequence of Adriano Celentano's "Azzurro" started to play.

Liz and Dillan watched on as the elder Tramonte moved his head to the music.

Detective Tramonte reached for his father's hand, and together, they started to sing.

CHAPTER 35

The midday sun beat down on the arid, rust-colored land. Michael picked his way forward, his feet sweltering in his brown leather boots. He stopped, examined the billows of dust kicked up by his footsteps, and watched the particles as they gently settled back down to the ground. He wiped his forehead with the back of his hand and peered into the distance. Against the glare of the sun, his eyes narrowed as he searched for his rendezvous point. The small wooden hut came into view. He rubbed his wrists and took four quick strides. Lifting his arms skyward, he leapt into the air, willing himself to fly. But his launch was feeble and his feet barely lifted before pounding back down onto the dusty earth. Flying wasn't going to work, at least not in this dream. He was going to have to walk the rest of the way.

Aware of the quietness around him, Michael looked up at the exceptionally clear, deep-blue sky. High above him, two parallel vapor trails drifted behind a small, silvery jet. He observed the plane as it silently inched across the sky, then trudged on toward his destination. The hut now looked more like an old ramshackle barn, its weather-beaten planks crooked and riddled with cracks and holes. He looked up again; the jet and its white vapor trails were gone. Michael approached the barn warily. The door was partly open, but it was the paisley-like pattern of washed-out grays and blacks in the wood grain that caught his eye.

He hesitated, studying the barn and his surroundings before pushing the door with his fingertips. To his surprise, it opened wide without the slightest creak. "You're in the right place!" a man called out. "Come in!"

Michael entered. Sitting at a table in front of him was a bear of a man sporting a hoary chinstrap beard that fused into wild, bushy sideburns. His head was bald and as big and round as a pumpkin.

"It took you a little longer than I expected, Mr. Kohler," the man said, his voice deep and gruff.

"I tried to fly but couldn't."

The man leaned back in his chair and chuckled. "Of course you couldn't. This is, after all, more my dream than yours. Wouldn't you agree?"

"Of course, Mr. Mihalovitch. I thought it was worth a try."

"Would you be so kind as to close the door?" he said, pointing a pudgy finger at the entranceway behind Michael. "And please, call me Ivan."

Michael pushed the door closed and turned back to Mihalovitch, hoping to get a clue as to what to expect, but the man's steel-blue eyes held only bemusement.

"I assume we can dispense with the tests lesser lucid dreamers usually want to engage in," Mihalovitch said.

Michael nodded. "Thanks for agreeing to meet with me."

"Please, have a seat."

Michael pulled out a chair, dragging its legs across the wooden floor.

"Tell me, Mr. Kohler, what do you think of the chair? Did I get the feel and weight right? What about the sound it made? Convincing?"

Michael sat at the table. "Yes, everything is remarkably realistic." He stomped his boots on the floor. "You even got my shoe size right," he added with a nervous laugh. "I'm trying to remember what I was doing before I walked here, but I'm drawing a blank." He examined the inside of the barn. Although beams of sunlight shone through the nooks and cracks in the walls, it was the bulb in a socket hanging from the rafters that provided the main lighting—a simple fixture with a long golden pull chain.

"You noticed it," Mihalovitch said, looking up at the bulb.

"The cord makes it look like an electric bulb," Michael said, "even though there aren't any sources of electricity here."

"And yet it works!" exclaimed Mihalovitch. "Care to see it in action?" He reached for the cord with an open hand.

"That won't be necessary," Michael replied, fearing some kind of trick. "I don't doubt your abilities."

"As you wish, Mr. Kohler. Now, I understand you're in deep shit and hope to stay alive by volunteering for one of our experiments. Is that about right?"

"Yes. I think I have what it takes."

Mihalovitch smiled. "We'll see soon enough. But the people you work for, they've lost their trust in you."

"I told the woman everything. I don't know who got to the boy or how anyone found out."

Michael turned in his chair. Someone outside was fumbling with the handle on the door. It creaked open. A tall man stepped inside, his shoulders hunched as if weighed down by the coat that covered his body down to his bare feet. Michael stopped breathing.

With slow and labored movements, the man in the dark suede coat made his way toward the table. He stopped and stared at Michael. The gray halo that had once circled his irises was gone, his eyes now luminous and white. Ivan cleared his throat and using his foot pushed out the chair next to him. The man slumped into the chair and lifted his seemingly cumbrous arms onto the wooden table. Michael stared. The man's left hand was missing. In its place was a coal-colored stump.

"I hope you don't mind my inviting the Priorate," Mihalovitch said. "I thought it'd be good to have your recruiter sit in on our meeting. Don't you agree? He is, after all, one of those who believe your life should have been terminated."

Michael processed the question. "Yes ... of course."

The Priorate sat in silence, his eyes iridescent and unblinking.

"Mr. Kohler was telling me that he doesn't know how someone could have gotten to the boy before we did."

"I was told where Vincente would be sleeping," Michael explained, "and took the drugs exactly as planned. But I don't think he ever went to sleep that night. There were no dreams for me to spy on."

Mihalovitch stared at Michael and after a short pause said, "Why don't you tell us about *your* special dream? The one you had before taking the drugs. You do, after all, have a dream you like to create before diving into these kinds of situations. Isn't that right?"

Michael responded with a slight nod, one meant to conceal his thumping heartbeat. "It's a tool I've been using for some time," he said. "A sort of recurrent dream in which I get to talk to my alter ego. A part of my unconscious, but in human form. It always takes on the same persona: me as a hunched-over centenarian. Our exchanges allow me to consider details I may have missed while awake."

"Where do you meet this alter ego of yours?" Mihalovitch asked.

"We always meet at the same place," answered Michael. "At a small bar I've created dozens of times in my dreams. It's something I've come to master. I always sit at the counter, first stool on the right. He always walks in through the front door using a cane for support then makes his way to the stool on my left."

Mihalovitch looked up at the light bulb. "You're sure nobody else could have infiltrated your dream?"

Michael's face tightened. "I would have felt it."

"So you say. But the only people who knew of the plan, other than you, were our lovely lady, whose heel mark still graces your jaw, the Priorate, and the men hired to kidnap the boy—a group most loyal to us. Under the circumstances, you can appreciate how tempting it is to point a finger in your direction. If, as you claim, you didn't speak to anyone about this while awake, then your dreams must have been the source of the leak. Who else was at the bar?"

"I always create the same scene. There's a bartender behind the counter who's a replica of a bartender I knew as a student. He takes my order, brings me my drink, then keeps to himself. There's also a drunken cowboy farther along on my left who's based on a movie character. He always wears the same oversized cowboy hat and drinks almost nonstop, but his glass is always half full. Neither of them are sentient, of course. They're just background. I've had them in place for years now."

"You know what I think?" Mihalovitch said. "I think you got complacent with these dreams of yours. I think you failed to properly monitor the background elements in the bar. And I think someone other than your so-called alter ego infiltrated your dream."

The man in the suede coat dragged his arms off the table, leaving inexplicable streaks of chalk-colored liquid on the wooden surface.

"I'm always careful," Michael hurried to say. "I'd have known if there was an intruder. I would have felt it."

"You're sure about that?"

"Yes."

Mihalovitch stroked his jaw. "Well then, you leave me little choice."

The light bulb overhead flickered. The Priorate's eyes appeared incandescent as he rose from his chair and let his heavy coat slip off his shoulders and onto the floor. The man's body was emaciated and hairless, his skin yellowish and dotted with festering sores, his external genitalia withered to a rumpled plum. Mucus oozed from his fingertips and stump, giving off a putrid smell.

The Priorate raised his arms above his head and dove over the table. As he soared through the air, he morphed into a leathery reptile with sharp claws and formidable outstretched wings. The beast knocked Michael over in his chair and pinned him to the floor. Its inhuman head moved close to Michael's and flashed a mouthful of rotting teeth; the stench from the creature's breath was stomach-turning. Outside the barn, frenzied howls filled the air. The beast sprang from Michael's chest, latching on to the rafters with all fours. Splinters of wood blasted into the room as a pack of wild dogs smashed through the walls. Two canines tore into Michael's calves and ankles. Michael kicked and screamed, but their jaws ripped his flesh and snapped his bones.

Everything went silent. Over Michael's right temple, a wild dog froze with a retracted upper lip, its sharp white teeth ready to dig into his skull. In the midst of the fixed scene, Mihalovitch sat in his chair, arms crossed over his belly, smiling.

The action resumed: the noise, the frenzy, the fear. Michael's face exploded with pain as the snarling dog planted its incisors into his skull and tore at his face.

Michael woke up, heart racing and unable to catch his breath. He was sitting in a stone chamber, his legs spread-eagle, his wrists and ankles covered in lacerations from the shackles chained to the floor. A man bearing a torch walked in his direction. Michael tried to make out his face, but the light from the torch hurt his eyes.

"You tell me you're certain no one could've infiltrated your dream," the man said, "yet you failed to recognize the illusory nature of the Priorate in our shared dream. How then can I possibly trust your judgment about what may or may not have been real in your own dreams?"

Michael couldn't speak; he was paralyzed with fright. Then, in a shadow near a wall, he made out the eyes of the Priorate.

"The boy," the Priorate whispered.

The words rang off the walls and resonated in Michael's head. He felt queasy and disoriented, drowning in panic. "You're right!" he said. "I can't be sure. Maybe someone was in my dream after all."

"That's disappointing," said Mihalovitch. "For a while I thought you might have been of use to us. But you're not up to the task."

Mihalovitch turned to look behind him. Someone was unlocking the chamber door.

The glowing eyes of the Priorate hovered closer to Michael and vanished into a blink. A cold wind blew into the room, driving the flames of Mihalovitch's torch into a frenzied dance before snuffing them out.

Darkness. Michael yanked on his chains. "Ivan, where are you?"

"He's by my side," said a woman's voice from the far end of the chamber.

Michael heard the woman close the door behind her and walk toward him. Although her pace was slow and deliberate, the sound of her heels striking the floor grew louder with each approaching step. She stopped a few feet away from Michael's shackled body, but the scent of her skin continued to journey forward. A fragrance of wet autumn leaves reached Michael, conjuring an image of barren trees in a shadowy field. The image vanished, supplanted by the sound of a sword being pulled from its metal sheath.

"This time," the woman said. "It's *your* hands I want."

"No!" Michael yelled. "Wait!"

He heard her step closer. She whispered, "Where's the vase?"

"I don't know!"

Then he felt it: the ice-cold blade hacking into his right hand, through his skin, tendons and bones. Blood shot out of his stump and onto his writhing body. He screamed, his maimed limb flailing in the air.

The woman planted the heel of her shoe in his cheek and thrust his head against the wall. Warm blood pooled inside his mouth.

"I'll ask you one more time," she whispered, easing her heel off his face. "Where is the vase?"

Michael spit out the blood and caught his breath. "I don't know, I really don't. Maybe in the Dolomites, away from where Santilli was found. I don't think she'd have taken her son near it. If not there, then maybe by the monastery where she trained as a kid."

Michael's back teeth came loose. Soon the rest of his teeth were falling out, spilling into the pool of blood amassing in his mouth.

He gagged and reached for his mouth with his stump, desperate to dislodge the mess choking him, but the woman drilled her heel back into his jaw, pinning his head against the wall.

He was losing consciousness. A thump-like sound pierced his ear as the sword sliced into the side of his neck. Its heavy blade, lodged several inches into his flesh, was pulled out and then came another blow, and another. Dizziness. A muffled voice. Then his head broke loose.

* * *

Michael's body snapped back in horror as he awoke in the dark. He was sitting in a stone chamber, his legs spread-eagle, his wrists and ankles tightly shackled to the floor. Other than the sound of his own gasping, the room was silent, and his captors nowhere to be seen. A rat stood over his fingers, gnawing at his hand. Michael squirmed and tried to flick it off, but his movements were too restrained to be effective and the rat too hungry to stop. Out of a corner of the room, a man bearing a torch appeared. It was Mihalovitch.

"Please," Michael begged. "You've made your point. I'm not ready for this."

"Oh, come on now, you're not going to give up so easily, are you?" Mihalovitch took a series of short, heavy strides and sent the rat scurrying with a swing of his torch. "Lucid dreamers usually pride themselves on recognizing false awakenings. Don't worry, though, this time you really are awake, and lucky for you, you still have your hands—and your head."

"What do you want from me?"

"You have this all wrong, Mr. Kohler. It was you, not me, who requested this meeting."

Mihalovitch knelt by Michael's side and examined his face. He scooped a small drop from Michael's cheek with his finger and tasted it with the tip of his tongue. "The interplay between dreams and wakefulness is so fascinating. Your dream-self cries in a distant world, yet it's your earthly body that sheds tears."

Michael recoiled as Mihalovitch placed the torch by his temple, briefly searing the side of his head.

"Being able to control your lucid dreams is child's play. But once you get involved with people harboring inscrutable pasts, once forces you know little about start seeping into your mind, once you willfully accept to enter another man's dreams, once you do that, you'd better know what the hell you're getting yourself into."

"I misjudged things. I understand that now. Give me a chance. Let me go after a *taurine*. I'll die if I have to."

"A *taurine?*" Mihalovitch burst into laughter. "There are so many things you don't know, Mr. Kohler. And thus so many ways for you to screw up as you straggle into worlds whose nature you don't understand."

"When you asked if someone could have entered my dream," Michael pressed to say, "I was too scared to admit my doubts. The lady in heels was clear. My only hope of staying alive was to convince you of my worth."

"Iris," said Mihalovitch.

"What?"

"The woman in heels. Her name is Iris."

Michael let his head drop and began to laugh.

"Do share, Mr. Kohler."

"Iris is the name of the Greek goddess of the rainbow … of the sky and sea. She was also an envoy for the Olympian gods and carried a pitcher of water from the River Styx."

"And why is this so amusing?"

Michael looked up at Mihalovitch. "She used the water to put anyone who'd perjured themselves to sleep. It's fitting irony, her thinking that I've somehow perjured myself, then allowing me to be put to sleep and killing me in a dream."

"You're smarter than I gave you credit for. Alas, you've given me no reason to recommend that you be kept alive." Mihalovitch turned and began to walk away.

"Wait! I know I can defeat a *taurine*."

"You? You almost shat yourself because of some imagined dogs. Please, I don't think so."

"I already fought one, years ago. When I was a kid."

Mihalovitch snickered. "If you had, you wouldn't be here speaking to me. You'd be long dead."

"I swear it's true. I did more than study the hidden world of dreams. I entered it once."

"Do continue."

"I was nine at the time. I dreamt that I was standing on a see-through flooring, like the curved top of a glass dome. Beneath me was a black sea. I saw a dark mass moving on the horizon, and just by the feel of the dream, I knew it was something formidable. I became so cold, even my bones ached. I didn't dare move. I lost sight of the creature, and then it happened. It grabbed me by the throat. The fear was overwhelming. Having it that close, its flaming eyes peering into mine. I remember thinking this was going to be an extraordinary way to die. I don't know what I did or thought, but something changed. It was as if something greater than the dream had taken over, and I was one with it. The fear was gone. I knew I could win."

Mihalovitch smiled. "You didn't, though, did you?"

"My sister heard me moaning in my sleep. She shook me out of the dream before I could fight the creature. I know what I'm up against. All I'm asking for is a chance."

"You're a desperate man. Why should I believe you?"

"Look under my T-shirt," Michael said. "On the left side of my chest, you'll see a scar. It's from the *taurine*, from the liquid it drooled on me."

Mihalovitch came closer to Michael, pulled up his T-shirt, and lowered the torch to get a better look. He slowly ran his index and middle finger back and forth over the scar, then lifted his gaze. "This changes everything. If you were to meet that creature again, you might be able to kill it. I can make that happen."

"Really?"

"Yes. I could train you. Show you ways of entering the *anumia*. Given what you've told me, I assume you know what that is."

Michael nodded. "It's been called different names throughout history. It's a secret dimension of dreams, one inhabited by creatures and forces from other worlds. Like the *taurines*. Many consider it a sort of Holy Grail, proof of the existence of a world beyond this one."

"Proof indeed," Mihalovitch said with a grin. "But the *anumia* is much more than the secret world of dreams. It's infinitely more powerful—and dangerous."

"I'm not sure I follow."

"The *anumia* lies within the deepest reaches of the dream world. It's its beating heart. The forces and creatures you mentioned, they all draw their powers from this living core. Not a year goes by without a handful of people stumbling onto one of its distant, outer shores, often during a childhood dream, when their minds are still open to the unknown. Reaching the *anumia* itself, however, is a whole other matter. The paths that lead to it are well-guarded, as you saw for yourself. Those who make it there are unusually gifted—or cleverly drugged," he added with a smirk. He then looked Michael in the eye and said, "Tell me, why did you accept to work for the Priorate?"

"After I'd glimpsed the hidden dream world, I spent my life trying to find my way back inside. I trained hard and became proficient at lucid dreaming. I even experimented with dream intensifiers, stuff like choline, ibogaine, and galantamine, but never managed to find a portal. The Priorate promised me drugs that would make that possible."

"In exchange for?"

"Putting my dreaming skills to his service. I didn't know what I was getting myself into. That I'd be working for a monster. Other than drugs to observe people's dreams and some feeble REM enhancers, he never gave me shit. Only orders and threats. He said he wouldn't hesitate to kill my sister, as well as my parents. I believed him."

"As you should have. But he did pay you, and well too, from what I've been told."

"I was never in this for the money. I was in it for the dreams."

"Does he know about the scar?"

"I was too afraid to tell him."

Mihalovitch raised an eyebrow. "Why?"

"I knew he'd tried all sorts of things to induce lucid dreaming, everything from direct transcranial magnetic stimulation to the latest experimental drugs. I also knew that what he was really after was a way into the hidden realm of dreams, probably into the *anumia* itself from what you've just said. I never told anyone about the scar when I was hired. And then it was too late. I became afraid that if he ever found out, he'd have me killed—or worse."

"A likely outcome," Mihalovitch said. "Your recruiter was once the head of a multinational conglomerate and part of a small, affluent group interested in new technologies, including drugs being developed for lucid dreaming. And like many people who tried these drugs, the Priorate became addicted. Not so much to the pills themselves, but to the dreams they enabled him to have. Soon things like flying and sex weren't enough. Bigger thrills were needed and more powerful drugs were developed. Your recruiter first pushed for the creation of drugs designed to intensify REM sleep, then to prolong it, then to stimulate skills normally absent during sleep, things like logic and memory. Now, after joining forces with Iris, he's on the verge of producing the kind of drugs he'd promised you. Cocktails that will allow people to enter the *anumia*. And that's just the start."

"Do the new drugs work?"

"Apparently. Although our subjects have yet to survive the experience."

"Why's that?"

"Even in sleep, you have to be careful about the gates you choose to open. Portals to ancient worlds are never left unguarded, and the *taurines* are ruthless. They are to the *anumia* what great whites are to the sea, and surviving an encounter with any of their kind is a rare, extraordinary event." Mihalovitch glanced at the door behind him. "We don't have much time before Iris gets back. I'll make sure nothing happens to you while you're here, but she can't know about the *taurine*."

"Whatever you say."

"You've insisted you didn't know where the Cellini is, and after the dreams I put you through, I'm inclined to believe you. A man of your intellect, however, must have some idea about the secret it holds."

"I think there's a substance or object inside it. Maybe a code or a formula."

"Go on."

"I think the secret has something to do with the hidden dream world—with the *anumia*. Maybe it can be used to defeat the *taurines*, or maybe to forge alliances. Either way, whoever gets hold of it will possess something unimaginably powerful."

The door to the chamber opened. Two guards, each bearing a torch, stepped inside. Right behind them was the woman in heels.

Mihalovitch turned around. "Hello, Iris. As always, your sense of timing is impeccable. We've just wrapped things up."

Iris remained motionless in the flickering shadows cast by the guards' torches.

"Was the meeting in any way beneficial to us, Ivan?"

"Indeed, it was. Michael here was very collaborative and his insights rather surprising. Quite valuable, in fact."

"So you've reached a decision?"

"I have, my dear. Kill him. And do it now."

CHAPTER 36

Detective Tramonte was walking toward the mountain hut when a breeze whistled through the pines. He stopped and looked over his shoulder. His father was gazing at the forested hills and adjacent peaks while Dillan and Liz stood silently behind him. The detective made his way to the top of the stone steps and pressed the latch on the wooden door of the *baita.* It wasn't locked. He pulled the door open and called for Vincente. No one was inside. He looked into the trees and shrubbery and called the boy's name.

"Detective!" answered Vincente.

Withered branches snapped under the boy's feet as he emerged from the woods. The second Vincente caught sight of Dillan, he sprinted to him.

"I knew you'd come!" the boy exclaimed, hugging the doctor. The detective walked over.

"I know you told me to stay inside, Detective," Vincente said, "but I wanted to see the sunrise. I didn't go far."

"That's okay," Detective Tramonte said. He introduced the boy to his father.

Vincente offered the older man a handshake. The elder Tramonte obliged and said something that made the boy smile and the detective laugh.

"He thinks Vincente is your son," Detective Tramonte explained to Dillan and Liz. "Says you make a nice family." Dillan gave Liz a smile then noticed the boy staring at the elder Tramonte's black hiking boots. "Everything okay?"

"Mama had the same boots. She rarely wore them, though."

"I have no idea where they came from," the detective said. "He had them on when I went to get him." The detective headed toward the *baita* with his father. "We'll be inside."

Vincente kept his eyes on the senior's feet as he walked away then turned to Dillan and the redheaded woman by his side.

"Vincente, this is Liz, a great colleague from Montreal and one of my best friends."

Vincente examined her face. "I like your hair," he said, shaking her hand.

"That's sweet of you to say, Vincente."

"Are you also a sleep doctor?"

"I'm a software engineer. I help James with his projects at the lab."

"Are you the one who puts the electrodes on people's heads?"

"No, but I develop programs that help people analyze the signals picked up by those electrodes."

"Sounds fun."

For the first time since he'd met Vincente, Dillan thought the boy looked content.

"It often is," Liz said.

* * *

Sitting around the table, the group had failed to reach a consensus as to what to do next. Vincente insisted that Dillan accompany him into the Dolomites to help him find whatever it was his mother had wanted to show him. Detective Tramonte opposed the idea, judging it to be short on specifics and high in danger. Dillan was wavering. As much as he wanted to help the boy, the detective was right; Vincente had little idea of where in the mountains they needed to go.

Detective Tramonte rested his forearms on the table. "You said your mom may have been taking you to a small *refugio*. Even if you are right, there are probably over half a dozen huts in the area. It would take us two days just to get to where your tents were."

Vincente looked as if he was about to cry.

"Do you know how many more days you and your mom were supposed be in the mountains?" asked Liz.

Vincente shrugged.

"Think about the food you had with you, or the quantity of fuel for the stove, or when you were supposed to be back at school. That could help us narrow down the area where the hut might be."

The boy looked at Liz. "I'm not sure about the food, but Mama said I'd probably miss two or three days of school."

"That's good. You left on a Saturday morning, so if you had turned around after setting up camp on Sunday, the earliest you could've been back was Tuesday. It's possible that you were only a day's hike from wherever your mom wanted to take you. That would have meant missing three days of school."

"So the *refugio* has to be somewhere near there," Vincente said.

Detective Tramonte shook his head. "The hut could be deep in the mountains or along difficult routes used by rock climbers."

Domenico Tramonte, who had fallen asleep in a chair at the far end of the room, woke up amid the discussion. He glanced out the window beside him then rose and walked over to the table.

Detective Tramonte offered his father a chair and explained their quandary about the location of the mountain shelter. The elder Tramonte muttered something to his son, who got up and went into one of the two small bedrooms. He came back out with several green maps, which he laid on the table while examining their titles. He unfolded one of the maps with the help of his father, who smoothed the creases with the palm of his hand.

"This is where the tents were set up," Detective Tramonte said, pointing to a spot in the upper right quadrant of the map. He took a pencil from his pocket and traced a jagged semicircle on the map that extended away from where Santilli and Vincente had camped. "If your mom had planned to hike somewhere and back in a day," he said, looking at Vincente, "then this is about the area she could have covered."

Domenico Tramonte studied the map and slowly ran his index across the area bound by the pencil marking. He stopped, tapped his finger, and said something to his son.

"My dad says that only two shelters were built in this area. One of them was destroyed years ago by an avalanche and was never rebuilt. The other one should still be there, right where his finger is. It should not be hard to reach by one of the main trails."

Dillan glanced at the map then looked at Detective Tramonte. "Are you sure we can trust his memory?"

"About something like this, yes. He knows these mountains like the back of his hand."

"Does that mean we can go?" asked Vincente.

Dillan was uneasy. "I'm not sure we have what we'd need to spend a couple of days in the mountains."

"You are right, *Dottore*," Detective Tramonte said. "But I might be able to get you up there and back down in a day."

"How's that?"

The detective discussed something with his father while they studied the map.

"There is another way up," Detective Tramonte said, turning the map toward Dillan. "The red dotted lines are trails, and this one here is the one Vincente took with his mom. Other than a short section requiring metal cables—a basic *via ferrata*—it's a fairly easy climb. But there is another, unmarked way to get up there."

Dillan didn't like what he was hearing.

"Right here, on the western flank of the mountain," the detective said, pointing to some contour lines on the map, "there should be a functional lift."

"Functional?" repeated Dillan, as if he'd misheard.

"It's like the open gondolas you see on some ski hills. This one was used to carry materials to higher areas of the mountain. Things like wood, tools, and stones."

Dillan was liking the conversation less and less. "So it's not meant for people, is it?"

"It's a simple system," said the detective. "Does not matter what it carries, as long as the weight limits are respected. People have ridden it, of course. Even my dad."

Dillan began to think about the gondola's age and its current state. "How long has it been there?"

Detective Tramonte shrugged. "Probably forty, fifty years. Maybe more."

"And it still works?"

"It should. My dad knows where they used to hide the key. Hopefully it's still there."

"Is it far?" Liz asked the detective.

"About an hour's drive."

Vincente's eyes lit up. "Can we go?"

Dillan's chest tightened. "I've never been up mountains like these."

"If my dad is right about the hut," the detective said, "then most of the route will be along marked trails. They will still be muddy from the snow, but nothing dangerous. I probably have something you can wear, maybe even an old pair of trail runners, and things like knapsacks, headlamps, and gloves."

"Would you be hiking with them, Detective?" Liz asked.

"I can't. Captain Battista gave me some leeway because of my father, but I need to get back to the station."

"Maybe I could go with them," she offered, glancing at Dillan.

"That would be good," the detective said.

"What about you, Vincente? Would you mind if I came along?"

The boy responded with a half-hearted shrug.

"I know we've just met, and I'd understand if you'd rather not have me there."

"It's not that."

"What is it then?" Dillan asked.

"Doctor Dillan is the one my mom spoke to me about. I think it needs to be just us two."

Although Dillan would have preferred Liz join them, he sensed he had to respect Vincente's wish. "Would that be okay with you?" he asked, turning to Detective Tramonte.

"You need to promise me two things," the detective said, addressing the boy as well as the doctor. "First, that you will check in every hour. You might not get cell reception everywhere, but if you move away from the rock walls, you will be okay. Second, you go to the hut and back. That's all. No detours. Agreed?"

Dillan and the boy nodded.

"Do you know how to use a compass and map, Vincente?"

"Since I was six."

"Good."

"Where do you want us to meet afterwards?" Dillan asked.

"Wait for me at the top of the lift. I will be there by five at the latest."

Dillan turned to Vincente. "Looks like you and me it is. I have to warn you, I'm not much of a mountain guy."

The boy smiled.

"Ms. Parks, you are welcome to stay here if you want," Detective Tramonte said. "Or I can drop you off in Trento and get you on my way back."

"What about your father?" she asked.

"I will drive him to the residence untill I'm done."

"Going to Trento would be good," she said.

"We are all set then," Detective Tramonte said.

CHAPTER 37

D illan was sitting on a rock with his head between his knees and his eyes fixed on the overly tight trail runners the detective had lent him. He was trying to calm his mind, but his nerves were not getting the message. The ride up on the cable car had made him nauseous, and he still felt as if his insides were swaying over the precipitous drops.

Vincente took a step closer. "Are you going to be sick again?"

Dillan looked up, forcing a weak smile. "I told you I wasn't much of a mountain guy."

"Is it the thin air?"

"I have a fear of heights. It gives me vertigo. Do you know what that is?"

"It's like dizziness, only worse."

"You're right. It's as if everything inside you is spinning out of control."

"Have you always been afraid of heights?"

"Pretty much."

The boy surveyed the snow-capped peaks and jagged spires on the horizon. "Thanks for coming with me."

"I made you a promise, Vincente, and I intend to keep it."

Dillan and the boy watched the shadows cast by low-lying clouds glide across the wind-scoured expanse, transforming argent boulders into glum mounds of stone. Winding across the rock-strewn plateau was the trail they were about to take.

"My mom always said that there were no other mountains like these."

"I think your mother was right," Dillan said. He heaved.

* * *

Although parts of the footpath were covered with gray slurry, making the steeper sections slick, Vincente and the doctor were advancing at a good pace. Dillan's shoes, however, were squishing, since the doctor had slid on one of the declines into a pool of stagnant water. Vincente stopped to check their position.

"There's another cairn up ahead," Dillan said, pointing to a pile of rocks stacked several feet high.

"I saw it, but this is where we need to leave the trail to head east," Vincente said, appraising the pale gray hills and karstic terrain before them. He took a swig from his water bottle and showed the doctor where they were on the map. "You should drink," he said. "It'll help with the altitude."

"I'll wait. My stomach is still sensitive." Dillan checked the reception on his smartphone. The signal was weak but serviceable. "We need to give Detective Tramonte an update."

Trail is muddy but fine. Now at first junction. All good. Dillan pressed "send" and waited until the message was marked "delivered."

"You should wring out your shoes," advised the boy. "You don't want to get blisters."

"You're right." Dillan scouted the area for a suitable rock to sit on. His cell buzzed. *Buono. Driving to Trento with L and my dad. Stay safe,* read the text sent by Detective Tramonte.

Another text bubble appeared. *Hi Dr J! Hugs to you and Vincente. Liz. PS: Try to relax and enjoy the ups and downs* :)

"Detective Tramonte and Liz say hi," Dillan said, putting away his phone. He sat and tried to take off his shoes. His wet laces, however, wouldn't come undone. He took a pen out of his knapsack, forced the tip into the knot, and wiggled it loose. One shoe finally came off, then the other.

"You're doing well," the boy said. "I mean, for someone who's not much of a mountain guy."

Dillan favored his good arm as he wrung out his shoes and socks. Stuffing his feet back into them, however, was trickier than expected. His dank skin clung to his socks, and his shoes, already a half-size too small, refused to stretch over his heel.

"Need any help?"

"You mean with the stupid socks or the smelly shoes?"

They laughed, and in that klutzy moment, Dillan realized how deeply he cared about the boy. It went beyond Santilli telling her son that he could be trusted. What he felt was commanding, visceral. Something about Vincente reminded him of Daniel. *You can't let anything happen to him.* The two exchanged a silent gaze, after which Dillan continued to pull, twist, and yank on his ill-fitting shoes till they were back on his feet.

"Ready?" Vincente said, amused by the doctor's efforts.

Dillan reached into his knapsack, pulled out his water bottle, and took a sip. "There. Now I'm ready."

The boy set out at a brisk pace up the gradual incline, with the doctor right behind him. "Is Liz your girlfriend?"

"Not really."

"But you like her."

"Yes, a lot."

"She seems to like you too."

"I think she does."

"So why isn't she your girlfriend?"

"It's hard to explain. Maybe I wasn't ready."

"Ready for what?"

"I'm not sure."

"You're not making sense."

"I know."

They came to a rise in the trail and slowed as they ascended the barren, rocky slope.

"Can I ask you something else?" said Vincente.

"Of course."

"When do children start remembering their dreams?"

"That's a good question. And a tough one. Children first need to understand what a dream is, which isn't as easy as many people think." Dillan stopped and took a few breaths. "Storing dream experiences into long-term memory requires a certain level of brain development, and children need sufficient verbal skills to—"

"I just want to know at what age."

"You're looking for a simple answer to a complex question."

"My question *was* simple. You're the one who's making it complicated. You did the same thing when you tried to explain why spinning in dreams works."

"You're right… So, some children start remembering basic dreams, including scary ones, around the age of three. But it usually takes several more years before their dreams are similar to those of teenagers and adults."

"In what way?"

"In how long their dreams are, in the range of emotions they experience, in how dream characters behave and talk. Dreaming is complicated. Your brain has to create a 3D virtual world and not only have the dreamer move within it, but also other characters, be they people, animals, or weird creatures. Then there are all the things we see, feel, and hear in our dreams. That's why the kind of dreams children have depends on their mental development."

"You're making it complicated again."

"But you understand what I'm trying to say."

"Yes … three years old."

The trail had become faint and much rockier since they began climbing the steep, snaking switchbacks. Above them, a band of loose scree waited to be crossed, and beyond that stood a soaring rock wall, its jagged points rising from behind the barren crest.

Dillan exercised caution, focusing on where he was stepping while keeping his eyes away from the dizzying rubble-choked gulley to his right.

"When we spoke the other day," Dillan said, "you mentioned that your mom had told you some things about me. Can you tell me more about that?"

"I'm not sure you're ready."

Vincente's answer left the doctor perplexed. *Ready for what?* "When do you think I'll be ready?"

"Soon, I hope."

Dillan and the boy kept plodding upward. As they approached the ridgeline, the wind picked up and whistled in their ears. Ahead were large clouds, including one shaped like an anvil. Dillan studied the dark tessellations at the base and the bulging mass of whiteness above it. "Do you think it's going to rain?"

"Not for a while."

"Can you be more precise?"

"The clouds we saw earlier are changing into cu … mu … lonimbus clouds."

"I'll have to trust you on that one. The name sounds menacing, though."

"It usually means it's going to rain," said the boy, "but they're moving sideways, not toward us."

Dillan smiled. "So you're saying we'll be fine."

The boy nodded.

The doctor clapped Vincente on the shoulder. "Let's keep going then before those fancy-named clouds decide to head our way."

After a final rise, they crested the hill, entering the lunar-like landscape at the top. The trail followed a gentle gradient as it wound through bleached scree and a long stretch of gravelly earth that leveled into a rocky basin. Rising from the far side of the basin were the sheer walls they had seen earlier as well as long, sloping wedges of rock, several of which harbored late-lying snow. With the wind gusting into their side, they left the exposed crest and began their descent.

"If children start remembering their dreams around the age of three," resumed Vincente, "at what age do you think people should start training them in dreaming?"

"What do you mean by training?"

"What we talked about. Turning falling dreams into flying dreams. How to become a lucid dreamer, how to explore dreams, stuff like that."

"I'm not sure there is an age. I mean, people don't train their kids how to dream—not in Western societies anyway. Why are you asking?"

"My mom said it was important to learn how to dream and that to become a good dreamer you had to start young, like musicians and athletes. She said that one reason why most grown-ups don't have lucid dreams is because they're not taught as children how to keep having them or why they're important."

"Your mother was probably right. Did she give you this sort of training?"

"My mom had me remembering my dreams before I went to kindergarten. When I was about six, she started teaching me different techniques for lucid dreaming."

"Like what?"

"You know what the word *sogno* means?"

"It means 'dream' in Italian," Dillan said.

"My mom had me write an *S* for *sogno* on the back of my hand, and every time I noticed it, I had to ask myself if I was dreaming. I mean really ask myself and stop to think about it. I'd look to see if anything around me was unusual. The sky, people, the season, my clothing. I'd try to remember what I'd been doing right before I noticed the *S*, how the day had started, how I'd gotten to wherever I was. It got me used to thinking in a certain way. Soon I was asking myself these questions in my dreams too. That was one way I learned." The boy slowed down. "There are other ways. And different tests to see if you're dreaming. The important thing is to keep practicing till you find what works for you."

"What kind of tests do you like to use?"

"I try to fly in my dreams. I've gotten good at that. I also try things like reading. I usually can't, and if I look away from the page and then back again, the words are all different."

"That's a good test," Dillan said. "Some scientists believe that reading is difficult because there's no physical book or text in your dreams. Your brain needs to create all the words and sentences you see, and if you look away and back again, it needs to recreate the text exactly as it was before. That's hard." The doctor stopped to catch his breath from the short climb.

"You're getting better," the boy said.

"Better at what?"

Vincente looked back at the doctor. "At explaining things," he said with a grin. "What kind of tests do *you* use?"

"I don't often have lucid dreams," Dillan said, "but one thing I try to do is turn on a light. It almost never comes on."

"Why's that?"

"When you turn on a light in a dream, everything around you has to brighten and take on whole new shades and tones. And it has to be instantaneous. Perceptually, it's a hard thing for your brain to do. It's much easier to have a light malfunction or make everything go dark when you turn a light off."

"Hmm." Vincente didn't look convinced. "So you think dreams are just things in our heads?"

"I think they can seem real while we're in them, but yes, dreams are virtual worlds created by our imagination."

"So you don't think dreams can be real."

"Real in what sense?"

"That some of them actually exist. Like this world, only different."

"Not physically real, like this world, no."

"Okay," the boy said, resuming the hike.

"Okay what?"

"Just okay."

Dillan walked behind Vincente, puzzled by the curtness of the boy's response.

"What aren't you telling me?" he finally asked.

"I think some dreams *can* be real," Vincente said while slowing his pace. "And I think some people in our dreams are real too."

"I need to stop for a second," Dillan said.

The boy turned around. "Are you okay?"

"I'm feeling light-headed. Probably the altitude." The doctor crouched down and sat on the trail. The second he closed his eyes, scenes of his brother drowning tore through his mind. He opened his eyes. Vincente was by his side.

"Do you want some water?" the boy asked, reaching for his flask.

Dillan took the bottle and splashed his face before taking a sip.

"What happened?"

Dillan remained silent, waiting for the anxiety to subside. "I'm not sure."

"Maybe we were walking too fast."

"Maybe…" Dillan reached into his front pants pocket and took out a bottle of pills. He went to snap off the lid when the bottle accidently flipped out of his hand. It bounced off a rock, rolled down the steep path, hit a bump, and disappeared over the trail's edge.

The doctor got up and took a few wobbly steps, but it was too late. The bottle had fallen down a ravine.

"Shit! I needed those pills!" He took a step back and sat down on the trail again.

"Were they some kind of medication?"

"Yes…"

"For your vertigo?"

"Sort of…"

"Well," said Vincente, "I'm not sure you really need them."

"Why do you say that?" Dillan's tone was more fraught with anger than he'd expected.

"I saw you take a couple of those pills before we came up in the gondola."

"And?"

"They didn't seem to help much. I mean, with all the puking and stuff back there. Maybe you should try something else. Like breathing exercises. At least while we're up here together."

"Maybe you're right. Besides, looks like I don't have much of a choice."

"You'll be okay then?"

Dillan gave the boy a faint smile and a nod.

Vincente examined the sky. "The clouds are moving away from us. The weather shouldn't be a problem." He turned to face the doctor.

"What is it?" Dillan asked.

Vincente appeared to be gathering his thoughts. "I think what you said about dreams is wrong."

"It's certainly possible. I'd like to hear what you think."

"I think that some dreams have a special energy, one that goes back in time, to our ancestors. Those dreams can be as real as this world. Sometimes it's not the whole dream that's real, just something in it, like an animal or a person."

"You mean real ... like you and me?"

The boy nodded.

Dillan wanted to dismiss the boy's view as nonsense, the kind of dream psychobabble espoused by quacks and charlatans. But Vincente was no charlatan.

"How can you tell which dreams, and which things in them, are real and which aren't?"

"That's part of the training," the boy said.

"What training?"

"The training you need to become a good dreamer."

Dillan was intrigued. "Did you receive this kind of training?"

"I started. You need to know a lot of other things first."

"Like the things we talked about a while ago?"

"Yes."

"Let's say you're right. You still haven't told me how we can tell dreams with real people or things from ones that are strictly products of our minds."

"They feel different. Real people don't look at you the same way. It's like you *know* you're being looked at. You can feel it."

"Do you think you've had real dreams or that some of the people or things in your dreams have been real?"

The boy's answer, barely audible, was "yes."

"When you told me you could turn falling dreams into flying dreams, you said it was important to remain calm and to remember that nothing can harm you. If dreams can be physically real, does that mean that something in those dreams could harm us?"

"That's why you have to believe in your powers. I mean really believe it, right there in the dream. No matter how scary it is. If you have doubts, the dream can hurt you. Even kill you."

Dillan took a moment to think about what the boy had said. "All kinds of things can go wrong in people's dreams. It's hard to overcome your fear when you're falling off a cliff or being pursued by some monster. Some would say impossible. I don't think I could, no matter how hard I tried."

"That's your problem right there. You're already doubting yourself. You have to learn to trust yourself, to believe in your powers in the dream. It takes time, but it's possible."

"You've learned these skills?"

"Some of them. When Mama was my age, she already knew a lot more about dreams than I do."

"Do you know if someone trained her when she was a child?"

Vincente gave a light nod.

"Domenico Tramonte was under the impression that your mother might have been trained by a priest or a monk. Do you know if he was right?"

"It was a monk," the boy said. "A blind Tibetan monk."

Dillan was stunned, almost queasy. "Your mom told you this herself?"

"Yes…" Vincente looked down and dragged the tip of his shoe across the ground, making a small groove in the pebbly dirt. "There's so much more I needed to learn…"

"I'm sorry."

The boy kept his gaze to the ground and dragged the tip of his toe back along the groove he had made. He looked up at the doctor. "We're not far from where it happened."

"You mean where you and your mom had set up camp?"

"I'd like to go back."

"We promised Detective Tramonte."

"It won't take long. There's a spur that goes over that hill." Vincente motioned with his chin to a small, craggy knoll about halfway down the trail. "I can show you on the map."

Dillan drank some more water. "I believe you. But why do you want to go back?"

Vincente appeared to hesitate. "It's a feeling I have."

Dillan was unsure of what to say next. In the end, he said the only words the boy needed to hear. "Okay, but we'll need to be quick about it."

* * *

Vincente sat down on a large, flat stone, his hands in his pockets, and stared at the brown patch of soil. He remained there, motionless, a bleak expression on his face. That was where it happened. Where he saw himself enter his mother's tent.

"Is it okay if I join you?" Dillan asked.

The boy didn't blink, but he moved over on the rock to make room. "I need to ask you something," he said to Dillan. "I want you to tell me the truth."

"What is it?"

"Do you think I killed her?"

"I know you didn't," Dillan said.

"How can you be sure?"

"You'll have to trust me on this."

"What about what I told you?"

"You mean the images? Do you still see them?"

The boy lowered his head.

"Listen to me, Vincente. It's hard enough to deal with the loss of someone we love. But if on top of that we can't make sense of what happened, then our minds can make us see and think all kinds of terrible things. Even about the people we love the most. You understand what I'm saying?"

"I think so." The boy stared at where the tent had been. "What's the earliest dream you remember?"

The question caught Dillan by surprise. "It's not a nice one."

"Can you tell me about it?"

Dillan paused. "I've never shared it with anyone."

The boy turned toward the doctor. "It's okay if you don't want to talk about it."

"Maybe I should finally tell someone. And if I'm to do that, then I'd like that someone to be you."

The boy gave Dillan a faint smile. "I'd like that too."

"I was eight when I had this dream. I must have had other dreams before that one, but it was the first one to leave a mark. I can't count the number of times I've wished I could forget it. It's always there in my mind, as clear as the day I had it. But first I need to tell you about something that happened before I had the dream."

Vincente looked up at Dillan, an expectant, almost wary look in his eyes.

"I had a brother."

"What's his name?"

"His name was Daniel. He died when I was eight."

The boy looked away.

"It was an accident. My dad had taken us ice fishing. He'd cut a number of holes in the ice and had a fishing rod topped by a little red flag in each one. I was sitting on a plastic crate, tugging on my line. Daniel was sitting a few feet away with his own rod. My dad got up to check if the holes he'd made earlier were still free of ice. He told me to keep an eye on my brother. I felt a tug on my line and got distracted. It couldn't have been more than a few seconds, but when I looked up..." He paused and then said, almost in a whisper, "My brother had wandered off, not far. I called out to him, but it was too late. I saw him fall through the ice. We never saw him again. He was only six years old."

Dillan took a deep, slow breath. "After that," he said, "I started having a recurrent dream. A nightmare. My brother and I are inside a dark tunnel and we're falling, but we're each headed toward opposite ends of the tunnel. His arms are stretched up over his head, trying to grab my hand. I can see his fingers, even his nails. They seem so close. But no matter how hard I try I know I can never reach them. He's calling me, begging me to help him, but there's nothing I can do. We keep falling away from each other till I can barely see his body. I'm scared and cold. There's no real up or down, only darkness. That's when I realize that he's not falling. He's being pulled from below. Then, for a split second, I see what's pulling him down.... It's me."

Vincente looked stricken.

"I've had that dream over and over and, after a while, I started seeing these other images, even while awake. I'd have these flashes of me looking down at him flailing under the ice. I'm not trying to help him. Just watching, helplessly. It was my guilt talking. Those images haunted me for years, and in some ways they still do."

Vincente gazed at the rugged mountains. "Did the dreams ever stop?"

"They didn't stop as much as change over time. I still have other kinds of bad dreams related to what happened, but my brother is no longer in them, and my feeling of guilt isn't as overwhelming as it once was."

"So it's better now?"

"Yes, I think it is."

"Thank you."

"For what?"

"For sharing your dream."

"I'm glad I did," Dillan said, his eyes locked on the horizon.

They sat there, immersed in a pensive and strangely comforting silence.

After a while, Vincente pressed his boot onto the soil and said, "If I didn't do it, what do you think happened to my mom?"

"I think someone or something attacked her in her sleep."

"But the police said we were alone."

"Maybe they were wrong."

"Why do you think she jumped?"

Dillan looked at the boy. "Because she had no choice."

"What do you mean?"

"I think she knew she was about to die and that she was out of options. That's why she left you her phone, the edelweiss, and the message in the snow."

"Why didn't she wake me up? I could have helped her."

"To keep you safe from whatever was after her."

The boy appeared to mull over the doctor's answers. "You think something happened to her in her dreams?"

"Maybe…"

"Do you think whatever was after her could come after me?"

"I don't know, Vincente. There are many things I don't yet understand."

The boy remained still. Then he said, "Do you know a lot about dreams?"

"I know quite a bit about the science of dreams. Why?"

"Because of what my mom told me about you."

"You think I'm ready?"

The boy looked Dillan in the eye. "Mama said that if something happened to her, you'd be the one who'd help me with my training."

"Your training?"

"In how to become a good dreamer."

"I'm not sure I understand. The things I know about dreams, they're not the right kind of stuff. I don't think it's the kind of knowledge you're after."

Vincente smirked. "Don't take this the wrong way, but I think you probably have more to learn about dreams than I do."

"In some ways, I'd say you're right. What did your mother tell you, exactly?"

"She said that we were entering dangerous times—those were her exact words—and if something bad happened to her, you would show up. She told me that I needed to trust you. She said you'd know what to do and that together, we'd fight the evil growing inside people's dreams."

"When did she tell you these things?"

"When she showed me the picture of you and Kohler."

"Do you know why she thought something might happen to her?"

Vincente looked down at his shoes and shook his head.

"I'm sorry, Vincente. I promised you I'd do everything I could to find out what happened to your mom, and I'm trying to do that. But I don't know much about the kinds of things your mom wanted to teach you. Or why this training would be so important. Do you?"

"Mama said that one day I'd be helping the Dreamkeepers. Maybe even become one myself. Do you know who they are?"

Dillan felt his heart race. "Not really…"

"They're special. And important. They live in a hidden dream world. But everything there is real. As real as where we are now. Mama said that this other world had a name. She called it the *anumia*."

The word was unfamiliar to Dillan.

"It takes special powers to enter it," the boy said, "and even greater powers and training to become a Dreamkeeper."

"What exactly do the Dreamkeepers do?"

"They protect our dreams, our freedom."

"And I'm supposed to know how to help you train for this?"

"Mama said you had a gift. Maybe you just don't know about it yet."

Dillan gave a nervous laugh. "I'm sorry, Vincente, but judging from my nightmares, I don't think I have much of a gift for dreaming, let alone for protecting the dreams of others."

Vincente bit at his lower lip. "She wouldn't have said it if it wasn't true."

"You mentioned that your mom wanted to show you a special book. Was that to be part of your training?"

The boy nodded.

"Maybe if we find it, we'll know a bit more about what your mom had in mind."

The boy looked up at Dillan. "Do you know about the tooth?"

"What tooth?"

"The one in the rock over there."

"You mean the one from the prehistoric shark?"

Vincente made a face. "A shark?"

"Detective Tramonte told me about it. He said the tooth was from an ancient species of shark. They're extinct now, like the dinosaurs."

Vincente got up and headed over to the large, rectangular boulder. The doctor followed.

"It's right here," the boy said, pointing to the upper corner of the rock. Dillan examined the straw-colored tooth encased in the boulder. It was larger than he had expected. Its wide top and long shaft were clearly visible, but the sharp end was angled into the rock, making it impossible to see.

"A tooth from an extinct shark," Vincente said. "That's clever."

"What? You don't think it's true?"

"Give me your hand." The boy took Dillan's fingers and placed them over the fossil. "Now close your eyes."

The rock was unusually cold, and an odd tingling—not unlike a weak current—flowed through Dillan's fingers. He became disoriented. His arm started to hurt. He opened his eyes and pulled away his hand.

"You felt it, didn't you?"

"Felt what?"

"The cold," Vincente said. "I saw it on your face. Not everyone can feel it."

"Your mom showed you this?"

"The other day."

"Did she tell you what it was?"

"She said it was from a creature from the world I told you about. She said it might come back, and that if it did, people would die. She didn't say anything more about it. She did tell me what it was called, though. A *taurine*."

CHAPTER 38

T he taxicab had pulled away from the curb when Liz noticed a large man wearing a black-and-white chauffer's uniform sitting in the vehicle on the other side of the street. *Can't be much legroom behind him,* she thought with amusement. She headed off at a brisk pace, hoping the short walk to the Duomo would help her unwind and take her mind off James and the boy.

It was only when she rounded the corner that she started to feel as if someone was watching her. She looked around. Driving along the street were several cars, as well as two obnoxiously loud scooters. Behind her, a young child was eating an ice cream cone under the watchful eye of his parents. In front of her, an elegantly dressed woman walked her way with a small dog, followed by a trio of teenaged girls caught up in a giggly conversation. Maybe her apprehension was really about how Dillan would handle being in the mountains. Should she have insisted on going up there with them?

The chic woman with the dog passed Liz, leaving a trail of floral-scented perfume in her wake while the teenagers huddled around one of the girls' smartphones. A string of high-pitched yelps pierced the air. Liz turned and saw the woman pulling her dog by the leash away from a tall stocky man in a gray suit who looked eerily like the chauffeur. Liz resumed her walk and spotted a bakery up ahead. She stepped inside, the small bell above the door tinkling.

A woman behind the counter greeted Liz as she walked down a small aisle. She took her phone and pressed the detective's number. *Quick, pick up!* The bell above the door to the bakery rang again. The man was standing there. He walked up to the counter and ordered an espresso. No answer; only the detective's voice mail. This didn't feel right. She hung up and pressed a six-digit code. The phone was about to self-encrypt.

Liz walked out of the store and heard the woman call out good-bye as the bell rang above her head. She scanned both sides of the sidewalk and turned right, looking behind her. The man hadn't followed her out.

She looked for a quiet, safe place where she could try the detective again. Noticing a taxi driving toward her, she stood on the edge of the sidewalk and hailed the cab, but it didn't stop. Still no one behind her. She hurried to the next corner, rounded a building, and ran into a hulk of a man. It was the chauffeur. He grabbed her by the arm and pulled her against him. Liz kneed him in the groin, but the man hardly flinched. She swung at his head, aiming for an eye, but the man seized her wrist with one hand and her waist with the other. Like a boa constricting its prey, the man stiffened his grip, almost breaking her lower ribs. Liz let out a half-formed scream as a sharp object jabbed her in the neck. A flash of panic. Her legs buckled; her body wilted. Then the blackout.

CHAPTER 39

"There's one last bit of climbing ahead," Vincente said, looking at the map. "We should be at the hut in about twenty minutes."

They skirted around a rocky outcrop and resumed their hike along the plateau.

Vincente slowed. Perched at the top of a nearby hill was a cross. "I've been here before," he said. "When I was little. My mom took me to see it."

"The cross?"

"It's made out of steel. That's why it looks so shiny."

As Dillan examined the cross, a ray of light pierced the cloud cover, making the metal glisten. "The fact that you remember being here might be a good sign."

Vincente continued to lead the way.

The narrow trail, carved into the rocky escarpment, zigzagged up the increasingly steep grade. Although Dillan's legs felt strong, his lungs were laboring. Maybe it was the thin air after all.

Vincente waited for the doctor to catch up. "You remember the story of the moon princess?"

Dillan placed his hands on his hips and stopped to catch his breath. "Of course."

"My mom told me that the first moon flowers were planted in this area of the Dolomites. When I asked her if she knew the exact spot, she said she did and that one day I'd find it myself."

Dillan smiled. "That'd be something."

"She told me most of the edelweiss around here are great-grand-children of the original moonflowers, but that if I wanted to see where the princess had planted the first ones, I'd have to look where I'd least expect to find a flower."

"And where would that be?"

"I don't know. She never said."

* * *

As they wound their way through a jumble of pillars and boulders that led to towering walls of sulfurous limestone, Dillan began to wonder if they were in the right place.

"Over there!" Vincente shouted before sprinting toward the massive rock face. It took Dillan a few seconds to visually untangle the small hut from the ash-colored backdrop. He caught up to Vincente standing by the stone shelter. The boy lifted the metal latch on the door. "It's not locked."

Dillan stepped in front of the boy and pushed the door open slightly. The air inside smelled of burnt wood. In the middle of the dark room stood a table and bench, but the place seemed deserted. He opened the door farther, letting in additional light. Against the far wall was a makeshift bed—a wooden plank with a scruffy blanket—as well as a small iron stove with a few branches and crumpled newspapers on the floor next to it. To their right, affixed to the stone wall, was a shelf with several tins of food and a few utensils. They stepped inside.

In one of the corners, leaning against the wall, was a shovel with a rounded metal blade. In another was a pack of waterproof matches, two carabineers, and a roll of twine. They unfolded the blanket on the bed and examined the wooden plank as well as the space underneath it. They went through every item on the shelf, studied every section of the floor, ceiling and walls, and inspected the stove from top to bottom, inside and out. Finally, they went through the half-strewn newspapers looking for clues. All for naught.

Vincente stood by the table. "Maybe we should look outside."

"You can go, but stay close by. I'll join you in a minute."

Dillan sat on the bench and stared at the fissures in the tabletop. He reexamined the walls and floor then used a butter knife to chip at the mortar between the stones. He looked under the table and bench and pulled at their legs and lathes. Nothing. He took the shovel and stepped outside, where Vincente was inspecting the hut's exterior.

They continued to search, unsure of what they hoped to find. The area contained little more than rocks and boulders of various shapes and sizes. Although Dillan and the boy dug out, poked under, and turned over a multitude of rocks, their actions began to feel empty as disappointment waxed and eagerness waned. Dillan surveyed the soaring rock flanking the hut, behind which the sun, muted by darkening clouds, would soon disappear.

"We'll need to go soon," he said.

* * *

Vincente and Dillan were heading back the way they had come. The boy had been quiet, almost solemn since leaving the hut, and his slowed pace betrayed his disillusionment. Out of the blue, he hopped off the path and scampered in a new direction.

"Where are you going?"

"I'm following the butterflies!" yelled Vincente, accelerating, slowing, and speeding up again while zigzagging toward a looming rock wall.

"Wait up!" called the doctor, but Vincente continued his snaking dash. As Dillan hurried to catch up, he spotted two yellow butterflies fluttering in front of the boy. They were moving swiftly around one another toward a striking rock face capped by jagged bone-white points, curved upward like giant tusks.

Wary of tripping over the heaps of stones scattered before him, Dillan kept his eyes on the uneven ground.

"Come and see!" the boy hollered.

Dillan found Vincente crouching by a bulging rock formation that was as wide as a house and three times as high. "What is it?" he asked, catching his breath.

"Look."

At the base of the rock, a little more than waist high and maybe a few feet wide, was an opening.

Vincente turned to Dillan. "Do you know what this is?"

"No…"

"The last place you'd look for a flower."

Dillan grinned. "Cute."

"I'm serious! Just inside, there're some edelweiss!"

Dillan put a knee to the ground and tilted his head to get a better look. About three feet in, against a rocky side, was a patch of pale rosettes.

"Can we go in?" Vincente asked.

"It's probably nothing more than a big hole." Dillan put his hand on the cave's upper lid and stuck his head farther in. "Might be deeper than I thought." His words entered the grotto and faded into muted echoes.

"We have our headlamps," urged the boy.

Dillan scanned the ground, looking for a stick or rock. He picked up a handful of marble-sized pebbles, leaned into the gaping hole, and hurled them as hard as he could. There were a series of smacks, compounding echoes, then nothing. He pulled out his head and stood up again.

"We need to get back by the agreed-upon time."

"But the butterflies brought us here!" Vincente said. "Didn't you see them?"

"I did." Dillan took out his cell. No signal.

"Please, a quick peek. Then we'll go straight back. Promise!"

The doctor released a slow breath, put down his knapsack, opened a zipper, and took out their headlamps. Once in place, he turned on his light, ready to lead them into the cave. He got down on all fours and crawled along the narrow passage, sharp edges and angular planes scraping his hands and knees. The light from his lamp flickered, quivering up and down, left to right, from close surfaces to distant darkness. Everywhere, nothing but black rock. Farther in, the walls opened up and the space between his head and the immeasurable tonnage of rock above it began to grow. Dillan, however, would have preferred the whole thing to end in an impassable *cul de sac.* Now, he had to struggle to rid himself of the thought that mortal danger was not possible, but imminent.

They advanced, their beams flashing about like spotlights in search of a fugitive. Dillan stopped, flabbergasted, then carefully moved to the side to make room for Vincente.

"What is it?"

"I'm not sure…"

The boy's light bounced off a wall and fused with Dillan's. Caught in their beams was a small plant growing out of the rock. They crawled closer. Its densely woven base held a sandy-brown mass of interlaced sprigs, each one wrapped in countless golden bristles. Sitting atop it were five petals, silvery in color and with a plump, gelatin-looking texture.

Vincente put his lamp directly over the flower. "Can I touch it?"

"You shouldn't. It could be poisonous."

"It looks a bit like an edelweiss," the boy said, "don't you think?"

"Yeah…"

"How can it grow in here?"

"It must be a special strain," Dillan said. "One that doesn't require chlorophyll. Like some species of mushrooms."

Vincente stared at the plant, then at the shadows ahead. "Let's continue," he said, squat-walking past the doctor. They advanced slowly. "Two more!" Vincente exclaimed. His words echoed. They stopped to look at the twin plants before continuing on. Soon the tunnel began to widen and then widened even more and expanded until Dillan was able to stand upright. Neither he nor the boy saw any other sign of vegetation, or anything else of note, for that matter. Only shadowy rocks and black rutted walls.

"Can we turn off our lights for a second?" asked Vincente.

"Why?"

"I once dreamt of fireflies moving deep inside a cave. I wanted to follow them but was too scared. I stood there and watched until the flashes became so small, they disappeared. When I told Mama about the dream, she said that if I had followed them, I would have learned something about myself. She said that many things people look for are often hidden in the places they're most afraid to explore. I'm not scared right now, and I want that to continue, even in the dark."

Dillan turned off his headlamp without a word. The boy did the same, encasing them in impenetrable blackness. Speckles fluttered before the doctor as his eyes tried to adapt. He became aware of his breathing, his blinking, his heartbeat. A tension materialized and with it a rush of venomous thoughts. He inhaled through his nose to the count of four and exhaled through pursed lips to the count of six. It helped. His mind was quieting. He heard a noise. Vincente was going somewhere. Dillan reached for his light but left it off. "What are you doing?"

"Shh." The boy was still moving.

Dillan extended his arms out at his sides; the walls were beyond his reach. He tried to raise his hands over his head, but solid rock stopped him midway up. *Breathe.* Vincente wasn't stopping. His footsteps echoed but sounded sure, deliberate. Then silence. Dillan waited. A brushing noise.

"There's something here," Vincente said. "I'm turning on my light."

The beam shining over distant rocks provided the doctor with a needed dose of relief and enabled him to see how far the boy had wandered. He turned on his light and carefully started to walk. The boy was crouched on all fours, sweeping the ground with his hands, a cloud of particles dancing in his beam. Then he spied it: a square lid, maybe three feet by three, seemingly metal, and level with the bedrock. The doctor pulled the sleeve of his jacket down over his palm and rubbed some of the encrusted dirt off the metal.

Markings … no, letters. Gorgeously written letters. He squirted water from his bottle onto the surface and rubbed again, only harder. "How did you find this?"

"I followed the fireflies."

Dillan paused. "I didn't see any fireflies."

"Neither did I, until I closed my eyes."

Dillan was about to ask Vincente about what he'd said when he deciphered a phrase on the lid's surface. The water and scrubbing had worked, and while a small section of the calligraphy remained caked with dirt, there was no mistaking the phrase inscribed on the metal plate: *Vivimus in somnio.*

"It's not Italian," Vincente said, staring at the words, "but I think it says, 'We live in sleep.' "

"It's Latin, and you're close. *Somnio* means dreams."

"So, 'We live in dreams?' "

"That's what it says."

Vincente examined the square lid. "What do you think is inside?"

"I'm not even sure it opens." Dillan pressed his hands onto the different sides of the metal plate, pushing, pulling, and tugging, but to no avail. He tried to wedge his fingers between the metal and the rock, but his efforts were in vain.

"Here," Vincente said, taking Dillan's hand and pressing it on the top right corner of the lid. "Feel that?"

Dillan tried to make sense of the small, circular ridge under his fingertips.

The boy scratched the surface grime with his fingernails. "We need something else."

Dillan took the emergency kit out of his knapsack. The large safety pin would work. He unclipped the needle, pushed the spike into the center of the flange, and scraped while blowing away the loose dirt. He looked closer. "It's a keyhole." He angled the needle, pushed it farther inside and scraped some more.

"What do we do now?" Vincente asked.

"The plastic card holder with your mom's edelweiss. You still have it with you?"

Vincente unzipped the inside pocket of his jacket, took out the small two-sided holder, and held it up to the light. He took the thick silver key out of its sheath and put the edelweiss back in his pocket. Holding the key firmly between his thumb and forefinger, Vincente wiggled it into the slot. Once he had gotten it halfway in, however, he stopped. "There's something rubbing against it. Like sand." He carefully pulled it back out and watched Dillan clear the remaining debris in the hole. Second try. This time the key went all the way in but wouldn't turn.

"Push a little harder," Dillan urged.

"In what direction? I'm scared it might break."

The doctor hesitated. "Clockwise."

The boy applied more torque. The key appeared to be stuck, then moved a quarter turn. He forced some more. Another quarter turn. Something metallic fell inside. The key wouldn't go any farther.

Dillan tried to lift the metal lid and pushed on it, first sideways, then head-on. It moved away from him, not much, but enough to know that it might come off. "Help me," he said, wrapping his hands around the edge of the lid closest to him. "At the count of three."

After some grunting and huffing, they lifted the lid and managed to push it away from them. Recessed in the floor of the cave was a metal crate. They looked inside. Caught in their lights was a large book. Its cover was dark and covered in soot.

"Can you get it out?" asked Vincente.

Dillan slid his fingers down the sides of the book and carefully lifted it out. The tome, bound in soft, earth-brown leather, was surprisingly heavy. He sat on his heels, laid the book on his knapsack, and turned it toward Vincente. "I think it was meant for you," Dillan said.

The boy appeared hesitant. He ran his fingertips over the creased leather cover before lifting it. The first page was blank and discolored, the edges withered. He turned it, slowly. On the next page were two brief paragraphs, handwritten in black ink. The words were all in block letters. The boy scanned a few lines before turning to the next page. It contained similarly handwritten entries, one of which was considerably longer, and each was preceded by a date and short title.

"It looks like a journal," Dillan said, glimpsing the text. Too absorbed in reading, the boy didn't even look up.

Dillan trained his headlight inside the crate. He reached in and ran his fingertips down the sides. The metal felt cold and damp. The bottom was like dense parchment paper, only dark. He dug a fingernail into the top right corner and peeled it back.

"What are you doing?" asked Vincente.

"There's something else in here." Under the layer of wax-like paper was another book, similar in size to the first but thicker. Dillan wedged his index and middle fingers under the tome and lifted it out. Plumes of dust rose in the beam of light then dissipated into the shadows.

"You can look inside," Vincente said, returning to his own book.

The doctor wiped the black leather cover with his hand and opened it. The pages were covered with finely executed symbols, some elongated and some angular, along with subscripts and superscripts. The orthography resembled ancient Indic scripts he had once seen at a museum. Then, turning a page, he saw a drawing. He froze. Before him, illustrated in a variety of colors, was the beast from his elevator dream. The creature was standing on its hind legs, its thick forelimbs charging an invisible enemy, its wide-open mouth frozen in a terrifying roar. At the center of the creature's eyes was a fiery substance resembling molten lava. Dribbling down the sides of its mouth was the same yellow-green vomit that had splatted onto the glass elevator.

"This book," Vincente said, snapping the doctor out of his haze. "It's Mama's dream diary. She wrote it when she was a young girl." He clutched the volume to his chest. "I'm sure this is what she wanted to show me." Vincente was all smiles. "What about that one?"

Dillan flipped back to some symbol-laden pages and held them open for the boy to see. "It's written in a language I don't know. Do you recognize it?"

Vincente shook his head. "We have to take these with us."

"That's fine, but we need to leave." Dillan opened his knapsack, wrapped the tomes in the raincoats, and gently placed them in the main compartment. His heart was starting to race again. It was time to get out. "Okay, let's go."

Vincente, however, was on his knees, his right hand inside the crate, scratching at the bottom. "Do you have that safety pin?"

"Why? What is it?"

"I think this comes off." Vincente used the pin's rounded clasp to dig into the plate junctions. "I need something stronger."

Dillan looked at the furrow the boy had made between the plate and the metal wall. "We have the detective's multitool."

Of the half-dozen implements available, the cross-slot screwdriver appeared best suited to the task.

"Here, let me do it," Dillan said. He planted the screwdriver tip into the furrow, pushing and twisting until he wedged the metal point between the plate and the wall. Clasping the army knife with both hands, he angled the metal shaft for leverage and drove it farther under the plate. With each thrust, the side of the plate rose higher. Finally, he gripped the plate by the edge, tugged and jerked it until it broke away, sending clouds of dust rising and twirling into the dual beams. "Careful," Dillan said, lowering the plate to the ground.

The newly exposed stratum revealed an iron grill, and under the lattice of black transecting shafts, another layer of darkened parchment paper. Like a man trying on ten rings at once, Dillan slid his fingers as far as they would go under the grill and lifted it out, along with the sheets fused to its underside. He put it down while the boy removed the remaining parchment. Immediately below was the mouth of a vase.

"Is this...?" breathed the boy, reaching for the rim.

Dillan pulled him back. "Don't touch it. It could be booby-trapped."

They examined the top of the vase. Along the citrine-colored rim were two rows of olive-shaped patterns. The inner one slate-blue, the outer burnt orange. Below the rim, and poking out from either side of the bowling pin-shaped vase, were two golden handles. Dillan angled his light, trying to make out the bottom of the vase. The artwork was sitting in a wrought iron holder with three spear-like extensions running up the sides of the vase and three curved legs with elaborate curls and tresses.

"I don't think it's dangerous," Vincente said.

"What makes you say that?"

"My mom wouldn't leave me the key to something that could hurt me."

Not wanting to take any chances, Dillan picked up a few pebbles and dropped them into the crate. Nothing.

Vincente ran his fingers around the mouth of the vase. "We need to take it out."

Dillan's throat had gone dry.

"Please…"

"What was that?" he whispered to the boy. They listened. Silence. "I thought I heard something."

"I didn't hear anything," hushed Vincente.

They remained motionless, alert to the faintest of sounds, but could hear nothing except their breathing, and, in Dillan's case, the pounding in his chest.

"Come on," the boy said, "Let's take it out."

Dillan moved the metal grill to more level ground and tested its steadiness with his hands. He planted his feet on either side of the open crate, crouched down, wrapped his hands firmly around the handles, and pulled. The vase was heavy and made a dull, grating sound as it slid out of its iron base. He had it about halfway out when a jolt of pain shot through his arm.

"Careful!" Vincente said, trying to keep the bulky vessel from hitting the sides of the crate.

Dillan struggled with the vase and needed the boy's help to set it down.

They stood and stared. The vase was stunning. Its contours were soft and its surface covered with entrancing designs, from fields of flowers in intricate ovals to interlaced rhomboids, trapeziums, and polygons, all in striking greens, blues, reds, and yellows. The handles were in the form of a drawn-out face seized by dread, with large, protuberant eyes turned skyward. Below each pair of pleading eyes was a broad, flattened nose, and a mouth frozen in a wide-open scream. Their look of terror was eerily palpable. Behind the arched face was the hollow space forming the handle. Details that hadn't been visible from above were now apparent, including the line of warped teeth in the mouths of the figures and their long, forked tongues. And there, at the center of the vase, was a now-familiar pattern: five red orbs and one blue, on a shield of gold.

Dillan lifted his head in fright. This time the boy had heard it too. A light flickered off a distant wall. They turned off their headlamps. Specks flashed before the doctor's eyes and faded as the blackness around them thickened. Another glint of light. Then darkness. Someone was there. Dillan reached out blindly and pulled the boy against him. The cave began to reek. A revolting stench, like that of rotting carcasses, poisoned the air. Dillan became dizzy. Muffled steps. Someone was walking toward them.

Out of the blackness, two pallid objects emerged side by side. They were small, oval, and infused with an ashen glare. Dillan stared as they hovered in midair, vanished, and reappeared. Waves of panic rose in his throat. They weren't fireflies. They were someone's eyes.

The shuffling stopped. "I know you're there," said a sluggish, almost robotic male voice. The words hung in the air before dispersing in the cave like surf on a beach. The eyes blinked. The shuffling resumed.

The boy was silent, but his quivering body betrayed his fear. Dillan held him tighter.

A light appeared behind the man. A lantern. Someone else was coming. Someone with a heavy tread. They were about to be found.

"Who's there?" Dillan asked, his heart ready to explode.

The lantern swayed, the eyes, glowing ash white, broadened.

"People have been waiting a long time for this," declared the man. "And many believed this day would never come. But it has … it has…"

The putrid smell deepened. The light would soon be upon them. "Who are you?" asked Dillan, frantically grasping at the ground around him. The boy handed him the screwdriver.

The man's incandescent glare turned iceberg blue before vanishing into the darkness. "*Vivimus in somnio*," hissed the man.

Dillan held his weapon behind his back, aimed his headlamp at the shadows, and flashed on the light. The man before them was inhumanly frightening, an emaciated specimen with a skeletal head with ivory-white eyes recessed deep in their sockets. He was draped in a long dark coat, and the rumpled skin visible between the unbuttoned sides was sickly yellow and covered with boils.

The man behind him came closer. He was colossal. Even with his wide torso bent forward, his head was grazing the rocks above. In one of his hands was the lantern, in the other a gun. Dillan, the boy, and the Cellini were all within the arc of his light.

"What do you want?" Dillan said defiantly.

The man in the dark coat gave a derisive laugh, but his snickering quickly turned into a choking cough. He bent over and spat. A puss-yellow strand was left hanging from the corner of his mouth.

The man with the lantern came within a few feet. He cocked his gun and pointed it at the doctor's forehead.

"Okay, okay," Dillan said, tightening his grip on the screwdriver. He and the boy moved away from the vase.

The skeletal man raised a finger and pointed it at Vincente. "And you … you must be Santilli's boy."

Dillan could feel Vincente trembling. He pulled the boy against him and with the screwdriver still in his hand wrapped his arm around the boy's shoulders.

"Your mother was a worthy opponent," the repulsive-looking man said. "But a poor strategist. And a fool to have brought you into this." His ivory eyes widened, as if to better gauge the boy's reaction. "Women of her kind are a dying breed—dying being the key word."

Vincente jumped forward. Dillan tried to hold on to him, but it was too late. The man with the gun had already knocked the boy down. Vincente tried to get up on all fours.

"Should I kill them now?" asked the hulking man, kicking Vincente to the ground.

Dillan glanced at the vase. "Go ahead. Take it," he urged.

"Oh, I shall," said the skeletal man, his eyes aglow. "You still don't get it, do you, *Doctor* Dillan? I don't know what Santilli saw in you, but thanks to your dear friend Kohler, you, my bumbling idiot, have led me to the very treasure Santilli thought she could keep from me."

Vincente went to say something, but the towering man brought his foot down hard on his shoulder blades, cutting off his breath, reducing his words to a whimper.

The skeletal man released a jumble of coughs and laughter. Puss-like filaments spewed from his mouth.

Dillan steadied his grip on the screwdriver and took a step forward. His heart was beating like a snare drum.

The man with the gun flashed him a smile. "Go ahead, try me," he said.

Using the back of his long, spindly fingers, the skeletal man wiped away the slimy strands dangling from his lower lip. "The doctor here is no menace to us," he said. "He is but a broken man, haunted by inaction and guided by laughable hopes." The man paused. His eyes were like blazing embers. "Poor little Daniel," he said. "You can still see him being sucked into the icy water, can't you? His cold limbs flailing. His little lungs gasping for air. Drowning can be such a cruel, ghastly way to die. Even more so for a child, don't you think?"

Dillan was about to strike when something hit his temple hard. His head started to spin. The air around him was too heavy to breathe. He fell to the ground, the boy's scream ringing in his ears. Another blow. His skull exploded with pain. A warm liquid poured down his forehead, down the sides of his face, and out of his nose and mouth. Inside him, a sea of blackness beckoned, and into its rising tide he fell.

CHAPTER 40

Liz regained consciousness. Around her there was nothing but darkness. Her mouth was taped shut; her hands bound behind her back. She tried to calm herself, focusing on the air coming through her nose. She was curled up on her side, her legs tied together at the ankles. There was a slight vibration under her body. A sense of motion. *Cripes.* She was in the trunk of a moving car. She tried to wiggle her hands free and move her legs, but her efforts were futile. The car braked, propelling her forward, her head hitting metal. Blood trickled down her scalp. Her breathing became frantic. The car had come to a sudden stop, and someone had gotten out.

The lid to the trunk opened. The sudden flood of light hurt her eyes. A man reached down and grabbed her bound hands and legs, hauled her out of the car, and flung her over his back. He turned and walked away from the car, the gravel crunching under his feet. Lifting her head in fright, Liz saw some pine trees to her side.

The man brusquely lowered her to the ground, her buttocks, arms, and back absorbing most of the impact. He gripped her by the armpits and dragged her for several feet before propping her against a tree. Her eyes were starting to adapt to the sunlight. She was in a forest by a gravel road. Standing before her, in a now familiar dark gray suit, was the tall and burly chauffer. Not far behind him, closer to the car, was a similarly dressed and equally imposing man.

"Scream, and you're dead," the man closest to her said. He crouched down by her side. Liz noticed a fresh cut under his left eye. Then, in one swift yank, he ripped the tape off her mouth.

"How did you get the pictures?" asked the man, his voice deep, his accent German.

"What pictures?"

The slap across her face was as violent as it was sudden.

The man seized her neck with one hand. "I will kill you," he warned her, tightening his grip on her larynx.

Fighting her terror, Liz blurted, "I hacked them. They were on a server in Lugano."

"Who do you work for?" asked the man, his oversized hand still clutching her throat.

"Nobody," she struggled to say. "I work at a lab. A research lab. Honest. I'm helping investigate a murder."

The man released his grip on her neck, reached into his jacket, and pulled out a gun. He pressed the cold steel muzzle to her cheek. "You get one more chance." He pushed the gun harder into her flesh. "Who do you work for?"

The man collapsed, his head making a dull thump as it hit the road. The second man had also fallen to the ground, his limbs unmoving. There had been no gunshots, no sound.

Lips twitching, heart pounding, Liz stared at the man by her feet, her gaze immediately drawn to the side of his face. Beneath his closed lid, the man's eye was darting furiously back and forth. She stared at the flickering motion.

Footsteps. Not from the road, from the forest to her left. Liz put down her head and let her body go limp. The person was getting closer. Maybe two of them. They weren't talking. She heard only the twigs and branches crunching under their feet. In seconds, they were going to be standing next to her.

"I know you're faking!" yelled a man moving toward her. "So cut the act and let's get going."

Liz didn't move a muscle.

The man stopped by her feet, placed a hand under her chin, and raised her head. "*Now*, Princess."

Liz opened her eyes. Standing before her was a corpulent man with a large, bald head and a neck as thick as a bison's. Covering his round jaw line was a band of bushy gray hair that fused into his wild sideburns.

"You're coming with me," he said. His tone left no doubt as to the choice she had in the matter.

Liz glanced at the chauffeur lying on the ground. "What happened to him?"

"He passed out," replied the man gruffly. He took a knife out of his pocket and cut through the layers of tape wrapped tightly around her wrists and ankles.

Throbbing pain shot through Liz's hands and feet, the pulsing rhythm wedded to each beat of her heart.

"Let's go before they come to."

Liz felt a burning sting in her fingertips. She examined her left hand. The nail on her index finger was gone, the exposed flesh raw and bloodied. The one on her middle finger was broken across halfway down, the bottom section scarcely attached to the tissue.

The man glanced at her hand then at the chauffeur's face. "Looks like you gouged him pretty good! An inch or two higher and you could've ripped his eye right out its socket. What a sight that would've been!" The man let out a roaring belly laugh.

Liz was in a daze, her mind spinning wildly. Where was the other man she had heard walking in the woods? "Who are you?" she asked, her voice quivering.

The man stood up. Below his expansive chest was a bloated gut, round as a watermelon. "None of your concern, Princess. What you should be concerned about is the deep shithole of a mess you got yourself into. That and the fact that I'm the only one around who can get you out of it."

He held out his hand. His eyes were small and a piercing gray-blue. Liz took his hand and grimaced as she tried to stand, her legs wobbly and numb. She leaned to rub her thighs, mindful of her maimed fingertips, and as she did so, she glanced down at the chauffeur, at the eyes still darting under his eyelids.

"Something wrong?" asked the big-headed man.

"Shouldn't we be taking their guns?" she said, improvising an answer.

"Do you know how to use one?"

Her heart was racing. "No."

"Then we have no use for them, do we?"

The thought of escaping crossed her mind, of darting into the forest. But her legs were unsteady, her hand throbbing. If he could neutralize the chauffeurs, surely he would do the same to her—or worse.

They walked past the second chauffeur, still sprawled on his back, fingers twitching and eyeballs darting beneath his lids.

"They're not unconscious," Liz said. "They're asleep, dreaming. I can tell from the way their eyes are moving under their eyelids. It's as if they're under some kind of narcoleptic spell."

The man locked eyes with Liz and scowled. He remained motionless, studying her face.

Liz braced herself for an assault, thinking of how she might beat him to one of the guns.

The man took two steps toward her, stopped, and grinned. "There is such a thing as being too smart for your own good, Princess. Now listen up. Here's what's going to happen. I'm going to get you out of here and back to Trento, where you'll meet up with your doctor friend. Then you'll get yourself on the first flight back to Canada and forget what you've seen here. If, however, you insist on sticking around, I guarantee you that you'll be found by day's end. And next time, these gentlemen won't be so nice to you. You get me?"

"We'll be gone by morning."

"Your doctor friend won't be flying with you."

"Why not?"

"Let's call it unfinished business. You already know where he needs to be. And don't leave from an Italian airport. They'll track you down. Go to Innsbruck. I'll make sure you get through there in one piece. Let's get a move on."

* * *

"Six months." Those were the first words the big-headed man had said since parking the old clunker by the side of the mountain road, getting out of the driver's seat, and joining Liz in the back. He opened the black leather satchel at his feet, took out a first-aid kit, and began treating her wounds. Liz silently observed the man's bushy sideburns as he worked on her mangled fingertips, first disinfecting the raw nail bed with a clear gel, then bandaging her fingers with gauze.

"What about six months?"

The big-headed man kept his eyes on the roll of gauze as he wrapped it around her middle finger. "That's how long it'll take for them to grow back."

"I never thought about that," Liz said, still processing the information. "It's longer than I would have guessed."

"Toenails are worse," he stated matter-of-factly. "Up to a year and a half."

"You have medical training?"

The man checked the tightness of the final bandage. "Top-rate."

"From where?"

"Google," he said. He proceeded to clean the gash on the side of her head.

Although peculiar in appearance and behavior, he had given Liz no reason to be suspicious of him or the plan he had explained to her. Still, the knot in her stomach and flashbacks of her abduction made her uneasy. "Why are you helping me?"

"There's something bigger than any of us at stake here, Princess. Something you happened to get entangled in." He stopped to put his medical supplies back in the satchel. "Helping you was something I needed to do. Under different circumstances, I may have had to kill you." He chuckled. "My friends call me Ivan, but so do my enemies. You're welcome to ride up front with me if you want." He stepped out of the back of the car and climbed into the driver's seat.

Liz joined him up front. "Whatever your reasons, thanks."

The man put the key in the ignition and turned it. "I do what I think is best," he said with a smirk. "That's my reason for being." He put the car in gear and pressed the gas pedal. The front wheels spun on the loose gravel before gripping the asphalt with a sudden jolt. "That, and messing with people's heads."

CHAPTER 41

By the time Mihalovitch made it to the opulent room on the upper floor of the castle, the doctor had already set Iris's broken nose and was almost finished covering it with medical bandages. Having made eye contact with Iris, now sitting in a Queen Anne chair, arms folded across her chest, and her purple stilettoes planted on the marble floor, he opted to wait inside the room's large wooden doors.

"Aiia!" Iris yelped. "*Hai finito imbicile!*" she said, rebuking the doctor.

"*Si signora. Mi scusi signora.*" The doctor bowed his head, collected his supplies, and scurried out of the room, too timorous even to glance at Mihalovitch.

"Come in," Iris said.

Mihalovitch took a few steps. "Mind if I look?"

"It's a nasal fracture. I want him killed."

He came closer. The sides of her face were swollen, her eyes already bruised. "You're sure it was him?"

"I want him *killed*, Ivan."

"How could this happen?" asked Mihalovitch.

"*Che cazzo* do I know! It happened, and the only person who could've pulled off such a stunt is him."

"Straight into REM sleep?"

"From the guards to the workers in the kitchen. Every single one of them dropped like a sack of bricks. One second we were awake, the next fast asleep. I was heading down the stairs when the bastard struck. I tumbled head first. I could have broken more than my nose, Ivan."

Mihalovitch examined her rainbow-colored necklace and its attached pendant: a golden ewer filled with limpid crystals that appeared to flow out of its widening spout. "I'll take care of it," he said. "I'll need Kohler, though. As a trap."

Iris gave him an icy stare. "Just get it done."

* * *

Mihalovitch reached the bottom of the stairs then took a corridor that led to two massive wooden doors, each with elaborate ironwork bearing leaf patterns and lion heads. He pulled one of the doors open.

He stepped inside the dank chamber, took one of the lit torches off its holster, and walked toward a man shackled to the far wall. He appeared to be unconscious. Mihalovitch shook the man's shoulders then slapped his face. The man groaned.

"Can you hear me, Mr. Kohler?"

The man coughed, spat, and coughed again, only harder. "Not you again…. How did you know they wouldn't kill me?"

"It was an educated guess. Iris has always been wary of her allies, including yours truly. You were an important asset. She wouldn't have disposed of you so easily. Certainly not without being certain about what you may or may not have known."

"They asked me things I didn't know … secret locations … portals, about Santilli's son, the Cellini."

"I know these last few days may have been a little difficult—maybe more than a little. But you're about to get your chance."

"At what?"

"At entering the *anumia*." There was a pause. "I can get you into a lab more advanced than anything you can imagine," Mihalovitch whispered. "I can also get you a rare form of the drug, one even the Priorate doesn't know about."

"Why would you do that?"

"Two most excellent reasons. One, believe what you wish, but your skills are rare, and your potential even rarer."

"What's the other?"

"I need you to help me get close to the Priorate. He may have been less of a fool than we believed and his powers greater than we imagined."

"Whose side are you on anyway?"

"What a question, Mr. Kohler. It should go without saying. I'm on whatever side I need to be to win."

Michel coughed, hacked, and spat again.

"You help me get the Priorate, Mr. Kohler, and I'll get you into the *anumia*. A rematch with a *taurine*. Do we have a deal?"

"Yes…"

CHAPTER 42

The day was cold but bright as Dillan skated, alone, hockey stick in hand, on the outdoor rink. He glided by the wooden boards, snatched the puck with the blade of his stick, and dashed toward the net. He aimed for the right goal post and slapped a shot. PING! The puck ricocheted off the red metal post and somersaulted back onto the ice. Dillan cut a semicircle around the net, got hold of the puck, and rushed along the boards toward the opposite end of the rink. He glanced at the left goal post and with a seamless, almost slow-motion wrist shot, cast the puck at the target. PING! The clarity of the sound was startling. Dillan grinned as he corralled the twirling disc and sprinted again. He leaned into the shaft of his stick and took aim at the center of the crossbar. A flick of his wrists and the disk was airborne. PING!

Skating around the goalposts, he glided toward the puck. He cradled it in the heel of his stick, turned one hundred and eighty degrees and with his back to the far net shoved the disc blindly between his legs. He turned and watched, incredulous, as the puck glided slowly along the ice, its momentum barely sufficient to carry it into the left post. Ping.

He stared at the puck then crouched down, studying the lines and marks etched into the ice. He passed his fingertips over the frozen edges and grooves. Something wasn't right. He shuddered as he looked up. The rink was gone. In its place was a vast, frozen lake—ice, thick and ashen, as far as he could see. Behind him was a shoreline bordered by a forested hill. The trees were tall, leafless, and gray, their twisting branches stretching heavenward like arms pleading with the skies. Every segment of every tree, from the widest trunk to the thinnest shoot, was encased in clear ice. Storm clouds blew in, and dark shadows slithered across the frozen terrain. Something was coming, something terrifying. Dillan had to get to the other side of the lake. Now!

With blades carving into the ice, he tried to skate toward the horizon but met with powerful gusts that howled in his ears. He was no match for the unyielding wind. His limbs became heavy and slothful, as if moving under water. That's when he saw it: a massive globe emerging over the skyline. Like a gargantuan full moon, it crested the edge of the earth.

The ground rumbled as the sphere began to roll toward him, crushing everything in its path. Cracks ripped through the ice. He leapt over one fissure, then another, but it was no use; the lake was being torn apart. Violent waves heaved mounds of ice skyward as the sphere boomed closer. He fell on an ice float and grabbed onto the edge. Above him loomed a tower of darkness threatening to annihilate him.

The orb crashed down on the float, thrusting him deep into the glacial waters. His arms and legs frantically flailing, Dillan couldn't stop his violent descent. The turbulence quieted, the deafening noise receded, and the whirling stopped. Dillan was submerged in a cold sea of blackness, a world without ground, walls, or ceilings, without right and left, up or down. No air to ease the burning in his lungs.

A voice. Distant. Muddled. A young boy. He was screaming something. Dillan tried to surface, desperately stroking toward him. Overhead, a halo of light. The boy's voice became clearer. The child was calling out his name: "*James! James!*"

His lungs about to explode, Dillan thrust his body upward. The halo in the ice became a silvery opening through which he could see the little boy leaning close to the surface. It was his brother.

"*James!*" Daniel called out again before plunging his hand into the water. Dillan reached for his hand with outstretched fingers. He almost touched it. The light was getting brighter. One more kick, one more stroke.

"*Dottore, Dottore!*" called out a voice.

Dillan gasped. There was a bright light by the side of his head and water droplets falling onto his face. He turned and shielded his eyes.

"*Dottore!*" A hand moved from his shoulder to his forehead. "What happened? Where's Vincente? *Merda* ... you're bleeding."

Dillan winced as he lifted his head. There was another head-lamp, this one higher up and off to one side. "Is the boy here?" he said.

"No," Detective Tramonte answered. "Can you move?"

"I think so..."

"What happened?"

"I don't know ... we found this place by accident. Vincente dis-covered the crate in the ground. The vase was inside. Two men arrived. One of them looked—I don't know, inhuman. He knew about Santilli. As if they'd been enemies. They'd come for the Cel-lini."

A man spoke. It was the detective's father. He was crouched over the crate.

"You are sure about the vase?" Detective Tramonte asked.

Dillan leaned on his good arm. "Yes." There was a distant rum-bling. "What was that?"

"Thunder," Detective Tramonte said. "It's pouring outside."

The elder Tramonte called out to his son. Detective Tramonte retrieved something from his knapsack and took it over to him. He came back and continued to clean the wound on the doctor's head.

Dillan flinched.

"Sorry," Detective Tramonte said. "Were they armed?"

"One of them."

"I think a bullet grazed your head. You're lucky to be alive."
The detective paused, took another roll of gauze out of his emergency kit, and applied pressure to the wound. "There's a bad cut
at the base of your neck. Looks like you were gouged with a knife."
Dillan's thoughts were muddled, lost in a sea of emotions.

Detective Tramonte kept one hand on the gauze covering Dillan's wound and reached for a large plaster with his other. "Why
did they take Vincente?"

Dillan was overcome with guilt, with the unbearable feeling—
now bordering on panic—of having lost another child under his
watch. "I don't know.... One of the men, the grotesque one, knew
who Vincente was... I can't believe this is happening. Maybe we
can still catch sight of them."

"They are probably long gone," said Detective Tramonte.
"There was a report of a helicopter in the area. That was a few
hours ago."

Dillan rubbed the back of his head. "How did you know I was
here?"

"I didn't. My father insisted we come for you, even before you
stopped answering your phone. We hoped you were still at the hut,
waiting out the rain. When we could not find you anywhere, we
set out on a trail. I don't know how my father found this cave. He
said he didn't know about it, and it was almost impossible to see
in the rain. Once he spotted it, though, he was adamant that we
go inside."

Domenico Tramonte grunted. He was lying on his stomach
with one arm inside the crate. For a second, Dillan thought he saw
fireflies floating above the old man's head. He closed his eyes and
opened them again. The hovering lights were gone.

"Give me a minute," Detective Tramonte said. He walked over
to his father, lay down on his stomach beside him, and reached
inside the crate. Together they tugged on something. Seconds
later, they pulled out a cast-iron base with three hooked feet, a
thick, round platform, and three wide shafts, each with three

outstretched prongs in the form of spears. They set it down on the ground. "It was bolted into the rock," Detective Tramonte said. "That's why he needed my tool."

"I noticed the base when I was looking down at the vase," Dillan said, studying the artwork.

"We should go. Can you walk?"

Dillan pushed himself up onto all fours. "I think so."

The elder Tramonte picked up the iron base. "*Voglio portarla con me*," he said.

Detective Tramonte let his father carry it out. They lined up to leave, the detective at the head and the elder Tramonte at the rear.

"Wait," Dillan said. "My knapsack. Did you see it?"

"No."

"There were two books on top of the vase. I'd put them in my pack."

They scanned the ground and walls with their headlamps. The knapsack was nowhere to be found.

Dillan turned to the detective. "Where's Liz?" he asked, almost in a whisper.

Detective Tramonte hesitated. "She hasn't been answering her phone."

The men started to exit. They arrived at the tapered section of the cave, where they had to start crawling. Dillan swept the ground with his light, hoping to see the gelatinous flowers, but murky contours, angled rock walls, and fleeting shadows where all his beam would reveal. Then, scarcely visible against the black rock, he spotted one of the aphotic plants. His heart sank. The plant had been trampled, its petals flattened and mashed. Farther ahead, he spied the other flowers. They, too, had suffered the same fate. Beside them were a few milky-white and foul-smelling stains.

The downpour was heavy, with thick curtains of rain hanging in the distance. Dillan and the elder Tramonte pulled up their hoods and waited as the detective sprinted across the puddled terrain toward a crest, hoping to get a phone signal.

Domenico Tramonte gripped the cast-iron piece he had carried out of the cave and set it down by a boulder. Dillan looked on, marveling at the fact that Cellini himself may have created the artwork. The elder Tramonte removed his knapsack, took out a folded sheet of blue tarpaulin, and wrapped the base in it.

A bolt of lightning tore across the gray sky. Domenico Tramonte stared into the distance. His lips moved, as if he were reciting a silent prayer. Seconds passed. A loud crack ripped through the air, followed by a boom so formidable that the mountains appeared to tremble.

Domenico Tramonte turned to Dillan. He had a grave look on his face. "*Dovete andare nella foresta!*" he shouted over the driving rain.

Dillan wasn't sure he had understood. "*Cosa?*"

"*Dovete andare nella foresta! Nel prato!*" he repeated with greater urgency.

Why was it so important that Dillan go to the forest? To a meadow. And what forest was he talking about?

Another flash—this one brighter than the last—lit up the sky. Dillan glanced at the storm clouds. Thunder boomed over the massif and rumbled into the valleys.

Detective Tramonte came running toward them. "Still no signal," he hollered.

Dillan pulled his hood over the side of his face. "Your father," he shouted, turning his back to the wind. "He said I needed to go to some forest. He sounded serious!"

"He told me the same thing on our way here," the detective yelled back. "Not sure what that's about."

"*Andiamo!*" ordered the elder Tramonte. And into the cold, lashing rain they went.

CHAPTER 43

The white minivan had crossed the narrow, wooden bridge when Mihalovitch loosened his grip on the steering wheel and turned to Michael. "You're being awfully quiet."

"I was thinking about some of the things you told me."

"A most excellent use of your time, I must say." Mihalovitch pulled over to the side of the road and turned off the engine.

"If I do this," Michael said, "how do I know you won't take me back to Iris?"

"You can't. I will, however, let you in on a secret. I tricked her into asking me to go after the Priorate. I wasn't sure I could pull it off, but she experienced something terrifying. Something she thought was the Priorate's doing."

"So you're playing them against each other?"

Mihalovitch flashed him a smile. "When your allies are snakes and hyenas, it's best to keep your ear to the ground and your eye on the prize."

Michael considered what Mihalovitch had just said. "What happens if the Cellini isn't here?"

"The question isn't whether he has the vase, but whether what we're looking for was indeed inside it."

"You still haven't told me what it is we're after."

"What do you know about the origins of the Medici emblem?"

Michael shrugged. "Not much."

"The Medici claimed to be descendants of a great warrior. This fighter had defeated a beast that had been terrorizing the people of a nearby valley. During the battle, the beast swung a massive spiked club at the warrior, who blocked it with a golden shield. The Medici balls symbolize the dents left on the shield by the beast's weapon. The story, of course, is a myth. But myths often hold vital truths."

"I'm not sure I follow."

"The dents were real, Mr. Kohler, as was the shield. Only there was no spiked club."

"So what caused them?"

"Six blazing stones. Each of them infused with the darkest powers of the hidden dream world."

Michael's eyes widened. "How were they thrown at the warrior?"

"The only way possible. Straight out of the creature's mouth, like fire hurled by a dragon. It was a *taurine*, of course. One of the greatest and most feared." He stopped, as if to gather his thoughts. "The stones contained unimaginable forces," he added. "Once recovered, they could be used to poison the dreams of millions. It wouldn't take long for humankind to be plunged into a world overrun by fear and savagery."

Michael tried to make sense of what he'd been told. "To what end?"

"Power, my friend. For carved out of this chaos, a new world order will rise."

"If what you're saying is true, someone would need to bring the stones back into the dream world, into the *anumia*, where their true power lies. No?"

Mihalovitch interlocked his fingers over the steering wheel. His knuckles cracked. "You're a clever man, Mr. Kohler. That someone, however, would have to be exceptionally gifted. Some would say predestined. For a while, Iris entertained the thought of you carrying them back, aided by the new drugs, of course. Maybe still does... Somewhere within the mountains and chasms of the *anumia* lurks the ruler of even the mightiest of *taurines*. This creature wishes nothing more than to be reunited with the stones, to unleash their fury upon those who dare stand in its way." He paused for a moment, then he said, "The Priorate and your beloved Iris are locked in an otherworldly race. Whoever crosses the finish line first stands to receive a prize like no other—a pact with the master devil himself."

Michael remained silent as he tried to make sense of Mihalovitch's words. "What about you?" he finally said. "Where do you fit in all this?"

"I've told you before, Mr. Kohler. I'm not that fussy. I'll help whatever side I need to if it serves my interests."

"But you could take the stones back. Right?"

Mihalovitch gave a light chuckle. "Yes, I reckon perhaps I could—as do Iris and your crazed recruiter. But while dealing with the vile ways of these two can be rather titillating, I'm not so sure I'd enjoy working with the devil himself. Unless, of course," he added with a grin, "I knew I could outwit him." He stopped and gazed out of Michael's passenger window. "But now we must head into these woods," he said, pointing his chubby index at the forest on Michael's side of the car, "and find out if the Priorate is indeed in possession of these delightfully wicked gems."

"Do you know what they look like?"

Mihalovitch shook his head. "The last person to see them was probably Cellini himself. The vase must be in pieces by now. Your goal is to find out whether the stones were there."

"You said I might have to kill him. How?"

Mihalovitch reached into the glove compartment, took out a small tin box, and gave it a slight shake. "Here, open it."

Michael removed the lid. Nestled in the box was a glass sphere the size of a small egg. It looked like a tiny snow globe, only the viscous liquid inside was a dirty brown, and instead of white flecks mimicking a snowstorm, the particles floating within were rust-colored.

"What is this?"

"A concoction that should fry his body. You'll be using it to kill him, after you've found out about the stones. Go ahead, take it out. Carefully."

Michael placed his fingers on top of the small globe, turned the box on its side, and let the object roll slowly into his hand. It was surprisingly heavy, its outermost layer made out of a dense, rubbery membrane.

"You'll need to throw it at him. Hard, so that it breaks. Like a water balloon."

"Where do I need to hit him?"

"That part is up to you. Just aim hard and well. As long as the liquid hits his skin, you'll be fine. Doesn't matter if it's his face, arm, or skinny ass."

"Wouldn't it be simpler to shoot him?"

"He already has one foot in a world beyond this one. A bullet or two might do him in here, but not in the realm where it matters most."

Mihalovitch pushed open his door but remained seated and turned to Michael. "One more thing. There's a chance the Priorate might be able to turn himself into a semblance of the creature that attacked you in the barn."

"You're joking."

"If I were you, I'd leave my sense of humor out of this and assume everything I've told you is true. And I'd prepare accordingly."

Michael swallowed. "Okay."

"I suggest you think of this as a dream. With one difference, though. Waking up won't be an option."

* * *

It was almost dusk when the two men reached the top of the barren hill. They hunkered close to the ground, scanning the small bowl-shaped valley. At the center of the grass and rock basin was a dark oval pond and to the left a small rectangular barn. "He's in there," Mihalovitch said.

"How do you know?"

"I can smell him." Mihalovitch reached into the leather pouch strung across his shoulder and drew out the small globe. He held it up so they could both see it. "You'll only get one chance," he said before slipping it back into the bag and handing it to Michael. "A lot more than your fate rests on what happens down there."

"I understand."

"Be strong, Mr. Kohler. And don't let him spook you. This is one place where fear isn't your friend."

CHAPTER 44

O utside the car, the temperature had fallen, and a dense mist hung in the late evening air. Detective Tramonte, troubled and exhausted, drove on as countless silvery particles swirled in front of the headlights. Beside him, his father was fast asleep.

Dillan, looking on from the back seat, took another series of slow breaths, hoping for relief from the knot in his stomach. "Maybe we should try calling Liz again," he said.

Detective Tramonte reached for his phone and handed it over his shoulder to the doctor. "The speakerphone should work now," he said, tapping one of the steering wheel's control buttons.

Dillan pressed redial. As with previous attempts, an automated message came on stating that the person at that number was unavailable.

No sooner had the doctor hung up than the phone rang. The detective used the car's Bluetooth to answer. It was Captain Battista. Detective Tramonte lowered the speaker volume as the captain unleashed a barrage of questions and rebukes. The detective's curt answers and defensive tone indicated he was in trouble. There was a click. Battista had put an end to the lopsided conversation.

Dillan remained silent.

"He's right to be upset," the detective admitted. "I told him I would be back hours ago."

Dillan peeled off his raincoat, pain radiating down his right arm. Under his coat was the soft-shell jacket the detective had lent him for his hike. He kept it on and checked the pockets. The left one was empty, but not the right. Dillan was taken aback by what he found: the small double-sided card holder Santilli had left for Vincente. Tucked in one side was the edelweiss and in the other the silver key they had used to access the vase.

Dillan examined the items. Folded behind the pale flower was a piece of paper. He held the edges of the plastic holder between his right thumb and forefinger and pressed on them gently, creating an opening at the top. He reached inside with the tip of his pinky, carefully slipped out the small piece of paper, and unfolded it. It was too dark for him to make out the handwritten message. He turned on Tramonte's phone and tried to read by the light from the screen.

"What is that?" Detective Tramonte asked, looking at Dillan in the rear-view mirror.

"Vincente must have slipped this in my pocket when we were in the cave. It's a note, in Italian. I'm assuming from his mother."

"Do you know what it says?"

"I'm not sure."

"Can I take a look?" the detective said, reaching blindly behind him. He slowed down and glanced at the writing.

Dillan turned on the ceiling light and leaned forward. "Well?"

"I'm thinking about how to translate it … it says … sometimes, the bearer of a great gift is more valuable than the gift itself. Something like that."

The elder Tramonte grunted and stretched before turning toward the passenger door and drifting back to sleep.

CHAPTER 45

The first troubling thing Michael saw as he rounded the barn was the Priorate's chauffeur lying dead on his back. The man's hands—charred to a crisp—were clenched around his throat, and his mouth, wide open, was frozen in a noiseless scream. His right eye was missing and his left hidden under a strip of carbonized flesh that extended from the top of his forehead, down the side of his face, and into his jaw. Through the blackened tissue, the pale, rounded end of a bone stuck out of his cheek. The man's clothes, however, from his jacket down to his dress shoes, appeared intact. Even the white of the shirt around his scorched neck and wrists was untouched.

Something crunched the ground behind Michael. He whirled around. Less than a dozen feet away, staring at him through the dim light, was a small goat. It stood motionless, grinning. It took a step forward, shook its head, and bleated twice, as if mocking him, before staring at him again with the same creepy grin. The animal remained still as a statue. Seconds passed. Then it raised its head like a horse about to gallop and scampered halfway up the knoll from which Michael had come. It stopped, looked back for an instant, and continued to climb sideways until it reached the top of the hill and disappeared down the other side.

Silence. Not even a breeze. Michael looked at the corpse before him and studied the man's blistered hands and disfigured face. Poisoning and exposure to chemicals were the more obvious possibilities for cause of death, but the sight reeked of something infinitely more ne-farious. He reminded himself of Mihalovitch's words: *This is one place where fear isn't your friend.* He moved along.

The next troubling thing Michael saw was lying in a puddle, star-ing skyward. It was the chauffeur's blackened eyeball, a few strands of muscle still attached. The sight triggered a memory of the Prior-ate's driver—his eyes staring at him in the rear-view mirror. Swallowing what little saliva he had, Michael walked toward the en-trance to the barn. A metal latch held the wide wooden door shut.

Michael started to raise the lever on the latch but stopped, stepped back, and examined the door. Although harder to discern in the dying light, there was no mistaking the swirling, paisley-like pattern of grays and blacks in the wood grain. It was like in Mihalovitch's dream.

Michael looked at his hands, palm-sides up and palm-sides down, at his shoes, at the muddy ground around him, at the dark-ening sky. He scanned the horizon and tried to remember everything that had happened to him that day, including how he had gotten to the barn. No other test was necessary. This was no dream. Time to step inside.

Once he'd unfastened the latch, he grasped the edge of the door with his fingertips and eased it toward him. He took a peek. The space inside appeared murky and quiet. He pulled the door open a bit wider. The hinges screeched. Inside the barn, about five yards in front of him, stood an old farm tractor. Behind it was a door that had been left ajar. A faint sliver of light shone through the opening. He entered the barn, taking care to step only on the straw scattered here and there on the floor—as if it conferred some sort of protective magic—and approached the tractor. The body was covered with patches of rust and flaking, faded crimson paint. The front wheels, bald from use, were angled outward, while the tall, deeply grooved wheels at the back were caked in mud.

A voice. Someone—a man—was on the other side of the door, his tone strained and mechanical. Michael recognized it at once. But who was the Priorate talking to? What if others—maybe Iris herself—were there with him? He clasped his leather pouch, tiptoed over to the hinge side of the door, and listened.

"...your mother survived that first attack, but she knew the day would come when mere survival wouldn't suffice. The beast that almost killed her as a child would return, and this time, nothing short of victory would do for either side."

"You're not making sense! You're disgusting!" cried a boy. It had to be Vincente.

"I disgust you because my human side is rotting. In its place, however, grows a power you cannot understand. In the world of dreams, my little boy, I'm becoming a ruler—a king—and soon enough, I shall be immortal." The Priorate choked and wheezed before catching his breath. "Do you know why your tents were set so far apart?"

No answer.

"Your mother was all too familiar with the forces residing in these mountains and knew that what had happened to her as a child could well happen to you now. She knew that, with their powers, the *taurines* could draw anyone sleeping close to their victim into a single dream and, once trapped inside, attack everyone in a single raid. Two birds with one stone, so to speak. Maybe even a whole flock." The Priorate gave a weak laugh that quickly degenerated into a consumptive cough.

"Your mother, though ... she didn't trust your feeble skills. That's why she didn't want you pulled into a dream that could threaten you both. Not that she feared for her own life. She knew she could take care of herself. Or so she thought. It was *you* she worried about. But, my little boy, in the end, it was your very presence that caused your mother's death."

"I didn't kill her!" yelled Vincente. "I hate you!"

"It's not me you hate," the man said calmly. "It's the truth I speak. What your mother failed to realize was that it wasn't only a *taurine* that was coming back for her, but also yours truly. With the creature's power on my side, I was able to infiltrate your dream body and enter your mother's sleep in a disguise so perfect, it could trick even the most gifted of dreamers."

The man paused, as if to contain his excitement, then said, "After what happened to your father, I knew that, if forced to choose, your mother would just as soon see you killed than give up the stones. That's why I needed to confront her directly and show her who was boss. And so I did."

"Shut up!" The boy started to sob.

"Your mother fell into a dream she believed was real, a dream in which you came into her tent and woke her up. She had no reason to fear, for the person before her was none other than her own loving son. She let her guard down, and by the time I had jumped her, it was too late."

"Stop it! You're just a stupid monster!"

"Your mother had great discipline," continued the Priorate, "and her training was exemplary. What I hadn't counted on, however, was her being such a coward. When she realized what I could do in the world of dreams, she took a spineless way out. She chose never to dream again. Your mother did leave me a message before dying. A message laced with bravura. But I wasn't impressed ... I mean, when you're on your last breath, outwitted and beaten, such acts ring hollow and childish. Don't you think?"

On the other side of the door, Michael was trying to scan the room through the gap between door and wall, but he had a limited view. He pressed softly on the door. Standing at the far end of the room with his back to Michael was the Priorate, and sitting at his feet with his back against the wall was Vincente. Michael removed the toxic globe from its leather pouch and placed it in his front pants pocket, in easy reach of his right hand.

"I didn't want your mother to die that night," continued the Priorate. "I only wanted to know where the vase had been hidden. You must understand, my little boy, that I am the last of the great

Medici. Those stones are rightfully mine. Tell me where they are, and I promise to let you go."

"I told you! I don't know anything about your stupid stones! She only told me about the vase…"

"If, as you say, you have nothing to offer, then that leaves me little choice."

Michael stepped into the room.

With startling speed, the Priorate wheeled around. His ivory eyes grew wide as he saw who was there. "What are you—"

"I'm here to help," Michael blurted out.

"Stop right there!" The Priorate raised his right—his only—hand.

Heat flashed over Michael's throat.

"I thought you'd be dead by now." The Priorate pointed his index finger at his recruit. "Unless Iris sent you here herself. Exactly the kind of thing that bitch would try."

Like a man held at gunpoint, Michael raised his hands above his head. It was only then that he noticed the Cellini over by the wall to his left. What remained of it. Someone had used a hammer and a large rubber mallet—both instruments still lying on the floor—to break the vase. It lay in a jumble of fragments and powdered remains. He looked at Vincente, whose hands were tied in front of him and his legs bound at the ankles. The moment their eyes met, the boy unleashed a string of obscenities in his direction.

"You know this man?" asked the Priorate, turning to the boy.

"He's a jerk!"

"How do you know him?"

"*Vaffanculo!*" yelled the boy.

"That's enough," hissed the Priorate. He turned to Michael. "How did you know where to find me?"

"Iris sent me. To try to kill you. But I know she'll only kill me in turn. What I want are the drugs, and you're the only one who can give them to me."

"You're lying."

"I've fought a *taurine*, Priorate. In the hidden dream world. I have a scar to prove it."

"Yes … I read the stories in your precious little diaries, lies and all. Come closer," he ordered. "And do explain how you got here."

Michael wetted his lips and took three small steps.

"Closer…"

Three more. "One of her henchmen drove me to a wooded area," Michael said, "maybe an hour's walk from here. She told me you'd be inside a barn. That I had less than twenty-four hours to find you, and that I'd be rewarded if I did."

The Priorate looked at him with an air of distrust. "When did you last see Mihalovitch?"

"Yesterday. He was with Iris. I'd just met him in one of his dreams. It didn't go well."

"This scar of yours," the Priorate said, shuffling barefoot toward Michael. "You want me to believe that *you* were in the *anumia*?"

"I told you. I fought a *taurine*. The scar is from that fight, from its drool."

The Priorate swung his stump. A milky substance flew off his coat sleeve and onto Michael's pants. The smell was revolting, like putrefying fish, and the substance alive. Inside the viscous fluid were hundreds of squirming little worms.

The Priorate's head—skeletal and covered with drooping, diaphanous skin—was mere inches from Michael's. "Show me," he hushed. His breath reeked of urine.

"It's on my chest, on the right."

"Pull up your shirt—slowly." The Priorate took a step back.

Like a dream, only without the option of waking up. Michael held the base of his T-shirt with both hands and pulled it up to his chin. "The scar is always cold," he said, noticing the Priorate's scrawny ribs rise and fall.

The Priorate was transfixed, his excitement palpable.

"The stones," Michael said, glancing at the remains of the vase. "I could carry them back for you. Into the *anumia*."

"As only a fated dreamer could," muttered the Priorate. He raised his hand. A flash of heat burned down Michael's windpipe. "If this is a trick—"

"Touch it, damn it!" Michael yelled, battling the stinging pain. "This is no trick! You have the stones, but I have the know-how to carry them back to where they came from. Give me the drugs, and the stones will be yours. Not on this earth but in the hidden world of dreams, where their powers will make you a god."

Michael's heart was pounding, his hands, still holding up his shirt, shaking.

"The problem," said the Priorate through gritted teeth, "is that I don't have the stones."

"But you found the vase!"

"And *only* the vase…"

Michael pulled down his T-shirt, and as he did, he saw Vincente creeping toward the back of the man's legs, digging his heels into the floor and sliding his bottom along.

"I can help you find them," Michael rushed to say. "I overheard Iris and Mihalovitch talking about a second vase. Under a church near Florence."

Vincente swung his feet at the Priorate's calves, but frail as he was, the man's knees didn't buckle. Instead, he turned, and like Zeus about to strike down an enemy, raised his clenched hand high above the boy's head.

"Priorate!" yelled Michael.

The man whirled around, sending more gobs of fluid flying across the room, but Michael's throw was spot on. The globe hit the Priorate where his coat was open, smack in his chest. It burst, sending its contents onto the Priorate's skin. A fiery orange flooded his eyes, and his pupils morphed into vertical slits. His body shook, and his heavy coat slipped off his shoulders and onto the floor. The Priorate hissed like a crazed cat, stumbled forward, and fell to his knees. His mouth opened, and greenish-yellow drool dripped onto the floor, where it sizzled like butter in a red-hot skillet. His long, bony fingers began to stiffen and curve.

Vincente had gotten up onto his knees. He pounded his clasped fists onto the man's spine. It cracked. He struck a second time before falling back in fright. Something was quivering under the Priorate's skin.

Michael ran over and pulled the boy away. He grabbed the mallet from the floor and was about to smash the Priorate's head when he heard a loud voice.

"Don't touch him!" yelled Mihalovitch, entering the room.

Michael froze with the mallet above his head, his trembling hands ready to deliver the blow.

"Back away. And don't step in that goo."

The Priorate, or whatever he had started to turn into, fell face first onto the floor. His gaunt legs shriveled and his toes mutated into angled claws, like the talons of a raptor. Then nothing. The metamorphosis appeared to have come to a stop.

The Priorate slowly raised his head and tilted it horizontally, as if looking for something. A faint moan. The talons closed, grasping some phantom prey. The Priorate exhaled. His head fell.

Mihalovitch circled the body. The Priorate's head was turned sideways, resting by his shoulder, his eyes half-open. Mihalovitch watched their faint, orangey glow fade to black. He looked over at Michael and smiled. "You did well, Mr. Kohler. Real well."

Michael stood there, motionless, the mallet still in his hands.

"Pass me that thing," Mihalovitch said. He was about to kneel by the corpse when it heaved. Thick drool oozed from the Priorate's mouth, down his jaw, and onto his shoulder, where, with a faint hiss, it dissolved his skin.

Mihalovitch let the mallet fall to the floor and chuckled as he turned to Michael. "Why so glum, Mr. Kohler? You should be rejoicing."

Jubilation, however, was the furthest thing from Michael's mind—and heart. He wiped the worm-infested patch off his pants with his sleeve, sat down resting his back against a wall, raised his bent knees, and wrapped his arms around them. There he remained, motionless.

A few feet away, sitting on the floor with his bound hands covering his face, was Vincente, doing his best to muffle his crying.

Mihalovitch walked toward the boy. "You must be Santilli's son."

"His name is Vincente," Michael said without looking up.

"I know his name. What I don't know is what he can tell us about the stones."

Vincente jerked his body in anger. "*Vaffanculo!*" he yelled. "Both of you!"

Michael blinked. "I'm so sorry," he said to Vincente. "I had no idea what I was getting myself into. I never wanted this to happen … I only—"

"Shut up! Just shut up!" Vincente screamed.

"I wish I could tell you this was all over," Mihalovitch said. "But I'd be lying. And you'd know it too. But I *can* help you."

Vincente looked up at the large-headed man and gave him a long stare. Then he pointed his chin at Kohler. "What about him?"

"That man saved your life."

"I don't care. I don't want him near me."

"After tomorrow, you'll never see him again. Now, you have two choices. Behave, and you can come with me, untied. Or misbehave, and I'll carry you, bound and tied as you are. What'll it be?"

"Untied…"

"A most excellent choice." Mihalovitch picked up the hammer and used the claw to rip the duct tape binding the boy's ankles and wrists.

"That thing," Vincente said, wiggling his hands and legs. "Is it dead?"

Mihalovitch looked over at the Priorate, at what he was trying to become. "As dead as a doornail."

"He said his human side was dying."

Mihalovitch snickered. "As if we hadn't noticed."

"And that in the dream world, he'd soon be a kind of king, and immortal."

The smile disappeared from Mihalovitch's face. "I have to admit that what he showed us here was rather impressive. But in the world of dreams, that fool doesn't stand a chance. The true kings of those realms will have him for lunch."

"What he said wasn't true, then?"

"What else did he tell you?"

"He said I was the reason my mother died."

Mihalovitch got up, hammer in hand, and walked by the Priorate's unsightly feet. Without warning, he swung the claw-end of the hammer down onto the half-grown talons. He raised the hammer again and with the second blow cleaved one of the hooks clean. He picked it up and returned to Vincente's side. "Look at this," he said, holding the eagle-like talon in his hand. "Would you believe anything said by someone who had shit like this for toes?"

Vincente turned his head away from the repugnant nail.

"Listen to me. Dreams played a role in your mother's death. That much is true. But you sure as hell didn't kill her. You understand?"

Vincente nodded.

From across the room, Michael spoke in a low voice. "I don't want to be part of this anymore…" He glanced over at the Priorate's remains. "Everything's so fucked up." He stared straight ahead, his arms wrapped around his knees, his body rocking back and forth. "I want out, Ivan. Please."

The look on Mihalovitch's face turned sour. He raised the hammer over his shoulder and walked up to Michael. "I'm ready to crack your skull open, if that's what you want…. Two blows, maybe three, and it'll be over. Shall I?"

Michael felt his heart race. "No … don't."

"You entered this game of your own free will, Mr. Kohler. You knew there'd be no turning back, no magical rewind button. But listen. You did well. You kept your fears in check, and you got me the Priorate."

Mihalovitch put the cleaved talon in his pocket, walked to where the vase lay in pieces, and began to pluck and set aside the larger fragments. He cupped his hand and swept the powdered remnants of Cellini's artwork into a small mound.

"Unfortunately," he said, collecting some of the mix into his palm, "the stones weren't in there after all." He closed his fingers and raised his fist in the air, letting a fine ribbon of the powder run out. It fell to the floor like sand in an hourglass. He walked over to the boy.

"I'm going to ask you a simple question," Mihalovitch said, kneeling by Vincente. He stared into his eyes. "Where are the stones?"

"They were supposed to be in the vase."

Mihalovitch didn't blink. "I will ask you one more time. Where *are* the stones?"

"I don't know!" the boy cried. "My mom never told me! Only that they were important and somehow tied to that vase. I thought they'd be there."

"Were you here when they broke it apart?" asked Mihalovitch.

"Yes. It was the other man, the big one who did it. When they realized there was nothing inside, that monster over there went crazy and killed him."

Mihalovitch arched an eyebrow "How?"

"I'm not sure... He raised his hand and it was like the man's face caught fire."

Mihalovitch stood up. "We need to go. Others might be coming." He helped the boy to his feet. "You too, Mr. Kohler."

Michael released a sigh as he got up. "What happens now, Ivan?"

"Now? I'm going to deliver on my promise. All of it. The lab, the drugs, the know-how and, soon enough, an encounter with your beloved *taurine*. And if that's not worth living for, I don't know what is. We may not have the stones, Mr. Kohler, but then again, neither does anyone else. Now come along."

Vincente took a few steps. "Where are we going?"

"To a fancy lab," he answered, letting the boy walk past him. Michael, however, was behind them both. He'd picked up the mallet. He raised it high above his head.

Mihalovitch turned as the mallet struck him on the side of the head. He stumbled. Michael took another, even more forceful swing. It sailed over Mihalovitch's outstretched forearm, hitting and shattering his clavicle.

"Run!" Michael yelled to Vincente.

Mihalovitch moaned as he fell to the ground.

The boy started to run, stopped, darted over to a corner of the room, snatched the knapsack that had been taken from them in the cave, and raced out without looking back.

Michael raised the mallet above his head, ready for the kill. He froze, watching Mihalovitch writhing on the ground, listening to his lingering groans.

"You idiot," Mihalovitch moaned. "We're on the same side ..."

"No, we're not," Michael said. "You're as crazy as the rest of them."

"I saved your life ... you don't understand..."

"You only kept me alive because it suited you," Michael said. "I can't let you do to Vincente what you did to me." Without warning, he swung the mallet down onto Mihalovitch's right kneecap.

Ivan shrieked as his bones shattered under the impact.

"I won't kill you," Michael said, more to himself than to the man writhing and moaning by his feet. "But if I catch you, that sadistic bitch, or anyone else coming anywhere near the boy, I swear to God I'll kill you all."

Michael gazed down at his trembling hands, raised the mallet above his head, and let it come to rest on his shoulder. He then turned around, walked out of the barn, and into the growing darkness.

CHAPTER 46

Liz was sitting at the back of the cab that Ivan had called for her trip to Trento. The male driver, a young, lanky Asian, had yet to utter a single word. Liz took out the cell the big-headed man had given her and tried calling Dillan again. No answer. She tried the detective. One ring. Two.

"*Pronto.*"

"Detective Tramonte! It's me, Liz."

"Ms. Parks! We have been trying to reach you. Is everything okay?"

"I tried calling earlier, but I couldn't get hold of either of you."

"I'm right here!" Dillan exclaimed into the car's speakerphone. "We were getting worried."

"So was I. Where are you?"

"We're in the detective's car, on our way back."

"How did it go?"

Silence.

"James?"

"There were people up there…"

"What do you mean?"

"I can't explain now."

"Are you all right?"

"Sort of. Where are you calling from?"

"I'm near the Trento train station."

"I can have an officer accompany you to the police station if you want," Detective Tramonte said. "We could meet you there."

"I don't think that's a good idea, Detective. Could we meet at the park by the train station instead?"

"Are you in danger?" asked Dillan.

Liz fell silent, as if gauging something. "I think we all are," she finally said.

"Stay put, Ms. Parks. We will be there as soon as we can."

* * *

The pigeon cooing near Liz's feet took off with a flutter into the darkening sky. Liz took another look at the text Dillan had sent her, got up, and headed for Via Vittorio Alfieri. As she reached the street, she glanced over her shoulder. Nothing unusual. A car pulled up to the curb. Dillan stepped out. Although relieved to see Liz, he was shocked by her appearance.

"What happened?"

Liz closed her eyes and put her arms around his shoulders. Dillan held her close.

"Careful," she whispered. "My ribs..."

Dillan released her and eyed her disheveled clothes, bandaged hand, and gash on the side of her head. "Who did this to you?"

She started to cry. "I couldn't tell you over the phone."

Dillan touched her hair ever so gently. "Please, tell me what happened."

"Someone tried to kidnap me."

Detective Tramonte rolled down his window. "Are you okay, Ms. Parks?"

Liz took a slow breath. "I am now."

The moment she stepped into the back of the car, Liz noticed the detective's father in the front passenger seat. She also realized Vincente was missing. Dillan tried to contain his distress as he explained how he and the boy had found the Cellini, and how the boy and the vase had been taken. Her voice strained, her lips at times quivering, Liz then shared what had happened to her, from her abduction in Trento to the events following the arrival of the big-headed man. She told them how her unlawful access to the Swiss-based server had not gone unnoticed and how the men who had kidnapped her had wanted to know why she'd been after the pictures of Santilli, and who she was working for. Her voice faltered when she told them about the gun being held to her head.

* * *

Detective Tramonte exited the restroom and joined Dillan, Liz, and his father at the back of the small coffee shop on the edge of town. They went over the day's events and considered possible courses of action. During much of these discussions, the elder Tramonte sat silent at his end of the table, sipping a soda and doodling on an open napkin.

"The more I think about the two men who fell asleep on the road," Liz said, "the more I think something was done to them. Maybe with a drug or implant."

Dillan raised an eyebrow.

"What if someone had figured out how to plunge people straight into REM sleep?" she said. "Even from a distance."

"I don't see how that'd be possible," Dillan replied, "although it would explain what you saw."

Detective Tramonte twirled his spoon in his espresso and turned to Liz. "Are you sure the instruction to leave from Innsbruck is not a trap?"

"All I know is that if it weren't for Ivan, I'd probably be dead."

"He never told you where the *dottore* was supposed to go?" Detective Tramonte asked.

"He said I'd know. He may have been right." She looked at Dillan. "The codes on the medallions."

"What medallions?" asked the detective.

"When I stopped at the Duomo di Trento," Dillan answered, "I saw a painting of Saint Anthony holding the Baby Jesus—"

"Like on Santilli's pendant," interjected Tramonte.

"Exactly. Beside it were some display cases housing several medallions. I took pictures of them. Some were engraved with symbols."

"Alphanumeric codes," Liz said, "from the World Geodetic System."

"Like GPS coordinates?" asked Tramonte.

Liz nodded. "I looked them up. Two pointed to areas in the Himalayas, and one matched the location where Santilli and Vincente had set up their camp. But the pictures showed three newer-looking medallions. The code on one of them also pointed to where Santilli's tents were. Another had the coordinates of James's apartment in Montreal."

"You're sure about this?"

"One hundred percent," Liz said.

"What about the third one?"

"It maps onto a small clearing in the Puez-Odle region of the Dolomites," replied Liz. "It's in the middle of a forest, about thirty kilometers from where Santilli died. These aren't coincidences."

A look of dismay washed over the detective's face. He drained what was left of his espresso. "My father told me several times today that the *dottore* had to go to a forest. To a meadow to be exact. In the Puez-Odle…"

They turned to Domenico Tramonte, who asked his son why they were looking at him like that. A lengthy exchange in Italian followed.

"He insists you need to leave before dawn," the detective explained. "Or terrible things will happen. He says a little girl from the snow field told him this. He has seen her a few times in his sleep. This is what he has been drawing."

The detective reached for his father's napkin. Penciled on it was a child-like sketch: a tree-lined field with a few wavy lines marking the ground cover and dozens of little flowers peeking out from under what was meant to be snow. Near the trees was a small girl with her hands down at her sides.

There was a collective silence.

"Much of what is going on is hard to make sense of ... to believe," Detective Tramonte said. "Ordinarily, I would have both of you stay here until these things could be investigated."

Dillan swallowed. "I know this looks like we could have—"

Detective Tramonte held up a hand, cutting off *il dottore* in mid-sentence. "I said ordinarily. These past days, however, have been anything but ordinary. For any of us. I will drive Ms. Parks to Innsbruck myself. We can be there in a couple of hours, plenty of time for her to make an early flight. From there it's about another two hours to the Puez-Odle. We could be at the nearest trailhead by first light."

"You'd be driving all night," Dillan said. "And the captain is expecting you first thing in the morning."

"Don't worry about me. We can make this work"

"What about the captain?" Dillan said. "What are you planning on telling him?"

Detective Tramonte reached for his empty espresso and let his fingers rest where his gaze had fallen on the edge of the small saucer holding his cup. "I don't know ... the truth, probably. I want us to find Vincente. Then there's my dad." He turned to his father. "Something is going on with him. What he did today was incredible. He was so strong and determined. So lucid. He hasn't had a day like this in years."

* * *

As might be expected at that time of night, the road winding through the Austrian Alps was deserted. Unlike the elder Tramonte, who had once again fallen asleep in the front seat, and Liz, dozing off and on, Dillan was wide awake, his head swirling with questions. He leaned toward the detective. "There's something I've been meaning to ask you. It's about the shark tooth you told me about. The one embedded in the rock near Santilli's campsite."

"What about it?"

"Have you ever touched it?"

"You mean like put my hand on it?"

"Yes."

"I have. When my dad first showed it to me."

"Was there anything unusual about how the rock felt?"

"Not that I remember."

"So the spot with the tooth wasn't warmer or colder than the rest of the boulder?"

Detective Tramonte glanced over his shoulder. He looked perplexed. "No..." He turned to face the road again. "Why do you ask?"

"Just curious."

* * *

Detective Tramonte walked around to the back of the car and opened the trunk. An image of Vincente played in his mind like a wretched, distant dream. Dillan and Liz had gotten out and were helping him with Liz's backpack.

"I'll come and take a look around," the detective said.

The front passenger door swung open. The elder Tramonte climbed out, stretched his arms, and joined the trio. Together, they walked to the main entrance of Kranebitten International Airport and scouted the area once inside.

"Don't worry, Detective," Liz said. "I'll call you before and after clearing security, and when I'm ready to board."

"You have been very helpful, Ms. Parks," Detective Tramonte said. "And courageous. I'm sorry for what happened, but I'm glad we met."

"Thank you for trusting me," replied Liz, brushing her lips against both his cheeks.

She turned to Dillan. "Promise me you'll stay safe."

Dillan took Liz in his arms. Cupping the back of her head with his hand, he led her into a gentle kiss, at once desperate and beautiful. As they parted, he saw the light glittering in a tear in the corner of her eye.

"I promise," he whispered.

CHAPTER 47

As soon as Vincente cleared the top of the hill, he paused to catch his breath. He turned and gazed into the shadows, barely able to discern the contours of the barn below, then scanned the horizon, hoping to see a familiar peak or landmark, but the gray sky was already too dim. He bolted into the forest and continued to run, his footing unsteady and sense of direction hazy. When it became too dark to run, he marched. And when at last his legs became too tired to carry him, he laid his knapsack by a tree, sat on the damp soil, and pondered his fate.

With people likely still after him, sleeping was out of the question. The gloves and thin hat he'd found in the knapsack had warmed him, at least momentarily, and the raincoat he'd folded and laid down under his bottom provided some insulation from the frigid ground, but he was now shivering again. Despite the cold, he was struggling to stay awake, let alone remain watchful.

He got up to collect whatever branches and leaves he could find to help him stay warm. What he saw next lifted his spirits. Behind the upper canopy of nearby larches and pines, in an area where the clouds had retreated, the moon shone, its fullness illumining wide swaths of the forest.

Vincente picked up his knapsack and raincoat and found a spot not too far away at the base of a dwarf willow, where he could sit in the moonlight. He took his mother's dream diary out of the bag, held the tome to his chest, and gazed at the moon's silvery glow. He remained still for some time, then closed his eyes. A sense of calm infused the far reaches of his mind. Eyes still closed, he lowered his mother's diary onto his lap, pulled back the soft leather cover, and ran his fingers over the first page. He then opened his eyes and began to read the first entry—one that Giancarla Santilli had written at the age of seven.

* * *

Vincente had read about twenty of his mother's dreams, some mind-bending, others terrifying, when he noticed a caterpillar inching its way over the top of the leather-bound volume. Fascinated, the boy looked on as the black and gold insect continued its undulating movements, creeping across the edge of the book and then wobbling down the very page he'd been reading. The caterpillar stopped and raised the first third of its body in the air, as if scouting the path ahead. It continued to crawl until what was under its body was not paper or leather, but the boy's lap.

Spellbound by the insect's progression and enchanted by how the color of its tiny hairs changed in the moonlight from bright shades of silver to vibrant hues of amber, Vincente watched the caterpillar crawl onto his chest. It continued, with stalwart determination, onto his arm, up to his shoulder, before disappearing onto the tree behind him.

Vincente edged away from the dwarf willow and looked back. There on the tree's furrowed trunk lay not one caterpillar but two. They were motionless, as if finally at home. The boy put away his mother's dairy, curled into a ball, and using the knapsack as a pillow, allowed himself to fall asleep.

CHAPTER 48

D illan was standing in a snow-covered meadow, a fresh layer of whiteness extending into the distant conifers. Peeking out from under the snow were hundreds of brilliant crocuses. He had seen the meadow before, probably more than once. The taupe-colored couch off to his right, however, was new.

Dillan moved with a deliberate gait, listening to the snow crunch under his feet. Not only was the doctor aware that he was dreaming, but his memories, recent and distant, were available to him. He also knew where he really was: in the back of Detective Tramonte's car, on his way back to the Dolomites.

As he approached the couch, Dillan noticed it was covered with fabric and not leather, as he had imagined. Then he saw something in front of the couch. There on the snow was a spiral-shaped mound of freshly picked crocuses, their petals craftily arranged to create a dazzling array of swirling blues, mauves, and golden yellows. Mere inches away from the arrangement were two small footprints, like those of a child. But other than the winding trail the doctor had left in the snow, there were no other tracks leading to or from the solitary pair of footprints.

Dillan walked over to the couch and ran his fingertips over the top of the backrest; the fabric was coarse and cool. He sat down and smiled as a cold dampness penetrated the backs of his legs. Rarely, if ever, had he been so poised in a dream, so keenly observant, so in control. This was his long-awaited chance.

He stared at the spiral arrangement of petals, wondering how to make Victor materialize. Lifting his gaze, he stared into the distant conifers. That's where he could come from. He closed his eyes and imagined the scene: Victor walking out of the woods, hands at his sides, eyes fixed straight ahead, feet pushing through the snow. The image became so clear, so real, that not only did Dillan begin to believe in his own powers in the dream, but also in Victor's. He opened his eyes.

A man was walking toward him. He had come not from the woods but instead from the center of the meadow, out of the whiteness of the snow. It wasn't Victor, though. It was an older man who appeared to be looking for something or someone. The man, dressed in a beige jacket, brown pants, and dark boots, came closer. Dillan recognized him. It was the detective's father.

Domenico Tramonte stopped to examine the mound of multi-colored flowers, then he spoke to Dillan in a language the doctor had never heard yet understood as if it were his mother tongue. "When I last saw her," the elder Tramonte said, studying the interwoven petals, "the little girl told me she'd be leaving soon, but I was hoping to see her one more time. This arrangement, however, was left for you."

"I don't think I ever saw the girl you speak of. How do you know the flowers were meant for me?" Dillan wasn't sure if he had spoken the words or only imagined saying them. No matter. He knew his friend had understood, for they were speaking the same language: that of the dream.

The elder Tramonte walked over to the couch, sat to the right of the doctor, and rested his forearms on his thighs. He clasped his hands before him and said, "She told me she wanted to see you and that when she did, she'd give you some of your favorite flowers—crocuses. I guess you missed her too."

Dillan rested his gaze on the kaleidoscopic display. Crocuses were one of his favorite flowers. "Who is she exactly?"

"I don't know her name. I've only met her a few times. Always in this meadow."

"Where was she going?"

"Home, I guess."

Dillan stared at the prints next to the flowers that the child—a little girl, if the elder Tramonte was to be believed—had arranged on the snow for him as a gift. "There are only two footprints," he said. "How did she leave?"

"She left as she came," replied the elder Tramonte. "Not from the meadow or the snow or even the forest. But through a door. If you do see her, though, please tell her I have what she asked me to find."

"What would that be?"

"The bearer of a great gift." And with those words, the old man stood and walked away, stepping in his own tracks, the snow under his feet giving a muffled crunch.

Domenico Tramonte did not hurry or slow down. Nor did he look back. He simply walked straight ahead until, in the space of a single stride, he vanished into the whiteness of the snow.

Dillan marveled at the dream and how his mind had used a line from the note Vincente had slipped into his pocket to construct the elder Tramonte's final words. Unlike many of his previous lucid ventures, Dillan accepted these events with an open mind and a sense of calm, for he knew the dream wasn't done with him, or he with it.

"Hello, James."

The voice of the man standing behind the couch was unmistakable, as was the touch of the muscular hand that came to rest on his shoulder.

"It wasn't easy getting here," Victor said.

Dillan kept his eyes on the flowers. "Why don't you come and sit?"

"I've always liked crocuses," continued Victor, electing to remain where he was. "Such a compelling way to announce a change of season. Never saw an arrangement like this one, though. It's stunning. The blues in particular look so lively. As if they were about to take flight. Don't you think?"

"Yes," Dillan answered. "The yellow ones too." The hand lifted from his shoulder.

Victor came and sat where Domenico Tramonte had been moments before. Dillan eyed his friend's black boots. They looked like the ones he had seen on the elder Tramonte.

"You've never noticed them before," remarked Victor, waving his right foot. "I'm quite sure I've been wearing these for some time now." He lowered the boot back onto the ground. "The thing with sleep is that so many details escape our attention. They trickle out of the mind and get washed out to sea, where, like weights, they sink into the deep waters of forgetfulness. The ones that harbor our forgotten dreams."

Dillan didn't move. This time he wasn't going to get trapped in a labyrinth of words. This time he was going to come away with answers.

"I don't want to play games, Victor," he said calmly. "I want an honest exchange. Can we do that?"

"Not only can we, we have to. There's a good chance we'll never see each other again."

The statement took Dillan by surprise.

"That's why I've been trying to find you," continued Victor. "And believe me, getting into the dream of someone zipping across the Alps at a hundred kilometers an hour is no small feat. But here I am, and you're clearly ready. What do you want to start with?"

"Did you know that Domenico Tramonte—Detective Tramonte's father—was here moments ago?"

"I saw a man disappear into the meadow as I arrived. I was going to ask you about him. He felt different from normal dream characters."

"In what way?"

"He felt real."

"Please, Victor. We agreed."

"I'm serious."

Dillan took a moment. "He told me the crocuses were a gift from a little girl hoping to see me. Does that make any sense to you?"

"He could have been onto something," Victor conceded. He studied the footprints the elder Tramonte had left in the snow. "I've long felt that a child was looking for me through people's dreams. It's the strangest feeling. Maybe it ties in somehow."

Dillan stared at the flower arrangement on the snow. "You know I messed up with Vincente."

"He needed to return to the Dolomites," Victor replied. "You made that possible."

"But they took him!" Dillan felt a tightness in his chest. His anguish was threatening to snap him out of the dream. He lowered his voice. "Do you know if he's still alive?"

"Thanks to you, he is."

Dillan looked over at his friend. "I don't understand."

"You acted on the warning I gave you. That saved Vincente's life. Yes, they took him anyway, but not before the two of you had a chance to be together in the mountains. I don't know why, but that needed to happen. What I do know is that you helped him come to terms with what happened out there. And that you'll see him again. As for the vase, nothing of value was found inside."

"How do you know these things?"

"You can learn a lot from being in other people's dreams."

"So Vincente is fine?"

Victor nodded. "For now."

Dillan fired his next question point blank. "How did you get into Michael's dreams?"

"What do you mean?"

"I read an entry in his dream diary. It was just as you had said: the bar, Michael, the man with the cane. Even the drunken fellow with the black cowboy hat. You really were there."

"Of course I was. I'm the one who told you about it when we met at the park. It's you who refused to believe me."

"Let's assume I'm ready to believe you now. That you live in people's dreams, including my own. Where do you go when I wake up?"

"Me?" Victor frowned. "I don't go anywhere. It's you and your dream that disappear."

"So the dream vanishes, I wake up, and you…"

"I remain in a world I hope you'll come to believe exists."

"You expect me to believe that?"

"No, not yet. But you asked."

The doctor remained silent.

"This wouldn't be the first time something you doubted turned out to be true," Victor said. "When you woke up from your dream in Florence, your body was positioned exactly as I said it would be. I was also right about the vase, and I was, in fact, in Michael's dreams. What I'm telling you now is also true."

"But it doesn't make sense."

"Only because you've wrapped yourself in the way you view the world around you, in how you think things work."

Dillan gave a strained smile.

"When your patients tell you they sometimes feel an evil presence around them as they wake up or fall asleep, you think about sleep paralysis, abnormalities in REM sleep, or misfiring in the brain. But what if some of those phenomena were real? What if there *were* entities watching over people, hovering inside their bedrooms, waiting to reenter their sleep, their minds?"

"I'll need to think that over once I'm awake."

Victor raked his hand through his hair. "Fair enough. But consider this. I need to get out of people's dreams, including yours."

"To go where?"

"To the same world you return to every time you wake up."

Dillan let Victor's words play in his mind. "If I understand what you're saying, you've been living in other people's dreams for some time now, but because their dreams aren't yours, you can't wake up from them."

"That's about right."

"But Maria could somehow get you to do it?"

Victor gave him a nod. "With your help, yes."

"Tell me again. Who is Maria?"

Victor hesitated. "My wife, I think."

"How can you not be sure?"

"It's when you wake up that memories of dreams start to fade. But when you live your life through the dreams of others, it's your memories of waking life that vanish with time."

Dillan considered the reasoning behind Victor's words. "You've always said I needed to help you find her. How am I supposed to do that?"

"I think she'll come to you, provided you're ready."

"What if she doesn't?"

Victor appeared pained by the question. "Then I'm afraid you'll see me again in your dreams."

"Where else could I see you?"

Victor picked a handful of snow off the ground and patted it into a ball. "You tell me. What other options are there?"

"I don't know," Dillan said. "Maybe I could come into *your* dreams."

Victor smiled. He got up, flung the snowball straight up in the air and caught it as it dropped back down. He turned to Dillan. "What if you saw me in your waking life? Like at work or in the subway. Could you handle that?"

Dillan laughed. It was a genuine laugh, devoid of nervousness. "I doubt it."

"Where do you think Maria will come looking for you?"

"What do you mean?"

"Would it be in waking life? Or in a dream?"

"In real life, I guess."

Without warning, Victor threw the snowball straight at Dillan's torso. It smacked him in the chest and burst on impact.

"What was that for?" Dillan said, brushing the snow off his lap.

"Is waking life all that's real to you? What about that snowball? Didn't that feel real?"

The doctor took some of the remnants of snow in his palm. It was soft and cool, and as he closed his hand over it, he felt it melt.

"At any given moment," Victor said, "the only world that matters is the one being created out of the billions of connections inside your brain. Ultimately, isn't that what you believe reality to be?"

"Yes..." Dillan scooped up a fistful of snow, packed it tightly, and raised his arm above his shoulder in readiness. "Now let's see what your brain makes of this."

Victor stepped back. "You wouldn't..."

Dillan aimed and fired. The snowball hit Victor smack in the hip. The doctor scooped up more snow as Victor took off in a sprint.

The men zigzagged across the snow-covered meadow, laughing. Dillan pursued his friend, who was constantly changing direction to avoid being hit. Dillan aimed and let go. This time the snowball exploded on Victor's shoulder. He stumbled in a feigned display of anguish and let himself fall flat on his back, his arms and legs splayed. "Truce!" he pleaded.

"Truce accepted," replied Dillan. He came closer and lay in the snow beside Victor. There they stayed, still and silent, gazing up at the gray sky.

"I remember having snowball fights with my brother," Dillan said, breaking the silence. "Once, after a snowstorm, my dad helped us build some snow forts. My brother and I spent hours attacking each other with snowballs. When we got too tired to continue, we would lie side by side in the snow and stare up at the clouds, like we're doing now."

"You're lucky," Victor said in a low voice. "I've gotten to a point where I'm no longer sure if the things I remember from my childhood are real or if they're memories from other people's dreams."

"Do you remember your parents?"

"I sort of see their faces, but the memories are vague. Distant. Same for where I grew up. I have images of snowstorms and warm sunny days, laughing while barreling down a hill on a toboggan, riding a red bicycle along a cracked sidewalk, a school with long, empty corridors. But I have no way of knowing if any of those recollections are actually mine."

Dillan remained silent. Then he said, "Tell me again about your last memory of Maria."

Victor slid his hands under his head. "It's summertime. We're making love in a meadow. I remember the flowery scent of her skin. The softness of her lips. The warmth of the sun."

"Do you have any idea how long ago that happened?"

"Three, maybe four years ago. Before I met you."

Dillan felt a knot in the pit of his stomach. "You've been in my dreams for more than a few years, Victor."

"Really?"

"Yes."

"How long?"

Dillan took a slow breath. "More than ten."

Silence.

There was no need for Dillan to look at Victor. He knew that his friend was on the verge of tears. And with that realization came a rush of emotions. "I'm sorry it took me so long to believe you," he whispered. "I want you to have your life back. If I can help make that happen, I will. I promise."

"I'm sorry too," Victor said. "I should have tried to explain things to you earlier."

"It wouldn't have worked. I wouldn't have been ready. I barely am now."

A beam of sunlight pierced the cloud cover.

"There's something important you need to know, James. About you and Vincente. Vital things are about to happen to you both."

Dillan turned onto his side to face Victor. "What things?"

Victor sat up, cross-legged. He was about to speak when his eyes focused behind the doctor and widened in fear.

"What's wrong?" Dillan said, whirling around. The meadow was empty, the distant conifers silent.

"No!" Victor screamed. He pushed Dillan onto his back and threw himself over him, covering the doctor's chest with his body. Something off to the side emerged from under the snow. Something large. Dillan glimpsed a dark creature with massive claws. There was a dull thud. Victor gasped. A giant stinger, like a scorpion's, was sticking out of his back.

Dillan woke up in the back seat of the car. The elder Tramonte was leaning toward him, shaking him by the arm.

"Are you okay?" the detective asked. "You were groaning."

"Yes…" Dillan said, collecting his thoughts. He gazed at the elder Tramonte. "Detective, did your father sleep at all during our drive here?"

"He may have. Why?"

"Can you ask him if he remembers dreaming or anything else from his sleep?"

Detective Tramonte questioned his father. The elder Tramonte appeared puzzled, looked back at Dillan, and shook his head.

* * *

"I'm still not sure this is a good idea," Detective Tramonte said, making sure the map, whistle, first-aid kit, and headlamp were all inside Dillan's knapsack.

"You said yourself this is an easy, well-traveled trail," Dillan replied, trying to quell his own apprehensions. "And I have the cell if there's anything. I'm more worried about you, Detective. Sure you're okay to drive back?"

Tramonte put on a brave face. "I'll be fine."

The elder Tramonte walked over to Dillan and, as he had done the first time they met, gently caressed his cheek. "*In bocca al lupo*," he said.

Dillan looked over at the detective.

"It means good luck," he explained.

"I thought he said something about a wolf's mouth."

"He did. Enter the wolf's mouth. It's an expression, like break a leg. You're supposed to answer *crepi il lupo*. It means may the wolf die. That way it cannot bite you."

Dillan looked at the detective's father. "*Crepi il lupo*," he said with conviction.

The elder Tramonte gave Dillan a smile. He looked serene.

"I need to head back," the detective said.

"Try to get some sleep."

"I can promise you one thing, *Dottore*."

"What's that?"

"When I finally do sleep, I will start paying more attention to my dreams."

The men gave each other a firm hug.

"*In bocca al lupo*," Dillan said.

"*Crepi il lupo*."

CHAPTER 49

The air in the moss-carpeted forest was damp and cool. Dillan climbed the wide switchbacks cutting through tall Norway spruce, larch, and scrub mountain pine, and, after a final rise, reached a partially exposed crest. Below him, encircled by tall coniferous trees, was a field of straw-colored grass. He began his descent.

As Dillan reached the open meadow, a warm breeze swept over the field, sending the taller blades of golden needlegrass into a slow, undulating dance. He scanned the trees before him. Something moved at the edge of the forest. A young girl—no older than nine or ten—in a white dress stepped out of the woods. The drawing rendered by the elder Tramonte had come to life.

She waved. Dillan waved back, hesitantly. She started to walk toward him, her blond curls bouncing off her shoulders and her dress swaying in the wind. Strung over her right shoulder was a small, silvery purse.

Dillan advanced. They met in the middle of the meadow. The girl's skin appeared soft, almost satiny, and naturally pale. She had a small, delicate nose, rounded cheekbones, and a radiant smile. But it was her striking emerald eyes that captured Dillan's attention. They had an unusual depth to them and exerted a mesmerizing, almost hypnotic pull.

"I'm so happy to see you," said the girl. "I wasn't sure you'd come."

"Do we know each other?" Dillan asked.

The girl smiled but didn't answer. She eyed the doctor. A look of concern washed over her face. "What happened to your arm? It must be hurting."

Dillan was dumbfounded. "How do you know it's injured?"

"I can see the crack in your bone. Below your elbow. You must have hurt it in a dream." She extended her hand toward his arm. The doctor, fearful, stepped back.

"Don't be afraid," the little girl said. "I can help you."

"It's impossible for you to see my bones," Dillan said.

The girl looked sad. "You don't know who I am, do you?"

"No, I don't."

"I was hoping you'd remember."

Dillan stood silently, unsure how to respond.

"Let me help you," she said.

He let her touch his arm.

"I can't see all your bones," she said, gliding her palm over his elbow. "Only the ones injured in dreams. You were hurt in other places, too."

"Like where?"

"Your shoulder, ribs, and ankle. They're bruised."

Dillan reined in his apprehension. "You're right. It happened in the same dream."

"It must have," the girl said. "Dreams with those kinds of powers don't happen often."

"I fell from a great height," Dillan explained. "But didn't wake up before hitting the ground."

The girl closed her eyes.

"I then fell off the couch where I'd been sleeping, but not hard enough to hurt myself like this."

The girl continued her healing motion. "You could have died," she said matter-of-factly.

"From the fall?"

"From whatever it was you were trying to escape."

"It was a monster."

The girl opened her eyes. They were now luminous green and even more beautiful than before. "They're called *taurines*," she said.

A shiver shot up Dillan's spine. That was what Santilli had called the creature whose giant tooth he'd seen—and felt—in the boulder.

"They're embodiments of evil," continued the girl. "And very powerful. They appear to us in different forms. Human-like monsters are the most common, but they can also be wild animals: pumas, vultures, sharks, even insects. They all have one thing in common, though."

"What's that?"

"Their eyes. You can see the evil in them. Like a swirling fire." The girl stopped her gentle, gliding movements. "Try moving your arm now."

Dillan flexed and extended his elbow, then pressed his ribs. "The pain's gone. What did you do?"

The girl smiled benevolently. "I made it better."

"Thank you. I don't think I know your name."

"My name's Juliette. But my mom calls me her little princess."

Dillan gave her a half-smile.

"What's wrong?" Juliette asked.

"What do you mean?"

"When I told you my name, your eyes became sad."

Caught off guard, Dillan remained silent. Then he said, "You're right. Juliette is a name that carries a special meaning for me. Do you know my name?"

She nodded. "James Dillan."

"Did your mom tell you that?"

"Yes."

"Am I supposed to know her?"

The girl appeared surprised by the question. "I'm not sure," she said. "I do have something she asked me to give you, though." She reached into her purse and drew out a pale, fibrous-looking flower with five petals, each covered in dense, silvery felt. The flower appeared to glow in her hand. "Take it," she said. "It'll help you."

"It looks like a type of edelweiss," remarked Dillan.

"Close. It's a moon flower."

Dillan smiled and thought better of his question about the flower's origin. "What am I supposed to do with it?"

"Keep it with you," she instructed. "Especially when you sleep. If you get hurt again, it'll help you get better, a bit like I did now."

Dillan took the flower and examined it closely. The glowing appeared to have been an illusion. He gently tucked it in the front pocket of his pants then looked back at the girl.

"A man called Domenico Tramonte told me I needed to come here. Do you know who I'm talking about?"

"I'm sorry," she said, "I don't think I know anyone by that name."

"He's an older man. Said he met you in a snowfield."

"Oh! Of course! He was so sweet. He did say you'd come."

Dillan tried to make sense of what the little girl was telling him. "But the snowfield. It doesn't exist."

"It does. In his dreams. And also in yours."

"But this—us—this meadow. This *isn't* a dream."

The girl giggled. "Of course not. You say the funniest things."

"I dreamt about Domenico Tramonte on my way here. He was looking for you and said that if I saw you, I should tell you he has what you had asked him to find. He called it the bearer of a great gift."

The girl's eyes lit up. "He has it? I knew he could do it. I knew it!"

Dillan froze. The image of him and Vincente staring down at the Cellini flashed through his mind. The bearer of the gift wasn't a person. It was the cast iron base that had cradled the vase over the centuries. It was more important than the gift itself. The secret that people had been searching for had never been in the vase, but rather in the metal base designed to hold it. It was exactly the kind of thing a man of Cellini's ilk would do. *L'uomo terribile.* A revenge worthy of his reputation. Dillan thought back to the handles on the vase: two drawn-out faces, each with pleading eyes cast upward and a mouth frozen in a wide-open scream. It made sense. Not only that, but if he was right, the secret was safe. He had watched the elder Tramonte carry the sculpted base out of the cave, into the rain, and all the way down to his son's car.

"Are you okay?" asked the girl.

"I was told of a secret hidden inside a very old vase. Now I think it was inside the metal base in which the vase had been placed. The same base I saw Domenico Tramonte carry out of the Dolomites. Am I right?"

The girl nodded.

"Do you know what the secret is?"

"Of course. Inside it are six stones. They were brought back from an ancient world. Five of them have the power to infect people's dreams, to poison their minds."

"How?"

"It's not something that can easily be explained in words," Juliette said.

"What about the other stone? The sixth one?"

"That one's different," she said. "In the right hands, it can be used to protect people's dreams."

"From the evil forces you mentioned?"

"They're getting stronger," she said in a low voice, "but we can't let them take over our dreams. We just can't."

"I'm trying to understand what's happening—what you're telling me—but I don't know why I'm here."

"My mom said that if you came, you'd be able to help us. That's why I'm so happy to see you."

"Help you with what exactly?"

"With keeping our dreams free." Juliette looked down at her hands. "Here, let me show you something." She held out her right palm before him. "There's nothing in my hand," she said, showing him both the front and the back. "But if I close it like this," she added, making a fist, "and concentrate, I can make something special happen." She kept her fist clenched for a moment then slowly opened it. Nestled inside her palm was another moon flower. This one was considerably larger than the one she had given Dillan, with dozens of silvery petals shooting out from its bristly core.

The doctor stared at the unusual, almost prehistoric-looking flower, then looked at the girl. "How did you do that?"

"You really don't remember, do you?" she asked.

"Remember what?"

"We practiced this in your dreams."

Dillan furrowed his brow.

"You may think you've forgotten," Juliette said, "but the lessons are there inside you. I'm sure of it." She gave Dillan a soft smile. "You were getting good, too. You have a gift you don't yet know about. My mom said so herself. That's why we need you to help us."

"To keep our dreams free?" he asked tentatively.

"My mom's never lied to me." The little girl put the flower in her purse then placed her fingers around Dillan's right hand and lifted his palm toward his chest. "You try it," she said. "Make a fist and work with the moon flower I gave you. It's right there in your pocket. Not far from your hand."

The doctor curled his fingers into a fist.

"You might want to close your eyes," Juliette said. "It's easier that way. At least it was in your dreams."

Dillan did as the girl suggested.

"Don't think," she whispered. "*Feel* the flower ... will it into your hand..."

A dozen seconds passed. Then a dozen more. "Well?" the girl asked. "Is it there?"

Dillan opened his eyes and unfolded his fingers. His palm held nothing but air.

"Don't worry," Juliette hastened to say. "I didn't get it for a while either. It'll come to you, though. I know it will. And so does my mom."

Dillan stared down at his empty hand. To his surprise, he hadn't felt the least bit foolish trying to do something he knew to be impossible. Or was it? He let his hand drop to his side. "Where's your mom now?"

"She left on a trip."

"Do you know where she went?"

"She went to find Dad." The girl's face turned doleful. "It's not the first time. She always comes back alone, though." She paused for a moment. "I've never met him ... I don't even think he knows about me."

"I'm sorry to hear that. How am I supposed to help?"

"You're easy to underestimate. And you don't feel strong. Don't take this the wrong way, Mr. Dillan," she said, "but you actually come off as being rather feeble. The powers menacing us won't give you a second look. But if you surprise them, you can make them blind with hatred. And that might be enough."

Dillan was more confused than ever. "I'm not sure I understand what you're telling me."

The girl shrugged, then smiled. "Don't worry about the details," she said. "They're not that important. The moon will never be too far, and my mom said that when the time came, you'd know what to do."

Dillan's mind was swirling with questions. He focused on a simple one. "What's your mom's name?"

Juliette looked at Dillan for several seconds. Her emerald eyes appeared to shimmer. "Maria," she said.

Dillan lay down slowly on the grass.

"Are you okay, Mr. Dillan?"

His mouth went dry. "Yes..."

A buzzing amplified his dizziness. The ringing wouldn't stop.

"I think you should answer," the girl said.

Dillan lay on his back, lifted the right side of his buttocks, and took his cellphone out of his back pocket. He squinted at the number. It was Ms. Petridis, his former landlord and still downstairs neighbor.

"Hello?" he said, sounding like a man gripped by a hangover.

"Dr. Dillan? Is that you?"

"Yes." He closed his eyes.

"I'm sorry to call you like this, but there's someone here with me. A woman. She says she needs to speak to you. I wouldn't have called if I didn't think she—"

"What do her eyes look like?"

"Her eyes? They're beautiful. A sort of translucent green. Do you know who she is?"

"I might. You did well to call, Ms. Petridis. I'd like to speak with her."

"One second."

"Doctor Dillan?"

"Yes."

"Thank goodness you're there. Are you with my daughter?"

"Yes."

"Did she give you the flower?"

"She did."

"Good. Do keep it with you at all times."

"Including when I sleep. Your daughter told me."

"Especially when you sleep. Do you know why I'm calling?"

Dillan hesitated. "I have an idea, but I'm not sure I can put it into words."

"I need to get into your apartment, preferably alone." There was a short pause. "Do you think your neighbor could help?"

"Yes, that won't be a problem. Your daughter mentioned your name, but for a reason I can't explain, I'd like to hear it from you."

"My name is Maria. I think you first heard about me before Juliette was born."

His heart raced. "You're right... Can I ask you something, Maria?"

"Of course. What is it?"

"Do you know Vincente? Santilli's son?"

"He's a special boy. An old soul."

"Do you know what's become of him?"

"It appears he's back in good hands."

"Would you happen to know where he is?"

"No. But I know where he'll be."

"Where?"

"Wherever the butterflies take him," answered Maria.

Dillan opened his eyes. The sky was cloudless and remarkably limpid.

"Look for him in your dreams," she added. "Chances are he'll be waiting for you there."

"What do I do now?"

"The enemy is already among us," Maria said. "What you need to do now is no different from what we all must do. And that is to be ready."

"Is there really a battle being fought in people's sleep? Through their dreams?"

"All humans dream. It's universal. A given. Our dreams embody our deepest and often truest hopes and fears. Dreams can compel us to fly, create, discover, and love. They carry ancestral memories interlaced with personal histories. Once dreamt, a dream can never be erased, only forgotten. Imprison, or worse, envenom people's dreams, and the human spirit falters."

"I have so many questions, most of them without answers. How do I get ready?"

"Like dreams, the world around us is stranger than most people think, its complexity underestimated, and its nature misunderstood. Sometimes there are no answers, Doctor. Only doors, and the experiences they offer—if we dare to enter, that is."

Dillan looked at the little girl. "Would you like to speak to your daughter?"

The girl shook her head in a categorical no.

"Juliette hates phones," Maria said. "Do tell her I love her, though. And that she can expect to see me soon."

"Would you like me to watch over her until you get back?"

"That's kind of you to offer, but there's no need to worry. She's a ten-year-old moon princess. Meadows and dreams are like homes to her."

CHAPTER 50

V ictor was feeling unwell. His head was spinning, his stomach in knots, and his footing uncertain. A sharp pain sliced through his upper back and into his shoulder blades. He lurched toward the big carmine leather chair and lowered himself into it, clutching the rounded armrests. He closed his eyes, but the dizziness persisted. Acid bile rose in the back of his throat. He put his head between his knees and breathed deeply. The spinning seemed to lessen.

He glanced over at the Tiffany lamp and stood, bracing himself. His legs were rubbery and his back ached. He took a few tentative steps toward the lamp, pondering its unearthly holdings, and switched it on. A melody of light materialized. He stared at the colors and patterns on the lamp, his mind lulled by their quieting, almost hypnotic effect. He ran his fingertips over the stained glass, caressing the silvery veins that held the reds, blues, and yellows in place. It all appeared so real. It *was* real.

He lumbered over to the bay window, the wooden planks creaking beneath his weight. There he looked out into the twilight, down at the handful of people strolling about the park. He made his way over to the oak desk, opened a drawer, and stared at the blank sheets of paper inside, then closed it. The spinning returned with a vengeance. He needed to lie down.

Victor stumbled into Dillan's bedroom and fell face down on the bed. There he lay, bilious and dazed. He slowly turned over, hoping for some reprieve. The apartment door squeaked open. Someone was approaching the bedroom. His heart raced as the door to the bedroom opened wide. Before him, in the shadows, stood a vision of beauty. A beauty he instantly recognized.

"Victor," breathed the woman.

Speechless, Victor tried to nod, but his body wouldn't respond. The woman came to sit beside him on the bed and caressed his face, her fingers lingering over his forehead, cheeks, and lips. Tears welled in his eyes.

"You're here," he managed to say.

"I never stopped believing, Victor. I knew this day would come."

His lips quivered as he smiled. "I didn't know for sure, Maria. I only hoped."

"Do you remember the last time we were together?" she asked.

A wrinkle appeared in the corners of his eyes. "We were in a meadow. We made love."

"We did. And that love came to life."

Victor narrowed his eyes.

"We have a daughter, Victor."

Silence.

"How's that possible?"

"When I found my way out of people's dreams and made it back to this world, I was pregnant with our child…. She's healthy, Victor. And beautiful."

"So she was…"

"Conceived in the dream."

Victor's eyes gleamed. "What's her name?"

"Juliette."

"Juliette," he repeated.

"Don't you remember?"

"What?"

"That was your mother's name."

"I'm sorry… There are so many things I don't remember."

"They'll start coming back, now that you're here."

Victor took Maria's hand in his. "I never forgot your eyes. Even when I couldn't remember your name, or how we met, or your promise that you'd come back."

Maria lifted his hand and pressed it to her cheek. "I only wish this day had come sooner."

"It came. That's all that counts. Where's Juliette?"

"She's waiting for you. In one of her favorite meadows. She's been waiting for a long time to see her father, to hold him in her arms, and to be held in his."

Victor took a long, deep breath. "Does she have your eyes?"

"From the day she was born," Maria whispered.

Victor grimaced as he sat up in bed.

"What's wrong?"

"My back. I was hit with a barb in Dillan's dream. There was a *taurine* lurking under the snow cover. I tried to protect him, but it struck me before he woke up."

Maria helped Victor lean forward and lifted the back of his shirt. "It missed your spine," she said, examining the wound between his middle vertebrae and right shoulder blade. "We'll need to take care of this soon."

Victor slowly pulled down his shirt. "Did you see Dillan on your way here?"

"No, but I did speak to him."

"Is he okay?"

"He was."

"Why the past tense?"

"Because he's about to open the gate and stare into the other side."

Victor bit at the edge of his lower lip. "He isn't ready."

"No one is ever ready for this kind of journey."

"He'll be too frightened to enter, and even if he does, he may never find his way back. And without the stones…"

"It's out of our hands now," she said. "The hidden world of dreams is coming for him as we speak." Maria paused, her eyes fixed on Victor's. "As for the stones, they may come to him still."

"How?"

"I think Juliette should be the one to explain this to you. But if they do find their way to him, it'll be because of her doing."

"I don't understand."

Maria smiled. "You will. She is your daughter, after all."

Victor drew Maria into his arms and held her tightly, taking in her warmth and her floral scent. They listened to each other's unspoken words, their bodies sealed in an impenetrable embrace.

* * *

Entering the living room, Victor steadied himself and walked over to the leather chair, stopping to caress the back and armrests. The leather felt cool and supple.

Maria looked on as he approached the glowing Tiffany lamp. "It's stunning," she whispered. "To think that it holds remnants of the shield…"

Victor stared down at the colors and patterns. "It's even more beautiful than the one in Dillan's dreams." He closed his eyes and slid his fingers over the lamp's surface. He felt the warmth, the ridges of the strips of lead running down the sides, the texture of the stained glass. He opened his eyes and, with trembling fingers, turned off the light.

CHAPTER 51

As soon as the taxicab drove away, Liz closed her eyes and felt the cool Montreal rain on her face. She was relieved to be home. As she turned to head to her apartment, she noticed a dead seagull on the ground by the sidewalk. The bird, only a couple of yards from her feet, was on its side, its visible eye—a small black pupil encircled by an orange-tinted iris—wide open. Liz stared at the creature as the rain washed away the trickle of blood from its beak. She rushed up the steps leading to her building.

It was only when she reached the entrance that she noticed a couple standing on the opposite side of the street looking at her from under a black umbrella. Liz studied them for a moment. The woman, maybe in her early thirties, was holding a taller and slightly older-looking man by the arm. Neither of them appeared menacing. On the contrary, there was something appeasing about the way they stood there, silent, in the rain. The man's physique reminded Liz of Dillan. In fact, he appeared to be wearing the same red and white McGill varsity jacket she'd seen the doctor wear in the past.

Liz let herself in. She headed for the elevator then decided to take the stairs and climbed up to the third—and highest—floor. All was quiet. She opened the stairwell door and peeked into the hallway. Nobody. She made a beeline for her apartment, opened the door, and locked it behind her.

Leaving the lights off, she walked into her bedroom and over to one side of the window. She pulled the curtain back from the wall slightly, scanning the street below. Walking away in the rain was the couple with the umbrella. Liz kept her eyes on them until they disappeared into the night.

CHAPTER 52

The elevator began to rise. Dillan steadied himself against a wall to his side as the glass carriage accelerated. This time, however, there were no cables or soaring edifice in sight: the entire contraption was hurtling upward like a missile into the sky. He glanced downward. There were no pedestrians, cars, or buildings receding below. Only a sea, black, deep, and boundless. Dillan scanned the walls, hoping to see a control panel, but there was nothing except a round, silver handle on the transparent door. His chest began to pound. He was trapped. The glass boomed and shook as the elevator continued its launch. Dillan fought his vertigo and glimpsed the dark sea miles below. The urge to look away was overwhelming, but he persisted, battling his innermost fears—his demons. The elevator began to decelerate, and his legs no longer threatened to buckle. His vertigo subsided, then vanished. Vincente's story of how he had learned to change falling dreams into flying dreams came to mind, bringing a faint smile to Dillan's lips. A comforting warmth spread over his right thigh.

Dillan reached into the front pocket of his pants. Inside it was the moon flower. He gently drew it out and held it in his palm. The elevator came to a stop. Along the far horizon, something gray and massive was approaching fast. It was a thick fog. Like a giant tsunami, it rolled over the glass walls, enveloping the hovering carriage in a dense, swirling haze. The flower began to glow. Dillan stared as the fog took on shades of lilac and darkening purple.

Within the fine, violaceous mist, tiny particles began to light up, an infinity of stars. Soon, the dazzling mass was whirling around him.

Then came a voice, faint and distant. Dillan recognized it at once. It was Vincente's. Maybe the boy's voice had been carried by the great fog, or maybe it had been brought to life by his own imagination. Either way, there was no mistaking the words whispered into his ear. *Believe in your powers...*

Dillan was leaning against the glass wall, contemplating the boy's message, when two flaming eyes flashed by the elevator, jarring him backward with fright. Panicked, he watched the two unblinking embers drop beneath his feet and vanish into the murk. The eyes were exactly like those of the creature he'd encountered in his last elevator dream. His heart still hammering, he picked up the moon flower, which had fallen out of his hand. It was still glowing.

Then, from the depths came a blood-curdling scream. All around him, the particles grew brighter and began spiraling with such speed that light trails appeared in their wake. From the dazzling and dizzying display emerged a low, pulsing hum with vibrations that rumbled through the elevator walls, ceiling, and floor. Another scream. This one more distinct—and horrifying. It was Vincente. Dillan needed to do something, quickly.

Clasping the flower in his left hand, he wrapped his right around the silver handle, turned it clockwise, and pushed the glass door open. The door immediately fell into the void, a vortex of purple swirls tracing its turbulent decent. The humming grew louder as a cold, humid breeze filled the air. Dillan stood there, stock-still, gazing at the countless points of light. Terrified, he brought the flower to his chest, peered into the unknown, and, eyes wide open, stepped into the abyss.

CHAPTER 53

The air was cold and dense. Dillan gasped as he spiraled out of control. He wasn't so much falling as being pulled downward at increasingly faster speeds. The twirling lights had disappeared. The humming was deafening. He forced his eyes shut and pressed his clenched hand to his chest. He was on the verge of passing out. Through the noise came a piercing and desperate cry for help. It was Vincente. Rashly, Dillan drew his knees to his chest and clutched them with his arms, making himself into a ball and quickening his precipitous descent.

The doctor opened his eyes. About two dozen feet below, he saw Vincente. They were both falling in a bottomless tunnel gripped by a coldness that stiffened his muscles and chilled his bones. He squeezed the flower with all his might, desperate to bring his spinning to a halt. He thought it, he willed it. His body began to steady. He spotted Vincente's arms stretched above his head, reaching up to him. The boy was calling out to him, pleading for help. Dillan was closing in; he could make out the boy's fingers, even his nails. He realized Vincente wasn't falling—he was being pulled from below. That's when he spied them—two fiery eyes, blazing with malice, looking up from under the boy's legs. Dillan clenched his teeth, thrusting his right hand down as far as he could. Their fingers touched, once, twice, then clasped. "Hold on!" he shouted. The human-sized beast was jolting Vincente by the feet, trying to shake Dillan loose.

"Don't let go!" cried Vincente.

Dillan gripped the boy's hand and pulled it hard while swinging his legs down toward the creature's outstretched arms and head. Time slowed as he kicked at the beast's arms, shoulders, and face. He became aware of the rhythmic pounding of his heart, the boy's trembling fingers, the creature's rancid smell. The beast let out an ear-splitting shriek as it lost its grip and faded into the blackness. The doctor clutched the boy's hands, and as if fighting a powerful current, he pulled Vincente up against his chest and wrapped his arms tightly around him.

Time resumed its natural course, and with it the frantic tumbling.

CHAPTER 54

D illan landed in the snow with a thump. He lay motionless, the side of his face resting on a cracked layer of frost and ice. He groaned as he came to. Lifting his head, he eyed the sea of white sloping upward before him. He had no idea where he was or how he had gotten there. His muscles were sore, his bones aching, his extremities cold. A rush of images: the booming glass walls and the dark sea; the fog, lights, and tunnel; Vincente's desperate cries and the horrid creature. Waves of panic rose to his throat.

He forced himself onto his knees, scanning the area in the hope of seeing Vincente. It was only then that he noticed the unearthly sky; swathes of pale mauves and deep violets were undulating overhead, slithering across the firmament. As he gazed at the eerie display, Dillan realized he was still dreaming, but this did little to ease his apprehension. There was something unnerving about the landscape, about the silence permeating the dream.

He slowly got to his feet and tried to jolt himself awake. When that failed, he closed his eyes and blinked rapidly, hoping to alter the views before him. The dream remained immutable, the mountains unchanged, his body strangely corporeal. He yelled Vincente's name, waited, and called out to him again, louder this time. Nothing. Nothing but a windless chill.

He looked behind him, down at the vast snow dunes extending into valleys, then up at the snow-covered grade leading to the higher mountainous grounds. No sign of life.

Dillan examined the higher reaches of the nearby peaks. Among the snow-capped summits were a smattering of dark entities, exposed rock faces and massive boulders in all likelihood. Then something else, closer to him, moving. Dillan strained his eyes, trying to make out the black silhouette shimmering against the niveous backdrop. It looked to be a man.

The doctor observed the figure with trepidation as it plodded down the slope through knee-deep snow. As the man got closer, Dillan could make out a beige jacket and dark pants. Folded over the man's arm was a shadowy object resembling a small blanket. Then Dillan recognized him. It was the detective's father.

Domenico Tramonte continued to trudge down the wintry slope, one measured step at a time, until he was but a dozen feet away. There he stopped and spoke to Dillan in a now familiar language: that of the dream. "This is for you," he said, holding up the blanket-like object. It appeared to be an old leather vest of a color that shifted in the light, from glimmering silvers to deeper amber-like tones.

Dillan started walking toward him. "Where are we?"

The elder Tramonte looked around calmly. "I think we're exactly where we are meant to be." He took another step toward the doctor. "It's the strangest thing ... out here, I can remember everything. Even my dreams." He paused, as if to appreciate the moment. "I came to give you this." He held the vest up for the doctor to see. Stitched into the left panel, at chest height, was a small rectangular pocket.

"What is it?"

"It's a garment like no other. It holds what the girl from the snowfield asked me to find and bring you."

Dillan's eyes were drawn to the wide bronze zipper running across the top of the pocket, then to the small rounded protrusions beneath it.

"I'm not sure I understand," Dillan said. "What did she ask you to find?"

Tramonte unzipped the pocket, reached inside with his index, and drew out something resembling a large marble, which he let roll into his palm. Dillan moved closer, his eyes fixed on the peculiar object. In Tramonte's hand lay a greenish-black stone. "There are six of them in all. You can hold this one if you like."

Dillan picked up the shimmery stone with his right thumb and index finger and held it up. Under the mauve sky, an uncountable number of golden flecks appeared on the stone's surface, along with faint striations bearing shades of silver and violet. The stone became cold and sent an electric tingling through his hand and into his arm. Dillan became disoriented. Ghastly scenes tore through his mind: a man thrashing under pounding waves, gasping for air; a gargantuan spider with fang-like jaws; a nursing mother pressing her infant's mouth against her breast until she realizes, horrified, that its lips are blue, its body lifeless; a young boy racing through a forest, looking over his shoulder and glimpsing the flesh-eating monster about to catch him; a field of gray, leafless trees, each bearing the limp body of a man, woman, or child, all hanging by the neck. Dillan fell to his knees, the stone dropping from his hand.

Domenico Tramonte stood by, motionless, staring at the doctor. "What did you see?"

Dillan was queasy. "Horrors," he muttered.

"That's a good thing. It means the girl was right."

The elder Tramonte reached down into the snow and retrieved the stone, its surface coated with frost. He opened the pocket, put the stone back in its rightful place, and closed the zipper. "What you saw were nightmares," he said. "Not yours, but those of others."

"I felt things..." Dillan said, getting back to his feet. He glanced at the vest pocket. "These stones, what are they?"

"I'm not sure. But the little girl said it was imperative I get them to you. They were in the metal base we carried out of the cave."

Dillan looked stricken. "That was real. This ... this is a dream."

The elder Tramonte smiled. "You're right. But this is no ordinary dream. That's why I wasn't sure I could do it."

"Do what exactly?"

"Bring them into this world, where she told me I'd find you." The old man's eyes twinkled. "She said she believed in me, that she knew I could do it. She was right. She believes in you as well."

Dillan stood there, speechless, struggling to grasp what was going on.

"Each stone is different," continued the elder Tramonte. "And one of them is quite a bit larger than the others—and more powerful. It's in here," he said, pointing to the pocket's rightmost bulge, "in its own slot. It can't be reached like the others. It was sewn right into the fabric."

"How do you get to it then?" Dillan asked.

"I wasn't told," Tramonte replied. He ran his fingers over the pocket. "The other stones are also protected. The zipper will only work in the right hands."

Dillan furrowed his brows. "Like yours?"

"Like *ours.*" Tramonte held the vest open at the shoulders. "You'll have to wear it. And keep it fastened at all times."

Dillan slipped his arms into the vest and stared at its shifting colors. He adjusted the garment over his chest, engaged the bottom of the zipper, and pulled it up. The vest was a perfect fit. There were three wide leather straps running horizontally from the right side that needed to be fastened into their respective silver buckles on the left. Dillan threaded the straps through the buckles and tightened them till they felt snug. Pressing lightly against his chest were the stones.

"It looks good on you," the elder Tramonte said. "The little girl had hoped to give it to her father one day, but finally understood that the vest and stones were meant for you."

"Her father? You mean Victor?"

"She didn't mention his name."

"What am I supposed to do with them?"

To this question, the elder Tramonte gave no answer. Instead, he scrutinized the nearby summits. A wary look washed over his face.

With an anxious knot growing in his stomach, the doctor fired another question. "Do you know where Vincente is? I was with him in another dream. Right before this one."

Tramonte turned to Dillan and released a heavy sigh. "You'll need to swim," he replied cryptically. "So that you don't sink as you get carried down into the valley."

"What are you talking about?"

"Try to swim uphill, and kick your feet as hard as you can. The important thing is to keep your arms and legs moving at all times."

The frozen ground beneath Dillan's feet rumbled.

"*In bocca al lupo, Dottore*. The Dreamkeepers will need you."

And with these words, Domenico Tramonte vanished as great sheets of ice and towering mounds of snow broke away from the upper reaches of the mountain and came thundering down toward him. The white wall hit him like a barreling train.

No longer aware of which way was up or down, Dillan flailed, scrambling to grab hold of anything, rolling backward and sideways inside the crushing onslaught. He clawed, kicked, and punched. For the briefest of seconds, there appeared above him a faint patch of mauve. Then darkness as layer upon layer of snow crashed over his body, entombing him. He tried to stay afloat, fighting his way toward the top of the current dragging him over unseen land.

The asphyxiating mass decelerated as thick layers of snow settled upon him. Dillan struggled to breathe in the blackness. He shoved his elbows out to his sides and twisted his fists in the snow, frantically trying to carve a pocket of air. He wriggled and wormed his right hand up to his mouth, cupping his fingers over his lips, but it was only a matter of seconds before one inhalation would become his last. He had to get out. But which way was up? He forced his saliva into a thick glob and spat it out. The liquid dribbled down the side of his face toward his ear. He punched his right fist in the opposite direction—against the pull of gravity—creating a small hole, which he enlarged by pummeling his knuckles into its sides. He tried to free his other fist, to no avail. He pulled himself up with his right hand, then twisted and jerked his right knee upward and kicked open a crevice higher into the snow. With his foot secured in the makeshift foothold, he pushed down hard with his leg; the maneuver brought him closer to the top. He tried it again; another inch gained. Shoving, pressing, and yanking his limbs, Dillan fought to haul himself up out of the shifting tomb. His right arm broke free. Another frenzied round of squirming and kicking and he'd dislodged enough snow to move his shoulders and force his left arm upward. He grimaced and groaned as he planted his right foot higher into the snow while his quavering arms worked at digging him out. His lungs were about to explode when his head popped out of the snow. He gasped, inhaling mouthfuls of air. He then jabbed and kicked until, wheezing and spent, he was out.

Dillan rolled onto his back. His heart was pounding, his lungs burning. He waited for the maelstrom to subside, then opened his eyes. Above him, bands of airy mauve snaked across the sky.

He marveled at the fact that although his body was aching, nothing appeared to be broken. As he studied his surroundings, Dillan caught himself hoping, against all odds, that the elder Tramonte would somehow reappear on the vast, downward-sloping field of snow. While the vest Tramonte had given him was still fastened, his shirt was frayed, his watch gone, and his left shoe and sock missing.

"Doctor Dillan! Doctor Dillan!"

He staggered upright. It couldn't be. At the edge of avalanche, maybe thirty yards below him, was Vincente, picking his way through the snowfield and waving his arms above his head like a castaway at a rescue plane.

"Doctor!"

Dillan limped down toward the boy with such excitement that he tumbled into the snow.

"You made it!" Vincente cried, moving faster up the uneven terrain "I knew it! I knew you'd make it!"

When they reunited, the boy hugged him with such strength that Dillan's ribs hurt. He held the boy's head and quivering shoulders gently to his chest. "I'll never let you out of my sight again," Dillan whispered, grateful beyond words for this second chance.

"Inside the tunnel … you saved me," Vincente said. He looked up at the doctor, a tender smile on his face. "I knew you'd come."

Dillan ran his fingers through the boy's hair, then down his cheek. "I had to," he said. "I promised. Remember?"

The boy nodded and glanced at the doctor's vest.

"The detective's father gave it to me," Dillan explained, answering the unasked question. "Before the avalanche struck."

"Where is he now?"

"I don't know… He seemed to disappear. I mean literally disappear, before the snow gave away."

"I saw the avalanche come down the mountain. I was afraid it might reach me. How did you make it out?"

"The detective's father told me I was supposed to swim and keep my arms and legs moving at all times. That's what I did."

The boy smiled. "See, I was right all along."

"About what?"

"You're more of a mountain guy than you think."

They laughed—a wonderful, genuine laugh.

"Do you know what this place is?" Dillan asked hesitantly.

"It's a kind of dream, only you and I aren't dreaming it. It's an actual world. A real one."

"Like the kind you were trying to tell me about?"

The boy nodded.

"But our—I was going to say real bodies—our *other* bodies are asleep right now, aren't they?"

"I don't know… I'm not sure we have other bodies. Not anymore. I think we were dreaming, and that those dreams led us here. But now…"

"What do you mean by not anymore?"

"There's something Mama used to tell me. I think it was from a book, but I never quite understood what it meant. She said there are things in the universe that are known, and things that are unknown, and that in between the two, there are doors. She said that one day it would make sense to me. The tunnel we went through. I think that was *our* door."

Dillan felt his muscles tighten. "Assuming you're right, how do we get back?"

"I'm not sure," the boy answered, avoiding the doctor's gaze. "Some people never return, you know. They get stuck here… Here, or in other people's dreams."

Dillan tried to calm his mind. "I think I understand what you're saying. We have each other, though."

Vincente took the doctor's hand and squeezed it hard.

"There's something you need to know," Dillan said. "I'm quite sure the secret from the vase is now in this vest. Right here." He ran his fingers over the zippered pocket.

The boy's eyes lit up. "You have the stones?"

Dillan nodded. "Do you know what they are?"

"I know they're important. There's so much we need to talk about."

"You're right, there are many things we need to talk about. So many in fact, I'm not sure where to begin." By now Dillan had abandoned any recourse to science, logic, or rationality, and for the first time in his life he felt ready to make peace with the unknown, with questions to which there were simply no answers.

Vincente surveyed the sky and the horizon. "I think we need to move."

"I agree. Where to?"

"I hate to be the one to tell you," the boy said, "but you're missing a shoe."

Dillan grinned. "I know, but come to think of it, I'd rather have one good shoe than two smelly wet ones." The boy giggled. "The strange thing is," Dillan continued, "I was cold and sore before. But I feel a lot better now. Even my foot."

"So you're okay to walk?"

"Of course. I wouldn't be a mountain guy otherwise, right?" Dillan studied the landscape. "So, which way do you think we should head?"

"I think we need to go into these mountains," the boy said, pointing his chin at the peaks and desolate crags rising before them.

"Why not down into the valley?"

"You see that big peak sticking out behind the others?"

Dillan gazed at the massive summit, marveling at how its upper reaches towered over the nearer sections of the mountain chain. "It's hard to miss."

"It looks like the mountain my mom told me about. The one from her dreams."

"You mean the one with hurricane-like winds?"

The boy nodded.

Dillan remembered Victor's drawing of Maria, with the snow-capped mountain on her left. "If that mountain is where you think we need to go, then that's where we'll go." The doctor tried to sound confident and determined, but he was wary of this place—this dream or whatever kind of world it was.

Vincente appeared to be studying the perilous terrain over which they would travel. "It won't be easy," he said. "It's not just the avalanches, it's also the crevasses. There are probably hundreds of them up here. Most will be hidden under snow, and many are wider and deeper than anything you can imagine." He paused. "Inside some of them…"

Dillan waited. "It's okay, you can tell me."

"That creature we saw in the tunnel. I think there are more of them out there."

A faint hum rose from the mountains. It appeared to be coming from above, or maybe behind one of the peaks. Dillan and the boy scanned the high horizon.

"There's something up there," Vincente said, pointing to a black, circular mark hovering over one of the summits. The hum quickly morphed into a loud, dissonant drone. "It looks like it's moving."

Dillan watched as the object swelled into an elongated disc. At its center was a gyrating mass of black specks.

Vincente gripped the doctor's arm. "It's coming toward us."

Dillan shuddered. The thundering mass had taken the shape of a twister, a spiraling fury that would soon be upon them. He realized what he was looking at. *God, no...*

"Get down! Get down!" he yelled. "Now!" The boy dropped to his knees. "Face down on the ground!" Dillan ordered.

Frantic, he shoved piles of snow onto Vincente's body, patting them down around his limbs. He noticed the boy's exposed ankles and rapidly tucked the bottom of his pants into his socks. Around them was a raging cacophony.

Dillan looked up. It was too late. "They're bees!" he yelled, covering the boy's body with his own.

The swarm hit them like a typhoon. The air churned. Waves of red-eyed hornets encased their bodies, ripping at their skin. They were everywhere: in their hair, in their ears, up their nostrils, and down their necks. Even their eyelids were under attack. The boy twisted and screamed, his movements futile, his cries drowned by the deafening noise.

Out of the chaos emerged a shadowy raptor with formidable outstretched wings. Dillan gasped as the beast landed on his back with full force. It clawed at his head, shoulders, and arms. Desperate to protect Vincente, Dillan kicked and thrashed, but his frantic attempts to dislodge the beast proved useless. Dillan convulsed as the creature pierced the backs of his legs with its talons, curling its claws into his flesh. With a few flaps of its massive wings, it hauled him away from the boy before dropping him face-first to the ground. The hornets attacked Vincente with a vengeance.

Hemorrhaging, ravaged by pain, Dillan pushed himself up onto his hands. The creature landed by his head. The raptor shrieked and moved its striking hooked beak toward his skull. A revolting stench, like that of rotting carcasses, poisoned the air. Dillan looked up. The creature's upper mandible was lined with snake-like fangs. He drew a breath as he caught sight of the fire churning in the creature's eyes. Inside the swirling flames he saw Santilli's mutilated hand, a skeletal head with glowing eyes, a mass of hornets ripping the flesh off Vincente's face.

Then came the scorching realization: the creature before him and the sickening, skeletal man in the cave were one and the same. Like a window exploding on impact, Dillan's body shattered. The beast had planted its jagged fangs into the side of his head, cracking open his skull. The shock ruptured his senses and untethered his mind. He'd become immaterial, a spectral presence drifting into a black, distant void. Looking down from a great height, he could see himself battling for his life. Flailing on the ground next to him was Vincente, raw and bloodied, his muted screams rising into the air.

As he faded into blackness, Dillan saw the beast circling the boy. An image of Daniel thrashing under a slab of ice flashed before him. His limbs jerked. The scene had jolted Dillan back into his body. He thrust his right fist into the air with all his might. The raptor turned toward Dillan and screeched. Its eyes widened and its monstrous beak opened as it headed straight at him. It swooped onto his raised fist and snapped off his forearm with a single, savage bite.

The beast recoiled and stumbled onto the ground. Like a startled mare, it reeled backward, its eyes widening with fear. Dillan's bloodied, severed arm was still pointing skyward. The creature leapt into the air and tried to fly away, but its head sagged and its wings went limp. It fell back to the ground, its body collapsing into a quaking heap. The thunderous noise deadened, and then, something utterly unexpected: it started to rain insects.

Soft, airy bugs were falling everywhere—by the billions. Dillan felt them land on his head, chest, arms, and hands, and even on his exposed foot. His entire body was inexplicably intact, his fist still raised in the air. A soothing, familiar warmth permeated the front pocket of his pants; it was the moon flower.

Covering the ground before him was a quivering sea of black, the bulging red eyes of countless hornets blazing within it. Sitting at his side in the thick morass of crawly legs, broken wings, and squishy abdomens, was Vincente. Dillan wrapped his arm around the boy as the fiery substance in the insects' eyes faded to black. Nearby, the creature wheezed, its talons raking the air before closing onto themselves. Dillan and Vincente looked away as the beast began to decay, its body overrun by mounds of white, squirming little worms. Within seconds the carcass had been reduced to a mass of sludge. The yellowish goo fizzed and bubbled, then vanished. The hornets themselves began to evaporate, dissolving into thin air, until a crisp gust swept over the field, blowing what was left of the swarm toward the valley below.

Vincente looked down at his body, then turned to Dillan. "We have no marks. But I felt them. They were everywhere." The boy's voice was raspy but poised. "Now it's all gone… What did you do?"

Dillan opened his fist. The largest of the six stones was in his palm, awash in a silvery glow.

Vincente looked mesmerized. "It's beautiful…" His eyes lit up. "You do know how to use the stones!"

"I did try something, but I'm not sure I can explain what happened after that, or why."

The glow from the stone waned, then vanished.

"I think it's part of your gift. The one Mama told me about."

Dillan closed his palm around the stone, relieved to feel nothing but its rounded weight. He willed the stone back into his jacket; it immediately vanished from his hand.

"That red thing in their eyes," Vincente said, staring at the doctor. "It was alive. And it wanted us dead."

"I know."

"What if it comes back? What if…"

"Shh…" Dillan placed his hands on the boy's shoulders. "Listen, whatever it was, it failed." He paused for moment. "A wise man once told me something very important, Vincente. Something I think we should keep in mind out here."

"What did he say?"

"He said you have to believe in your powers. Really believe in them." Dillan drew Vincente closer. "That wise man," he whispered, "was right."

Dillan stepped back but let his hands rest on Vincente's shoulders. "Now, you said we needed to head into these mountains. You still think that's what we should do?"

Vincente examined the sky. The swathes of dark mauve and violet had given way to a soft coral pink. "I'm sure of it."

"That makes two of us." Dillan fixed the high horizon, intrigued by the airy, rose-colored clouds slowly dissipating in a narrow portion of the sky. That's when he saw it: suspended over one of the mountain peaks was a massive, amber-colored moon. It was about three-quarters full, substantially bigger than the Earth's moon, and gave off a soft yet wondrous glow. The moon's contours were crisp and the surface shadows created by its giant ridges and craters clear as daylight. Dillan and the boy stood transfixed as the celestial body gradually vanished behind thickening bands of glimmering pinks and oranges. They remained stock-still, their eyes glued to the unearthly sky, immersed in a pensive silence.

"It was beautiful," Vincente said finally. "There were drawings of that moon in Mama's diary. This *is* the *anumia*."

"I'm still not sure I know what that means," Dillan said, "but seeing that moon made me feel a little better about this place." He cast his eye over the distant peaks, then looked back at Vincente. "So tell me, my great oneironaut, how do we figure out the best route across this field?"

At that moment, two butterflies appeared, glittering over their heads. They were golden, with striking sky-blue markings on their wings. As they descended before the two intrepid travelers, they fluttered one around the other, as if locked in a magical dance. Vincente smiled at Dillan, and together, they ventured into the landscape.

That night, the world slept a little better because of it, for there would be more sheltered sleep to be had and new, unfettered dreams to be dreamt.

THE END

AUTHOR'S NOTE

A ll facts on sleep and dreams provided by James Dillan are based on present-day science.

The Dolomites are a mountain range in northeastern Italy formed out of a unique sixty-million-year-old geomorphological history. Many legends associated with the Dolomites can be traced to the Ladin, one of the smallest ethnic minorities in Europe, who continue to inhabit the region's valleys. Ladin folktales recount the vicissitudes endured by wizards and ogres, the challenges faced by kings and princesses, and the battles waged by the forces of good and evil. In August 2009, the Dolomites were declared a UNESCO World Heritage Site.

Benvenuto Cellini, a preeminent artist of the High Renaissance, was born in Florence in 1500. A confidant of kings and popes, Cellini spent much of his career working for the papacy and aristocracy. His patrons included Pope Clement VII, Pope Paul III, Francis I of France, and Cosimo de Medici of Florence. In addition to being one of the greatest goldsmiths of all time—if not the greatest—Cellini was a man of questionable morals, a willing brawler, and a self-confessed murderer. He died in Florence in 1571.

A LETTER FROM TONY

R eading is what makes words and the stories they carry come to life. Without all of the wonderful readers out there, it would be impossible for the journeys, textures, and moods crafted in literary worlds to thrive. Thank you for choosing to read *The Dreamkeepers* and for breathing life into the places, people, and creatures that lie within it.

If you enjoyed the book, please consider leaving a review, even if it is only a line or two, on Amazon.com or Goodreads.com. Your help in spreading the word is gratefully appreciated, and reviews make a huge difference in helping new readers discover my work. To all of you who have already mentioned the book to friends or have taken the time to go back and write a great review, I say THANK YOU!

If you want to keep up to date with my latest projects and releases, you can sign up at my site at antonio.zadra.com.

Finally, I love hearing from my readers. You can get in touch through Twitter, Instagram, Goodreads, or my website. I hope you enjoy reading my books as much as I enjoyed writing them.

ACKNOWLEDGMENTS

Turning dreams into reality is never a simple matter and something rarely accomplished alone. A huge thank you to my first readers: Nicholas Pesant, Dominique Petit, Paul Cicek, and Giulietta Vicenzi. Your patience, feedback, and encouragement were exceptionally helpful. A special heartfelt thanks to Nick. Words cannot express how grateful I am for your willingness to share, listen, and discuss. Thank you, Elaine Kennedy and Josée Lafrenière. Your fantastic edits, comments, and support—especially in times of doubt—were vital in seeing this project through. *Merci,* Sidney Maynard, my always willing partner in folly as well as in crime. From hot desert valleys to freezing mountaintops, being with you is always a neuronal treat. Luke Ryan, thank you for reaching out, for your terrific insights and fleeting glimpse, and for your kind, supportive words. My wife, however, still doesn't believe you exist. Jeffrey Moore, thank you for opening my eyes to the intricacies of sentences and for your writers' ten commandments. One down, nine to go. Phil Harden, Alain Dagher, Drigissa Iles, and the rest of the Titans: thank you for your longstanding friendship and willingness to let me indulge in writer's mania. Thank you, Allister Thompson. Your polishing was superb, and your Lovecraftian queries spot-on. Thank you, Britanie Wilson, for your meticulous proofreading. *Merci,* Jacques Montplaisir, for being so open-minded and making possible those magical retreats by Lake Louisa. A big thank you to my agent,

Jessica Papin. I will always be grateful for your enthusiasm, candidness, and unwavering belief in the project.

My thanks also go out to my parents, my brother and sister, my two awesome boys, and my amazing wife, Anne, without whose tremendous patience and support this book could not have been written. I love you all.

ABOUT THE AUTHOR

Antonio Zadra is a sleep and dream scientist at the Hôpital du Sacré-Coeur's Center for Advanced Research in Sleep Medicine and professor of psychology at the Université de Montréal. He has published extensively on the science of dreams and is the co-author of *When Brains Dream: Exploring the Science and Mystery of Sleep,* from W.W. Norton. *The Dreamkeepers* is his first novel in a series blending sleep science with dream mythology. He currently lives in Montreal, Canada with his wife and two sons.

Made in the USA
Monee, IL
06 February 2021